The Thirteenth Echo

The Thirteenth Echo

To Mary – Thanks for being
so great!
Sincerely –
Chris Lambert

Aunt Mary,
Please enjoy!

Chris Lambert
James Backston

Xlibris

To order additional copies of this book, contact:
Xlibris Corporation
1-888-795-4274
www.Xlibris.com
Orders@Xlibris.com
51231

Dedicated to Ripley, Dad, and 4 a.m.

Prologue

God's Monocle. Maybe the Pentagon had named it that to let everyone know they felt God truly was on their side. There was even a rumor going around that some of the right-wing generals in command at the time of the satellite's birth felt like they had their own private deity on call. It constantly circled the Earth and protected America like some spiritual and moral Supreme Being. Others say it was named so for no other reason than the term seemed a sufficient code name. In reality it was nothing more than a spy satellite that orbited the Earth every ninety minutes at the height of five hundred miles.

High-ranking military officials tried to balance the Monocle's abilities against other satellites, but it was like comparing the vision of a soaring eagle swooping down upon its prey, to that of a blind man stumbling through a heavy rain without the use of his cane or aid dog.

The creators of this latest orbiting camera, technically designated as the Primary Camera, 1st series of the 21st century, boasted about its ability to identify certain pre-computed, oddly-shaped grains of sand out of a desert the size of the Sahara. As part of a test run from its berth in the sky, the PriCam 121 once picked out a single, thin dime among a warehouse floor covered with metal shavings, even going as far as relaying back information designating heads or tails.

The super camera also was capable of infrared chemical analysis and heat imaging as well as a host of other talents it used on behalf of the American government. Even the technicians who were in on the early phases of its development marveled at the degree of sensitivity it exhibited. Not only could the PriCam 121 sort out five different bodies based on their unique brand of heat signatures, but it could also delineate which ones had normal body temperatures and which ones might have been coming down with a fever.

Its specific, detailed sensitivity had come into play on one of its circles around the globe. God's Monocle had picked up a strange image deep within the borders of Northern Iraq, where U.N. soldiers were still fighting to restore normalcy to the area. The satellite registered a small, one-foot by one-foot area that transmitted back to its controllers as "hot." This wasn't hot as in body temperature, however, or even hot as in a rifle barrel firing repeatedly on the front lines of a battle. This was hot as in the slang vernacular that scientists relegate to fissionable material.

Chapter 1

Franklin Delano Roosevelt must have had hundreds of days like this during World War II.

President John G. Sumner stirred his iced tea and took a considerable drink that emptied a quarter of the glass. It wasn't exactly the etiquette he'd display at any public function the American populace might have cause to witness. Then again, not every Sunday afternoon was interrupted by one of his top generals with news of a dangerous threat to U.S. soil. Besides, he thought to himself, he was alone in his Oval office with most of the White House staff out enjoying what was left of the weekend, so who did it hurt?

The door leading to the Oval office opened quickly and quietly. It then closed in like fashion behind the military man who strode into the room. He took large steps and held a thin manila folder under his arm. To an interested onlooker, if any were allowed in the White House on a Sunday afternoon, it would have been a toss-up as to who exactly saluted, the man or the uniform. His fingers stopped at the brim of his hat. "Mr. President!"

Sumner waved one hand toward a nearby chair as he placed the glass of tea onto his desk. He leaned back in his chair and then motioned to the file under the General's arm.

"What have you got for me this time, Tabler?" He kept a lack of concern in his voice, but he was aware that General Tabler knew his well-known trick. As the Commander-in-Chief, he kept calm and steeled himself before he'd need to take action on a possible disaster. He remembered that Tabler had seen him use the method last year just minutes before he addressed the American people about the health-care riots in Detroit. Now, on a quiet afternoon, with just an audience of one, the trick held him in good stead once again.

"It's imperative, Sir." Tabler let the folder hit the desk with a slap and flipped the file open with his thumb. "The Monocle found something big within the last hour, Sir."

"Big, you say?" Sumner squinted at the paper before him. He reached into his shirt pocket for his reading glasses, placed them on his face, and let the crow's feet around his eyes relax.

"I know you need some time off, Sir. I wouldn't have bothered you, but this is of the uppermost importance." Tabler almost smiled, but forced the corner of his lips to straighten out into a more formal line of decorum and then added, "Sir."

Sumner did allow himself a quick smile and then leaned over the folder on his desk. "So what are you getting at?"

"Forget *weapons of mass destruction*, Sir," began Tabler. "The new key phrase around here is going to be *fissionable material*. At least that's what the media networks will hop on." He paused for a moment then added quietly, "If you let them."

"What do you mean by that last crack?" Sumner let an honest amount of curiosity creep into his voice without sounding annoyed.

"These pictures are from the Monocle, Sir." Tabler pointed to the first photo from the file. "Notice the heat signatures from a small group of men around a brighter colored image."

"Yes." His reply in a non-descript tone of voice showed no sign of emotion. Today was supposed to be his first day off in over a month. He'd slept in, eaten a large breakfast, and was getting ready to watch a movie when he'd received Tabler's call. As he stared at the satellite image in front him, he had a strange feeling that this was going to be a rough week—*and it was only Sunday afternoon.*

"They're soldiers, Sir." Tabler waited for what he obviously knew was going to be the President's next question.

"These soldiers are serving which country?" Sumner moved in for a closer appraisal. The satellite image not only showed a number of troops amassed in the desert, but a large number of tanks and transport vehicles. *Wait a second*, thought Sumner, *those are U.S. tanks . . . or at least they were U.S. tanks at one time.* He glanced back at Tabler, not sure he wanted to hear what he had to say.

"Two months ago, it would have been Iraq. But now it could just be another splinter group." Tabler was tense and professional. Generals weren't paid to have feelings. What good would that do in combat, especially if the Generals weren't the ones going to die?

Sumner took a deep breath before he asked the next question. He knew the answer, but he had to hear it from the military. "The extra bright image in the center of the men would be what exactly?"

Tabler didn't hesitate. "That would be uranium, Sir. I believe the exact number is 235, although it could be 237. Both would be ideal for use in a nuclear device."

Tabler paused for a moment while he watched his President take off his glasses, rub his hand over his face, and then replace the spectacles. Sumner felt weary, but he needed to continue.

Tabler seemed to read his mind and stated the facts plainly. "About ten pounds is what shows up on the photo here, Sir. That's more than enough to create a device."

Sumner shook his head. He understood exactly what type of device Tabler meant. So many people would die. He had to minimize the casualties.

Tabler continued, "I don't think the Iraqi insurgency has an underground nuclear power plant designed to power up a nationwide string of irrigation plants." He was silent for a moment and added in a very serious tone, "So we must act on the assumption that a device exists. Besides, if there were any underground plants, I think our inspectors would have found them before now, don't you think, Sir?"

Sumner leaned forward, surprise in his voice. "Are you suggesting that a pre-emptive strike is the solution?"

"We are still at war technically, Sir. Even though those who came before you might have declared victory over a half a decade ago. In fact if it were an ordinary military decision, I would have left it to our officers out in the field, but with us finding images of a nuclear threat, I thought it best to confer with you immediately."

"You were correct in doing so, Tabler," nodded Sumner. "Until I can think of a way to get us out of that country, we still are fighting another President's conflict. I want a team in there right away." He leaned back in his chair and thought about the previous administration's exhaustive search for weapons of mass destruction that yielded nothing.

"We have one slight problem, Mr. President." Tabler pointed to the next photo in the file. "If you'll notice the heat signatures on the middle frame photo. They show a massive build-up only a few miles to the east of the building holding the fissionable material, and another one five or six miles to the west of the building. That's where the Iraqi insurgent forces are dug in fighting our troops, Sir."

"Can't we muscle them out of there, overrun them, and bulldoze them flat?" As Sumner finished his statement, he cringed at how un-Commander-in-Chief like it sounded.

Tabler pulled a single sheet of paper from his breast pocket and placed it on the desk. "I suggest a quick strike Special Forces raid using the protracted fighting on either side as cover for the operation itself."

"How would the operation go down, exactly, I mean?" Sumner suddenly felt upset to his stomach. He put his hand on his temple and leaned over the images from the Monocle. *Nuclear material surrounded by our own goddamn military hardware, unbelievable.*

"High altitude parachuting in by way of pressurized troop transport planes. Two teams of six soldiers put down between the two battle points, take the building and administer lead foil to the material, thereby making it safe to transfer to a shielded canister." Tabler stopped long enough to take another breath and continued. "They make their way out, signaling a nearby Chinook helicopter for pick-up. At that point there would be no worry over the noise a lone helicopter would make amidst all of the other nearby fighting, since the mission would be wrapping up."

"You make it sound simple." Sumner looked up from the images and made eye contact with Tabler.

"It is." Tabler stared back at Sumner with an expression of supreme confidence plastered across his face.

"Let me make it clear; I want this operation to go down perfectly. The last thing I need is to be compared to Carter. We all know what happened when he sent the troops in to rescue the Iranian hostages." Sumner had preached time and time again that the Iraqi government was ready to take control of their country. He couldn't help but wonder what the political analysts would say if they found out about the nuclear threat.

"Eleven dollars worth of rusty bolts and poor upkeep of our machinery is not the type of military we run these days." Tabler sounded like he was annoyed by the Carter reference.

"Let's get in and out quickly. It's one thing to still be over there after all these years engaged in this bullshit, but to have a covert mission blow up in our faces and have to beg for the bodies of our own strike force just boils things inside of me that you don't want to hear about." As Sumner spoke, he recalled a lecture from the New England Historical Society on post war insurgency. Prior to his career in politics, he had been a history major at Boston College. His main focus had been on American foreign policies, and he was left to wonder how this particular chapter would end when it was finally written into history.

"I understand." Tabler was in total agreement. "You don't have to worry about losing track of any soldiers, Sir. The Special Forces are all tagged with a small transmitter located just under the skin at the top of their shoulders, very near the side of their necks. Each transmitter gives off a distinct signal. All twelve for this mission are located on the same frequency for better tracking."

"So I finally get to play the role of Commander-in-Chief in the Middle East." Sumner spoke quietly, almost to himself. *And I get to authorize a mission to prevent a nuclear incident as my first test. Is nothing ever easy?* He glanced down at the images once more. "Okay, General, how fast can we get in there?"

"I anticipated your thoughts. Taking into account the eight-hour time difference between Washington, D.C. and Baghdad, it's already two hours past sunset in Iraq. The plane is circling over the debarkation point now." Tabler sounded like someone who wanted to get a promotion. He'd already taken care of everything; the only thing left was the actual authorization.

"And what would have happened had you anticipated wrong, General?" Sumner asked.

Tabler retorted, "There is a recall button on the plane."

"I've known you a while, Chuck." Sumner finally allowed himself to be less formal. "If you can pull this one off, I'll let you run on the ticket with me for re-election in the next race."

"I don't think Vice-President Compton would like that, Sir."

"He'd still be the number-two man, I was thinking of having you take my spot and I'd be your campaign manager." *And,* Sumner thought, *you could handle all of the responsibilities of Commander-in-Chief.*

Tabler threw up his hands into a defensive stance with his palms toward Sumner. "Please, Sir, I'm a military man. Besides, I couldn't put up with all of the politics. I deal with enough red tape as it is."

"I've heard the rumors that have been floating around our armed forces. They think I'm too soft, waffling on too many of the commands concerning the war over there. Maybe they're right. Maybe I'm not as *hawkish* as the last guy who used this office."

"No, Sir, I've heard nothing of the sort. We think you're doing a fine job."

"But you know I am very concerned about Iraq turning into another Vietnam. Our country, our economy, and our people can't go through another ordeal like that one."

"No need to worry about that one, Sir," placated Tabler. "We won't let that happen this time." He finished with a smart salute and turned toward the door.

Sumner raised his glass in the direction of Tabler. "Send the team in. I want you to contact me as soon as the material has been retrieved."

Tabler stopped at the door and turned partially so that he could look the President straight in the eye. He stated two words before he turned back through the door. Both words were spoken with relish.

"We will."

*   *   *

SUNDAY 21:30 BST—SKIES OVER NORTHERN IRAQ

The small red bulb shone a dim crimson light throughout the inner fuselage of the transport plane. Captain Kyle Bradly peered through the glow at the eleven other soldiers that sat on the two rows of benches facing one another. He noted the deep shadows that fought the redness of the inside of the plane. He inwardly chuckled as he thought that the nearly rust-colored glow made the faces look as if they were peering out of a photographer's dark room. Including himself, that would be twelve sets of features trapped in a pan of fixative solution. Twelve sets of faces hoping to be turned from a negative image into a positive one, wishing that it could be done before the regular light might be turned on within the darkroom, dissolving their profiles forever.

Kyle knew he was being melodramatic, but he also knew the mission was an important one. The briefing of the exact details had finished just moments ago. He realized that if the word came through the cockpit within the next few minutes, he and his team of "Kodiaks" would be called upon to stop an enemy from the completion of another foreign nuclear threat.

Kyle allowed himself to lean back against the inside of the plane. *Everyone,* he thought to himself, *knew who the Green Berets were.* The Navy Seals were also well known because of the large number of books and movies that had featured them in the past few years. *The Seals*, thought Kyle. *Why name a strike force after something that usually gets eaten by a polar bear?* As he thought about the other Special Forces' titles, he couldn't complain about his team's designation. He was part of a new assault force created by the Pentagon based on the bear—code name *Kodiaks*. The Grizzlies were another name considered, but the generals responsible thought the name too common. So the less common name, Kodiak, the largest of the sub-species of Grizzly bears, was chosen. The men and women who became part of the group had to become as adaptable as bears. They had to be able to operate on ice, in water, run hard, climb trees, and take to the hills and mountains, all with equal ease. Yes, he certainly agreed that the Kodiaks fit the personality of this group.

Kyle felt a nudge in his left arm. The soldier next to him held out something between two fingers. In the red light it was hard to make out, but with a quick squint and a strain of his neck, he saw that it was a small piece of chocolate. He took the offering and popped it into his mouth. "Thanks."

"Anytime, Cap-"

"No names, no ranks, soldier," commanded Kyle. "I'm one, you're two. Numbers three through six are sitting here on our side of the plane. That's force designation *A*. The other designation is on that bench, numbers seven through twelve. And that's it. We want no enemy recognition of high ranking mission personnel."

A moment later, Kyle realized that the candy had been offered through the soft purr of a woman's voice. He stared into the face beneath the helmet. From what he could make out, she was at least ten years younger than his own thirty-five years of age.

"Number Two." Kyle leaned slightly forward in his seat. "State your credentials." The army trained Kodiaks separately so that any member could be dropped into any task force. Teams would complete missions without emotional attachments or friendships getting in the way.

"West Point, four years," retorted the female voice, this time with a harder edge to it. She continued, "I was involved in Navy Seal training for one year, Kodiak training for two. Of my four hazardous missions, Sir, I was responsible for eighteen enemies killed, none wounded."

Kyle was about to comment when Number Two continued. "Of the eighteen dead, sixteen were by gunfire, two by my own hand. I've also got a red belt in two separate martial arts."

"Okay, then on this mission—you've got *my* back." Kyle reached up with his fingers and tipped his helmet to Number Two before he leaned back against the side of the plane.

Number Two pulled up her right leg and braced it atop a large, wide-mouthed canister that sat before her and spoke once more. "As a designated Kodiak number two, I'm also trained to deal with hazmat missions, both containment and elimination."

"An area of expertise that I have no interest in." Kyle stroked his chin for effect. "Which is the reason that you're my second priority on this mission."

"What do you mean?" Number Two leaned closer to hear the answer without any mistake.

"I don't want to handle that crap, so I'll make sure *you* get to the 'hot' site." He then motioned to her with his thumb.

"Thanks, but I've never needed a personal escort." Number Two held up the automatic rifle in her arms. "I think my record shows that I can take care of myself."

"Don't worry; you're just another number on this mission." Kyle turned his head and faced forward again. After a few seconds of silence, he cocked his head back in the direction of Number Two. "But since you know how to safely handle radioactive items, you're an important number." He turned back and was quiet again.

After fifteen minutes of silence, not counting the humming of engine drone, the doorway to the cockpit opened. The co-pilot of the aircraft walked down the length of the plane until he stood between the two rows of soldiers.

"The word just came down from the highest source. This mission is a go!" He turned and headed back in the direction from which he came before he stopped momentarily. "You have six minutes before we're at the jump point. Good luck!" He continued on his way and disappeared back into the cockpit, closing the door behind him.

Kyle stuck his right arm into the air to get everyone's attention. He made circling motions with his hand and then pointed at his Adam's apple. Both rows of soldiers gave him their undivided attention.

"We chute down with night vision goggles in place and throat mikes on. Team One throat microphones will be at three-point-four. Team Two, set to three-point-six. Stay on your team frequency. I don't want any conversations overlapping and confusing one another. Remember, via satellite, Washington can hear both teams. They won't be able to speak to us directly, but they can hear our conversations. Digital audio files will be made from each person's microphone for the de-briefing sessions afterwards."

The Kodiaks adjusted their equipment, checked their ammo packs, and slipped their night goggles into the *on* setting.

Kyle added one last bit of advice. "Number Seven commands eight through twelve, I command two through six. This is a recovery mission. If we're compromised, call for the chopper and hold a firefight until we can get picked up. If we get separated, location finders are set to the exact frequency for all the chips in our necks aboard the copters, if you get lost, it shouldn't take much time to find you."

The central red light that beamed over everyone's head turned to a green hue at the same time a buzzer resounded throughout the plane. Kyle and the other Kodiaks all stood up and faced the back of the plane. Kyle watched as the rear hatch slowly opened to reveal the darkness of the Iraqi night sky.

One after another, they leapt from the rear of the plane, until only Kyle was left, perched by himself on the edge of the opening. He was always the last to jump, and when he did, he religiously brought to mind a line to remind him that all would be well.

"When can twelve soldiers take on an entire nation and win?"

He propelled out the rear exit and fell toward the earth. As he reached for the ripcord, he smiled inwardly and mentally answered his own question. "When bears fly."

Chapter 2

The Kodiaks hit the ground, immediately buried their black parachutes, and honed in on a small, temporary electronic beacon that buzzed on their belt monitors. Since the mission was uppermost top-secret, the buzz lasted for one-half minute, then stopped, then started again for another thirty seconds. After that, if any members couldn't meet up with the main task force, they were excluded from the mission. They'd need to fend for themselves for the next hour until extraction—never more than an hour since Kodiaks were only sent on quick strike, quick exit missions.

Kyle counted down through the first half of the second thirty electronic ticks, when the last of the team members gathered around him. They formed a tight circle as he clicked off the homing device.

"We all know the mission. Seven through twelve will head out in an easterly direction for a quarter mile before turning back toward the target. Seven leads the force. If anything happens, numerical seniority takes precedence."

The other team members briefly shifted their attention to the African-American leader of the second team. Number Seven gave a quick nod as Kyle continued.

"Watch the road on your right. There's been a lot of activity in this area."

Several members shook their heads in silent agreement.

Kyle continued. "My team is going straight in from this angle. We'll have protection on our right flank from Team Two. The American and NATO troop build-up should cover us on the other side. We'll run in five miles behind their front with no one the wiser. We pick up the stuff, contact our air exit, and then we're nothing more than another NATO recon chopper getting too close to the action."

Kyle rose from his crouched position and waved a finger through the air with a side-arm motion. "Start it up." With that command, the circle of soldiers broke into two groups and ran at a steady clip through the desert and rocky terrain.

*   *   *

General Tabler sat behind two technicians in sliding desk seats in front of a large electronic console. Three, very large, flat panel monitors sat directly above the console. A fourth screen was mounted to the wall just above the other monitors. It displayed an image of the globe that always reflected the real-time position and status for the Monocle. Tabler paced behind the technicians for a few moments before he glanced at his watch for the seventh time in the last four minutes. Finally, upon the last examination of his wrist-bound timepiece, he barked, "Okay, gentlemen, give it to me. What's going on, exactly when and where?"

The technician on Tabler's left pointed to a small window on the center monitor. It contained a single, straight, electronic line against a gray background. As he tapped the screen with his index finger, he spoke plainly to his commanding officer.

"The PAR application will give us every word from the team's throat mikes on a four to seven second delay due to their distance from us." The technician paused, pulled his hand away from the equipment, and patted another apparatus in front of him. "Although we can't talk to them, we'll receive every sound uttered by the team, and it will be stored digitally right here."

Tabler waited a moment as if to digest the information, and then bent forward slightly to identify the soldier's name tag. "I've been around a long time, PFC Bleeker, and I'm fairly up to date on most of our hi-tech equipment, but my current position doesn't allow me much time to keep up with the latest system acronyms. So if you'll kindly define 'PAR,' this General's lack of technical vocabulary won't give him away at the next Washington social."

Bleeker answered with a blank stare and monotone voice. *Personal Audio Recording,* Sir."

Tabler tapped the top of the machine. "In other words, what you have in front of you is a hi-tech tape recorder?"

"I think we're a little bit better than that, Sir." He smiled to give Tabler a show of confidence that he had in the system.

"Good." Tabler immediately turned to the soldier on his right. "What do you have for me, Corporal Price?"

"Something you've seen before, Sir. This is the satellite radar tracker for the microchips our people have implanted in the top of their shoulders. It's laid out over a grid of the map corresponding to their mission. Each white dot is a single soldier's chip beaming back his or her whereabouts. We use three different satellites to locate and triangulate their positions to within one foot."

"Yes," agreed Tabler. "I've worked with these before. They can be received by us here and picked up with a portable device locally by the retrieval chopper."

Price added, "There's also the heat imaging on the team we'll be getting from the Monocle every ninety minutes as the satellite makes its way around the globe. We'll receive pictures for ten minutes before it moves out of the orbit path of Iraq." He stopped long enough for another breath and continued his mild tirade of assurances. "But even without the satellite, General, even a blind man could hunt them down with this chip, Sir. It gives off an audio beep or *pinging* sound, and gets louder as the tracking signal gets closer."

"Just like a radar transmission, echoing off of an object."

"Correct." Price smiled as he answered Tabler. "We've got twelve of them right here that broadcast on frequency six twenty-two."

Tabler absentmindedly fingered one of the medals on his breast pocket, but for the life of him he couldn't remember which one it was.

"Then I guess for the time being, six twenty-two is someone's lucky number."

*   *   *

The second team of Kodiaks, numbers seven through twelve, had hit the deep end of their run in a northerly direction when they came across a four-cornered intersection. According to their mission goals, they were to turn west at the intersection to meet up with Kyle's force at the bunker.

Number Seven, the leader of the second team, held up his right arm and motioned to two large boulders near the road. The squad recognized the motion command, halted, and knelt down on one knee.

"Two hundred yards in that direction." Number Seven motioned yet again with his right arm. "Proceed at medium speed, and we'll be at link up in less than two minutes."

The leader rose from his squatting position and maneuvered between the two boulders with the rest of his team behind him. The squad had just exited from their momentary resting spot when they heard a noise from ahead and to the right.

"Scatter, drop, and freeze!" The whispered command was sent through Seven's throat mike with a sense of urgency. By his last word, the team was already motionless on the ground. Then another sound commenced, one of a metallic rumble and groan. Number Seven saw three canvas-covered trucks emerge from the darkness in convoy formation. A final squeal echoed, as brake pads in need of dire repair brought the mechanized unit to a halt beside the boulders the Kodiaks had just vacated.

In the exact moment the trio of vehicles were at a complete halt, Number Seven did a quick head count. "Where's Number Eleven?"

"Still behind the two boulders, Sir," retorted a faint reply.

"Then stay where you are and don't even breathe, the convoy is within feet of you." Number Seven's voice was calm and reassuring rather than agitated.

The passenger door on the lead truck opened, and a man dressed in drab garb, with strips of cloth wrapped around his face to hide his identity, dropped to the sandy soil a few feet below him. Without peering around, the man strode over to the first boulder. He spread his legs apart and undid the front of his pants.

"This doesn't look like the regular Iraqi army." Number Seven whispered into his throat mike. "This could be the renegade splinter group that has to do with our mission."

"This could also be a mission that's about to be compromised by some idiot who can't hold his goat's milk," said Number Eight.

Number Seven let the comment by Number Eight slide, instead he reassured his team. "Steady, let's play wait and see."

After the insurgent soldier was finished relieving himself, he shifted his private parts back into his pants and turned back toward the truck. Then for seemingly no reason, he turned back again and gazed out over the nearby desert.

"I said wait and see." Number Seven's soft voice was very smooth.

The soldier with the recently voided bladder seemed to squint.

"He can't see us, he has no night goggles, and we're at least ten yards away." Number Seven's voice had almost a charming quality to it now.

The man continued to squint.

"Like statues," came the gentle tone once more.

The man gave a shout in Arabic as he grabbed for the pistol at his side. He let loose with two shots in the direction of the prostrate Kodiaks when Number Eleven stepped out from behind the first boulder with his assault rifle at his side. He fired three times quickly in single shot fashion at the soldier's head. The slugs entered through the man's left ear and pushed out through the other side. The whipping of the air as the bullets zipped by made the loosely strewn rags around the man's head dance and jerk to the full length of the cloth and back again.

"I'm sure he'll have trouble hearing the word of Allah now," Number Eleven spoke aloud through his mike to no one in particular as he ducked back behind the boulder. As he did, all three vehicles in the convoy emptied themselves of soldiers, automatic weapons slung tightly around all of their shoulders.

Commence was the only word from Number Seven.

Almost as one, the Kodiaks opened a torrential volley of fire toward the three trucks, and for a few moments the Iraqi splinter group seemed to have been repulsed as several of them fell dead instantly. The sheer volume of men that poured from the interior of the vehicles, however, impressed Number Seven as one almost impossible to overcome.

Number Eleven popped back out from behind his place of security. He emptied his rifle's clip into a group of four soldiers that had just emerged from the second truck. They all went down before they could fire a single shot.

Number Eleven turned back again and rested against the first boulder as he dug in his pouch for another ammo clip. His pulse was still racing when he saw movement out of the corner of his eye and immediately remembered that the original soldier had come from the passenger side of the first truck, the one that was within an arm's distance to him. His jaw clenched as he saw another movement rustle in the shadow of the cab. He had not accounted for the driver.

The single shot from a hand sidearm blew through the front windshield of the lead truck, and the bullet buried itself in Number Eleven's larynx. His head snapped backward from the impact and his body slid down the boulder. As he hit the floor of the desert, a gurgling sound transmitted to the earpieces of the Kodiaks.

*   *   *

Fifty yards from the concrete bunker, Kyle propped himself up on one shoulder from his position on the desert floor. "Visual?"

Number Three brandished a pair of night vision binoculars and instantly scanned the low-slung, concrete building before them. "No guards, Sir."

"Anything else?" asked Kyle.

"An outside monitoring system seems to be in place, Sir." Number Three smiled as he rattled off what he thought was more vital data. "There is a camera technology that seems to have been perfected by a country we've already beaten in war, and that could possibly have been assembled in a country we will probably go to war with in the future, and is right now mounted atop a building in a country that we are currently trying to liberate."

Kyle allowed himself to return the grin. "What the hell is this type of technology doing out here?" He paused before adding, "Six, can you hit it?"

"Two words can describe how we can take care of this problem, Sir." Number Six laid down his automatic rifle and produced a silenced sniper rifle. He held up his index finger from his free hand. "*Lock.*" His middle finger emerged to join the other. "And *Load.*" He tapped the rifle with a smirk to finish conveying his meaning.

"Do it." Kyle watched Number Six line up his target.

A sound emitted from the gun not unlike that of a person clearing their throat, or maybe punching a soft pillow with all of their might. Tinkling glass was heard almost instantly.

Number Six lowered his rifle. "Done."

"Move in fast and hug the wall when you get there." Kyle ran down the slight slope that led to the shallow gully where the building was stationed.

Halfway there, with his strike force hot on his heels, Kyle dove to the ground. A split second later, the rest of the Kodiaks followed his lead.

"Something off to the west of us." Kyle spoke through his mike. "There's some kind of noise. Anyone else hear it?"

They all lay silent for what seemed like an eternity before Number Five's voice could be heard. "It sounds mechanical, sir. Tanks maybe?"

Kyle stood up quickly. "Number Three, put yourself on that sand dune to the west of us." Kyle's finger jabbed at the air in a westerly direction and gave Number Three no room for misinterpretation as to which dune he meant. "The rest of you gather around the door to that bunker."

Seconds later, Kyle did a quick head count of his troops and turned his gaze in the direction of the sand dunes. "What have you got, Number Three?" His voice was terse and clipped.

"Enemy mechanized forces, sir. It looks like they're fleeing, uh . . . that's retreating, Sir, from the front they've established against the U.N. forces."

"Great." Kyle thought about the U.N. troops. If they'd been able to push past the front in the first place, his team wouldn't have been called in.

"And unfortunately, Sir," said Number Three in a tired voice, "directly at us."

"Talk about a rock and a hard place." For the first time, Kyle sounded annoyed.

Suddenly, gunshots sounded and the entirety of the Kodiaks swiveled their necks in unison toward the east.

"Oh, shit, now what?" Kyle didn't even try to hide the fact that his annoyance was growing.

Number Two quickly speculated. "Sounds like shots from Team Two."

"A Kodiak fire fight, Sir?" Number Six questioned Kyle, although he thought he knew the answer already.

Number Four spoke for the first time since the Kodiak drop. "If they got intercepted, we're not going to have much time."

As they waited to hear Kyle's comment or next command, one of the team only uttered the plea, "Sir, what next."

"Forget about the hard place, we're stuck between a rock and another rock." Kyle pulled the tiny transmitter from his belt, the one necessary to call in the retrieval chopper. He toyed with the mechanism momentarily but left the *recall* button untouched.

"What's that, Sir?" Number Two shot back almost before Kyle had finished his sentence.

"Nothing," replied Kyle. "Let's blow this door."

*   *   *

As the renegade Iraqi splinter group advanced on the second team, most of the members had switched their weapons to automatic fire, all except Number Eight. He had used a random, single-shot technique since the battle had started. A quick turn to the left, and he put a round in one enemy's stomach, a turn to the right and he sent one over backwards with a slug to the head.

He continued back and forth with his method of delivering death before he took the time to specifically train his sights on one soldier. The soldier stood atop the cab attached to the third truck. Number Eight wanted this bullet to go in a certain spot. He wanted to give this renegade something to think about. He squeezed the trigger and grunted. The insurgent pitched forward and screamed horribly. As he fell from the truck, he clasped his hands to his groin.

Good luck trying to bang those afterlife virgins now, thought Number Eight.

Just then, several bullets raked the ground in front of him. Instinctively, he rolled to the left but noticed with disbelief that he'd failed to bring either his rifle or his left hand. His mind raced between a plan of action and outright shock as he continued to view the bleeding stump above his left wrist. He came to his senses and propped himself up on his left elbow. As he attempted to reach into his right pocket for his mini-medical pack, three more bullets struck him in the left side of his face. He fell onto his back and stared blankly at the dark, but clear Iraqi sky. Number Eight had one last thought as he closed his eyes, but it was a simple one.

I wonder if there are virgins where I'm going?

* * *

Kyle motioned his strike team through the opening where the door used to be. "Let's find the hazmat and get out."

"Geiger counter is on." Number Two waved the small portable detector.

After the last Kodiak had entered the bunker, Kyle slipped back to the opening and took a quick look outside. Number Three still manned recon duty from his position atop the ridge of dunes. "What's the status, Three?"

"They'll be on us in three to five minutes. Their retreat from the U.N. forces is turning into an advance on our position. Our people are chasing them right at us."

"I want to know when they're within fifty yards." Kyle turned and ran after Number Two. Within seconds he had raced past the line of Kodiaks who jogged in single file fashion behind Number Two. She held her counter out in front of her as she led the search for the radioactive material.

"What have you got?" The order from Kyle was stern but not harsh.

"I'm picking up fissionable material in a northeast direction from here." Number Two spoke with certainty as the low vibrations on her portable detector grew more distinct as the needle bounced into the red *danger* markings.

"Northeast would be ahead and to the right." Kyle pointed to the next hallway about to intersect their present course. He held up his arm and halted the team in mid-run. He closed his eyes and listened intently. "While I was talking to Number Three, did anyone run across guards of any kind?"

His team shook their heads to the negative, almost as one.

"No third shift available?" offered Number Two.

"They're trying to assemble the ultimate weapon, and they're not even trying to protect it?" Kyle shook his head in disbelief.

Number Two suggested another line of reasoning. "Maybe Team Two ran into a unit that was heading to the bunker."

"Could be," agreed Kyle. "And also," he added, "some of the guards could have been pulled away to help the insurgent front that's collapsing on top of us. That would make sense." He peered slowly around the next hallway corner and then turned back to the Kodiaks amassed behind him. "It's clear, let's go."

The segmented square tiles on the walls flew past their peripheral vision with Kyle and Number Two in the lead. As they ran down the hallway, their guns at the ready, Number Two's counter hummed at an ever-increasing volume of noise. *Good*, thought Kyle, *the louder that thing gets, the closer we are to out of here.* The deserted bunker still didn't feel right—regardless of what was going on outside.

As they passed a door with the universal markings for radiation, Number Two bellowed out, "It's in this lab."

The hum from the detector was now annoying. Kyle was about to ask Number Two to turn off the device, when the noise suddenly tapered off, then stopped altogether of its own volition. Kyle thought nothing of it until he saw the few clear spots of skin behind the paint markings on Number Two's face go pale white.

Number Two quickly pressed a button on the device, turned a switch several times, and then whipped out a small pencil-shaped object. She pointed it at the door then shook her head.

"I know these lab walls are lead lined, but this box should pick it up." She continued to adjust the detector as the rest of the team watched. "If not this one," she shook the black-box like device, "then certainly this mini-back-up." She wiggled the small pencil detector with the fingers of her opposite hand.

"What are you saying?" demanded Kyle.

"The uranium," stated Number Two nearly in shock. "It's gone!"

Chapter 3

The hand grenade landed so close that the ensuing explosion lifted Number Twelve's body into the air without time for even a scream. He was dead before what was left of him had settled back to earth to litter the desert with a dozen different parts.

Although it was contrary to his training, Number Ten allowed himself to get angry—very angry. That anger was pushed into an even higher state of agitation once he saw his fellow soldier's arm land with a final thud beside his leg. He finished preparing the grenade launcher and propped himself up on one knee.

"Flatten!" Ten heard the order resonate in his earpiece from Number Seven.

Ten pulled the trigger, and the middle convoy truck exploded into a ball of orange flame. The renegade Iraqi soldiers were sent sprawling by the force of the blast like cloth-topped bowling pins.

Number Ten shifted his aim and pulled the trigger again. A second later, the third truck exploded and sent the remaining renegades tumbling to the desert floor.

"Okay, fall back. They're off their feet," began the command from Number Seven, "but they're not all dead."

Number Nine jumped to his feet, his rifle at the ready. He walked backward and kept the renegade soldiers in plain sight. Whenever he saw movement, he lifted his rifle to snipe at it until he'd exhausted his ammunition. After his last shot, he quickly threw down the rifle and pulled his sidearm from its holster.

"Number Ten, fall back!" Seven rose to his feet and made his way toward Number Ten, who was still propped up on one knee, his launcher still pointed at the convoy.

"We've got a chance to get out of here." Number Seven reached Number Ten and grabbed him by the collar. The sudden movement made Number Ten slump forward, hit the ground, and roll over on his back. Number Seven realized that Number Ten wouldn't be seeing anything else, except maybe into eternity. A piece of metal shrapnel from one of the two truck explosions was lodged squarely in the bridge of his nose. His crushed eyes had become nothing more than collateral damage.

"Are there any problems, Sir?" The question originated several yards behind him from Number Nine, but the voice rang out in his earpiece as clear as if the fellow Kodiak stood beside him.

"No," Seven could only hope that Number Ten's death was instant and that he didn't suffer. As he turned away from the grisly sight, his thoughts were interrupted as his left arm jerked with an involuntary motion. He felt instant pain overwhelm the area of his elbow. The warmth of blood splatters on his face only confirmed his fears. He'd been hit.

He spun on his heel and raised his rifle with his remaining good arm. His finger tightened on the trigger and sent a spray of return fire in the direction of the enemy.

Number Seven turned around again and ran. As he passed Number Nine, he used his good arm to point ahead with his rifle. "Let's get out of here."

They sprinted and stationed themselves a few yards apart from one another. As they ran, they made sure that they changed their gait constantly. The more serpentine they moved, the harder it would be to hit them.

They ran for another thirty seconds when a spray of bullets kicked up the sand around their feet. Number Seven dove to the right as Number Nine rolled to the left.

Number Seven still hugged the sand face first. He kept his damaged left arm tight to his side, but his rifle had spun from his grasp out into the darkness. "Are you hit?"

A groan in his earpiece answered his question before his eyes registered the situation. He scampered through the sand on his knees toward Number Nine. He balanced with his one good arm as he went.

"Where did you get it?" Number Seven's voice was steady, but grim. He knew better than to give any false hope to a mortally wounded team member.

"A place where I'm going to have to stay, and you're going to have to get out of here." Number Nine moaned through clenched teeth as he pulled his sidearm from its holster. With his free hand he motioned to his shattered hip. Blood oozed freely from the wound to moisten the sand beneath him in a medium-sized pool.

Number Seven knew that Number Nine was right. There was no need to try and help him up. With Nine's current medical condition, he was going nowhere. He would be dead from loss of blood within a few minutes.

"Do you need a second gun?" Seven offered his weapon to the prostrate soldier.

"I've got a full clip. Keep those dunes between you and them. I'm going to buy you some time."

Number Seven didn't say a word. He nodded, rose from the desert floor, and staggered away.

Number Nine shouted over his shoulder to his departing leader. "Drink a toast to me when you get back."

Nine remembered the training he'd taken in pain management. They always advised to focus on some other object, event, time, or place to forget the aspect of the pain. He decided his designation number was a good place to start as he saw his armed adversaries rush out of the darkness. He focused on his number and cocked his weapon.

He sat up as high as he could, lifted his handgun, and aimed.

"I'm Number Nine!" he shouted loudly, squeezed the trigger, and an Iraqi renegade went down face first in the sand.

"I'm Number Nine!" He forgot about the pain momentarily. He pulled the trigger and another Iraqi died.

"Number Nine!" There was a third dead Iraqi.

"Number Nine!" And then another joined the third.

"Number Nine!" He felt the pain in his hip fight back. He yelled even louder and continued to pull the trigger.

"Number Nine!" Another shot issued from his handgun.

"Number Nine!" He noticed the flame emit from the barrel of his gun.

"Number Nine!" The gun bucked in his hand.

"Number Nine!" This time he wasn't even sure if he had hit any targets.

"Number Nine!" Click. The hammer fell on an empty chamber. Click, click, he continued to pull the trigger to make sure he was truly out of ammunition, and he used the only ammo left that he had—his defiance.

"Number Ni—"

The volley from three different weapons caught him in the legs, upper chest, and neck all at once.

He fell backward onto the sand as he continued to mumble, "Number Nine, Number Nine." He twisted his head and saw multiple pools of blood form around him. He thought for a moment how the desert must have been wetting its lips on the bloody beverage all his wounds were serving up as refreshment to the arid soil.

"Number Nine," he mumbled one last time with so little volume that it probably couldn't have been heard by anyone hovering directly over him. His thoughts grew fuzzy and dim, like a man being put under morphine after a painful operation. He thought it peculiar, though, that the last thought he had as he lay dying, was of his father playing an old, obscure Beatles song for him as a child, but playing it backwards.

*   *   *

Number Seven peered over the dune and saw the three remaining members of the renegade Iraqi convoy. They stood for a moment over the dead body of Number Nine to confirm he was dead. One of the three then fired a round from his rifle into the Kodiak's head to make their inspection a moot point.

Seven turned away and reached for his throat mike with his good arm. He flicked a switch on the device to change the frequency to that of the first team. Nobody on his team was alive to hear him talk anyway.

"Number One, if you can pick this up, this is Number Seven. I'm coming in alone in a minute or two, or not at all. I've got a few things to wrap up here and my squad's been taken out. Over and out."

*   *   *

Kyle removed his hand from where he had used it to cup over his ear, blocking out some of the noises his team was making around him. He had heard the message from Number Seven and shook his head.

Moments before, Kyle's team, minus their lookout, had blown open the door to the nuclear laboratory. They had used just enough to loosen the lock after Number Two had warned of setting off explosives within an arm's length of fissionable material. Once inside, the team quickly spread out, weapons at the ready. For the next few moments the only sound present was the shuffle of feet as each of the Kodiaks checked out another nook or cranny of the lab.

"Nothing," came back one verbal report.

"All clear," shot back another.

"We're all alone here," the last comment arrived in his ear.

Kyle depressed the button on the chopper recall box and placed the unit back into his pocket. *Team two was gone.* Things like this weren't supposed to happen to a Kodiak team—*they were better than this.* He thought back to his conversation with Number Two about her combat abilities. *I hope you're as good as you say you are.*

Number Two swept her radiation detection device in a slow, wide arc, when she noticed the pissed off look on Kyle's face.

"What's wrong?" The question was to the point as she continued with her wide arc.

"We have no flanking back-up. Team Two, except for its leader, has been terminated, and even the leader may not arrive."

"What?" It was Number Two's only word, spoken not in a tone of amazement or disbelief, but in one of calmness. Kyle understood what she meant completely.

"A convoy ran across them, or the other way around, who knows. Now we don't even seem to have a mission anymore." He waved his hand toward the middle of the lab. "If there's no hazmat, there's no mission. I've signaled the helicopter for pick-up."

"Believe me," she said and paused for a moment, "the stuff was here a minute ago." She sounded annoyed as she continued to sweep the room with her detector.

The three other Kodiaks returned from their search and stood before Kyle.

"Any orders?" the soldier closest to Kyle asked.

Kyle was about to issue orders when a voice in his ear spoke. "Number Three reporting in, Sir. I know you said to check in when the enemy arrived at the fifty-yard mark, but I thought I'd give you some leeway. They're about a hundred yards out and slowing down, but something's wrong. It almost looks as if they can't decide which direction to take, the one that continues on into the desert or the one that leads them right to us."

"Thanks," offered Kyle. "Keep me posted and don't get startled if one of our guys comes up from behind you. It's the Team Two link-up, only there's just one of them left."

"The firefight we heard to the east?" Number Three spoke in a hesitant fashion, as if he already knew the answer to his question but did not really want to hear his suspicions confirmed.

"Yeah, over and out." His team was now down to six, and it was his job to lead them out of this mess and salvage whatever he could from the mission. Something had felt wrong from the moment they hit the abandoned bunker, but the material vanishing from the lab was almost too much of a coincidence.

"I've got something here!" Number Two laid down her radiation meter and put her palms to the floor.

"Are you getting a reading on your counter?" Kyle approached and knelt beside her on one knee. *Now what? Could anything else go wrong?*

"No, but I've got a hollow sound in the flooring." Number Two turned her head to face Kyle's gaze directly. "There probably has to be some underground pipes for water in any cooling systems they use, but the hollow section's too wide for just that. This might be some sort of an escape tunnel, but I'm not sure. Uranium can't just get up and walk out by itself."

"Could it be a storage room to hide the material from United Nations inspectors?" Kyle made the suggestion for Number Two to consider.

"It could be. But couldn't this also be a tunnel that's used as a delivery system for loading and unloading radium directly into the lab?" Number Two's eyes grew wide as she believed she hit upon the solution.

Kyle agreed with her. He jumped up and ran through the door. "Follow me, everyone." They were going to need to move fast. The enemy troops were only a hundred yards away—and closing.

*   *   *

Guns at the ready, the Kodiak team raced through the well-lit hallways—clean, tiled walls to the right of them, more glassed-in laboratories to their left. The team followed Kyle as he wound his path through one turn after another heading in the general direction of the north side of the building.

The echoes of multiple footsteps resounded throughout the hallway of the most recent turn, when Kyle held up a hand. "Exit door ahead!"

Kyle picked up his pace and hit the metal bar to the door with his left foot. The door swung wide open and he poked his rifle barrel out in front of him.

He noticed a truck ramp off to his right that not only ran up to that side of the building, but from closer inspection, underneath it too.

Number Two appeared over his shoulder and tapped it to get Kyle's attention. "Flip your night goggles back on," she advised. "Isn't that a cloud of dust over there?" She pointed in the direction of the truck ramp's destination.

Kyle nodded, touched his throat mike and spoke to get his thoughts down on record for the tech teams back home that monitored their mission through the audio transmissions. "It seems someone might have heard us coming and got out the back door. Hazmat has been removed. Secondary team is possibly wiped out, and Team One is awaiting retrieval."

"That's probably burning some generals' stars right about now." Number Two made an odd facial expression and touched her throat. She obviously just remembered that her throat microphone was also being monitored.

Kyle exhaled and turned in the other direction. "Come on, let's get out of here, before a member of this team gets demoted."

It took only four minutes of re-tracing their steps through the winding corridors to make it back to the front hallway of the small nuclear compound.

As the team arrived at the entrance, Number Three staggered in through the doorway with the wounded Number Seven. As the group of Kodiaks approached the pair in the doorway, Number Seven held up the thumb on his good right hand. "I told you I'd make it."

"How?" Kyle was shocked that he'd made it safely to the bunker. "You said a few minutes ago that you might not survive."

Number Seven loosened himself from the grasp of Number Three and dropped to the floor. He spoke calmly and plainly. "The three convoy survivors knew they could catch up to me, but so did I. They didn't expect me to be waiting for them on the other side of the dune."

"Good." Kyle turned to Number Three. "Stay out there and flag down the chopper. Be ready for a fast pick-up.

"Yes, sir." Number Three responded instantly.

"The rest of you get outside and get ready to disembark." Kyle turned to look at his task force. It was a small consolation, but he was relieved to see that Number Seven had made it back alive. *Five Kodiaks were really gone.*

Kyle leaned over and offered Number Seven a pill he'd extracted from his belt. "Chew on this; it'll kill the pain until we get back." He then slipped an arm under the surviving team leader's armpit and helped him back to his feet.

As they walked outside into the desert they both heard a noise that offered the first sign of optimism since this mission had begun. The origin of the sound suddenly appeared overhead and cast a large, dark shadow as it placed itself between the moonlight and the ground.

"Chopper!" announced Number Three loudly.

Suddenly, along with the whirring of the blades and the shouting of Number Three, they heard another sound that puzzled them for a split second.

It was a hissing sound. The strike force had no time to pinpoint the origin of the hissing before it revealed itself to the group, as a trail of smoke appeared overhead and slammed into the helicopter.

The night sky lit up for a few moments, and the concussion from the ensuing explosion at such close proximity knocked them off their feet and to the ground. Debris whizzed close by, and Kyle issued a command through his throat mike. "Stay down until after it's clear, then move back inside the compound."

Kyle had just gotten the order out when a high-pitched scream resounded through his ear-piece. The main bulk of the flaming chopper fell on Number Three, who had been closest to the aircraft.

As the flying debris settled and calm was restored to the low-lying area in front of the compound, the sound of gunfire suddenly erupted from beyond the burning chopper. A hail of bullets cut a line in the sand that caused everyone except for Kyle to cover their heads and flatten further into the sandy earth. Kyle never took his eyes off of his team. Nobody else was hit, but now they were pinned down. He turned his head and stared across the sand dunes to find the source of the gunfire when an Iraqi tank appeared moments later and placed itself between them and their planned safe haven.

Number Two rolled over in the sand and quickly spoke to Kyle. "I don't want to have to write a book down the road, Captain, that is if we survive, about how I was able to put the ordeal behind me of being sodomized into a coma from half the Bedouin nation. If it comes to that, I can take a broken neck from you, alright?"

Kyle knew what she meant and slowly shook his head as enemy troops surrounded them. A few seconds later, the Kodiaks were held at gunpoint. They were forced to their feet and back into the bunker.

"I understand completely," he muttered to himself.

Chapter 4

SUNDAY 15:00 EST—WASHINGTON, D.C.

"I thought the mission was supposed to be a slam dunk." Sumner felt the veins in his neck constrict as his jaw tensed with anger.

"That *was* the plan, Sir." General Tabler stood at attention before his Commander-in-Chief.

"What exactly went wrong?" President Sumner's eyes narrowed as he concentrated his focus on Tabler's reply.

"A couple of things compromised the mission, Sir. The incident with the convoy happening across Team Two just happened to be a fluke. But the real mystery was when Team One reached the nuclear complex, only to find their hazmat objective suddenly vanished." Tabler mopped the perspiration from his brow.

"How?" Sumner wielded the one non-descript word like a scalpel, slicing through the tension-filled atmosphere in the Oval Office.

Tabler cleared his throat. "We picked up all their conversations through their throat mikes. We might even get visual confirmation, depending on whether or not the Monocle was overhead at the time."

"Can we contact the soldiers?" The muscles tightened further along the President's jaw line. His words carried the weight of his worries about his military decisions. He'd already reestablished many strained relationships with European countries—his diplomatic specialty. He was comfortable dealing with other leaders, but if he could choose one thing to delegate, it would be the role of Commander-in-Chief. He just wasn't comfortable, however, knowing that he was personally responsible for sending someone to his or her death.

Tabler's stance hadn't shifted an inch since he had alerted the President of the mission's unfortunate direction. He still didn't move as he unloaded another litany of bad news. "In the field, their mikes are only for inter-team, and depending on the frequency, inter-mission use; but we did monitor and record all of their conversations for post-mortem examination."

"Post-mortem?" Sumner felt a rush of anger surge through his body. He'd never had a problem with his blood pressure, but right now it had to be at the boiling point.

He felt his entire face tense up as he spoke. "Damnit, Tabler, this was supposed to be an in and out mission. Now we're counting the dead." He hated this role. *How did war time Presidents deal with this?*

"There is also the soon to be dead, sir. It seems the surviving members of both assault teams are now being held captive at the nuclear complex."

"We know this because . . ." The question halted with a pregnant pause that Sumner wanted Tabler to act as midwife to an acceptable answer.

"The PCI factor," said Tabler. "Remember that I told you before the mission about every soldier having the personal chip implant for monitoring purposes. Then every ninety minutes as the Monocle goes overhead, we can cross reference the echo signal that every chip gives off with the heat imaging that each body exudes."

"Yeah, that's right." Sumner seemed deflated as he spoke. "Let's just hope all of this technology can help us save what's left of our team."

Several seconds of silence elapsed as Tabler continued to stand at attention until Sumner snapped out of his momentary daze. "Okay, some troops are dead and some are now prisoners of war."

"I would have to guess," jumped in Tabler instantly upon the last words of his President, "that with the current state of mind of the Middle Eastern soldier, these are less prisoners of war than they are hostages."

"I'm aware of that," agreed Sumner, "as well as some of the things that can happen to prisoners at the hands of sadistic captors. A few American soldiers convicted of the same things are still in containment at the expense of the American taxpayers."

"Those weren't soldiers who committed those acts years ago, Sir, those were deviates." Tabler sounded defensive. He cracked one of his knuckles behind his back while he still stood at attention.

"Ask the Iraqi detainees if they felt any less violated or humiliated. Our side has done the same thing, and I want what's left of our task force out of there."

"It's understood, Sir." Tabler saluted and walked to the door.

"One more thing, General," added Sumner. "It may be no secret that I want our troops out of that country, but I'm not going to leave even a small task force high and dry. I don't blame you for what happened since our discussion of the mission, but I am going to charge you directly with using any military means possible to rescue the squad."

Tabler responded with a sharp salute and a vigorous, "Yes, Sir!"

Sumner continued. "Meanwhile, I'm going to see what I can accomplish through diplomatic channels." He leaned back in his chair and thought about his strength as a diplomat. He'd been in office just under a year and he'd already had two successful Asian summits to his credit. He'd also strengthened the U.S. ties with a number of South American countries in the hopes of further trade agreements. Maybe playing Commander-in-Chief *wasn't* the solution to this situation.

"If I could make a suggestion, Sir?" Tabler waited for Sumner to acknowledge his thoughts.

"Yes, go ahead, General."

"The Speaker of the House has multiple contacts in the Middle East. He might be able to help."

Sumner nodded his head in agreement. "Yes, Leamon Davis does have some business contacts over there, and he is considered somewhat of a mogul in various forms of the energy industry, needless to say which includes oil. With his contacts he may be able to get a lead on which splinter group is holding our soldiers by doing nothing more than calling in a few favors. Hell, for all we know, his contacts may be the ones bankrolling these bastards."

"So while you're trying a soft sell, back door approach, Sir, my troops will be reminding the insurgency that dealing with Davis might be the best way out of a bad situation." Tabler offered another smart salute as he headed for the door.

"Good luck, Tabler," threw out Sumner.

"We won't need it, Mr. President. God's on our side."

"General!" Sumner spit the word out like a rifle shot to get the high-ranking soldier's attention. "Adam and Eve were covered with fig leaves, not assault rifles and ammo belts. I don't remember America being mentioned in the Bible. This is war. God's on nobody's side."

"Yes, Sir." Tabler turned and was gone.

As the door closed, Sumner strode toward his desk and reached for the phone.

*   *   *

Within fifteen minutes of Tabler's departure, Speaker of the House Leamon Davis walked through the door to the President's office.

"Thank you for getting over here so quickly." Sumner was cordial but controlled as he stuck out his hand and grabbed Davis' in a genuine display of gratitude.

"You know I'm always at your disposal, Sir, but even more so under the circumstances." Davis almost bowed before he caught himself and merely nodded.

Sumner tilted his head and offered up the next statement. "I take it, then, you were briefed on the ride over?"

The tall, grey-haired, ruddy-cheeked politician nodded once more. "I've already seen the images that the insurgents have posted on the Internet, so I can understand your urgency, Mr. President. I'm not sure, however, how I can be of service, Sir. The Speaker of the House doesn't dictate foreign policy, doesn't command the armed services for a possible rescue attempt, and I'm sure as hell too old to pick up a rifle and be ready for the next regular draft."

If lives wouldn't have been on the line, Sumner might have chuckled at Davis' words. Instead, he just circled his desk and sat down behind it. "No, my friend, you don't think highly enough of your special skills."

"Which are?" Davis held up a hand, fingers outstretched with his knuckles pointed downward. It was as if he wanted Sumner to place the answer to his question directly into his palm.

"It wasn't that many years ago that you served another President as Secretary of Energy."

Davis nodded for a third time as he understood what the President meant and where he was going with the conversation. His family had dealt with the Arab world on the subject of energy for years. Their holdings included several hundred oil wells throughout the continental United States as well as shares in many oil companies located in the Middle East. His family's involvement in the original Alaskan Pipeline, solar manufacturing plants in Europe, not to mention an outright ownership of two nuclear power plants assured him of a certain grudging respect from the oil producing nations. If the respect wasn't present because of Davis' importance within the political hierarchy of America, then it certainly was on display over the his ability to foresee and meet future energy demands. He'd made his family, and sometimes the Middle East, richer with every move he'd made.

The President continued. "We've got a military option we're pursuing, but I want you to talk to your contacts over there, maybe back-door a contingency plan to get our people out of there through the people you know."

"I'll make some calls to my affiliates in the region, but in my dealings, I've found that these radical insurgents are rarely interested in any type of civilized negotiation." Davis paused for a moment before he went on. "Hell, Sir, what I mean is that those rebel bastards have our troops, a video camera, and access to the Internet. Anytime they have those three things at hand, it's an event to them that's bigger than sighting the moon during Ramadan. I'll try my best, Sir, but I'm not sure with the time frame at hand that conversation alone will make them release their grip on the balls of their enemies, which in this case is us."

"Look, Leamon." Sumner let some mild agitation creep into his voice. "I've been trying to get our entire army out of Iraq since I took office. Now it looks as if I'm escalating things over there because of the commando raid I authorized. I don't care if I personally look bad over this, but I don't want this country to look bad or any soldiers to suffer over decisions I've had to make."

"Yes, Sir, I understand completely." Davis had a look cemented on his face that conveyed that he truly did understand his President's dilemma. "I'll get on it right away, Sir."

Before Davis could place his hand on the doorknob, it seemed to open by itself as an aide entered the office.

"Mr. President." The aide didn't stop for a reply. "We've received word through our contacts that there's a live Internet video feed from the Iraqi insurgency concerning our captives."

"Already?" Sumner let disdain spill out along with his words. As he reached for his computer monitor with his left hand, he turned his head in the direction of the Speaker of the House and gave Davis a hard stare that was filled with urgency.

Davis halted before the open door long enough to disassemble the meaning behind Sumner's gaze. "As fast as I can, Sir." He turned and almost ran from the Oval Office.

"Thank you, Leamon." Sumner shouted the words of appreciation loudly, before he turned back to the monitor, which flickered with electronic life. His next words were muttered softly, barely audible but to his own ears. "I hope you're in time to save whoever's left."

*　　*　　*

SUNDAY 23:35 BST—NORTHERN IRAQ, BUNKER

The six survivors of the two Kodiak attack squads had been captured and herded back into the nuclear laboratory. In that hour the group had been searched, stripped of their weapons, had their hands and feet bound, and had their throat mikes taken from them. Most of the Iraqi soldiers who had captured them had since left, but a core of six insurgents stayed with the remaining Kodiak team members, their guns trained on them at all times.

One of the rebels walked in a constant radius surrounding the captured American force. As he continued to circle, he pointed a small digital movie camera at them as others shouted at them in Arabic.

Within another minute, only the cameraman and one gunman watched over them as two others paced back and forth in front of the nearest door. The final two, one covered in a rust-colored, overall type of outfit, and the last in a green shirt and dirty pants, talked heatedly in the far corner.

Kyle was stuck in a seated position like the rest of his team. He pushed against the tiled floor of the storeroom where they had been herded until he felt his back against the concrete wall. He tilted his head to one side and spoke softly to Number Two. "How are you holding up?"

"I'm fine." Her voice was quiet, yet seemed to be backed by an inner strength that kept her tone firm. After a short pause, she added, "By the way, my name's Laurel. My friends call me *RW*. That's short for *running water*. That is if you want to drop protocol."

"That's cool, *RW*, but I've got to ask you." Kyle turned his head toward the left to see her better. She was slightly smaller than some of the other woman he'd met in the armed forces, yet she seemed incredibly confident in her abilities. Even now, held hostage, her eyes were sharp as she stared back at him. "Why *running water?*"

"My last name's Crickowski. As a kid, my friends shortened it to just plain creek."

"Just like a small brook of running water." Kyle smiled slightly. "I think I'll just stick with Laurel?"

"That'll work, Captain."

Even though Kyle had been teamed with Laurel for more than six hours, he carefully took his first chance to see what she actually looked like. She had a petite frame that had obviously been sculpted by years of military training. Her short black hair was cut into a bob that framed her girl-next-door features, and although her last name didn't reveal it, her tanned olive skin and blue eyes must have meant that her mother was of Mediterranean descent.

"The name is Kyle. You can drop the Captain. Rank doesn't count for shit right now." Kyle shook his head from side to side as he spoke. He was probably a good six inches taller than Laurel, and except for a goatee, his light blond hair was almost non-existent due to his flattop military haircut.

A moan from his right brought his attention to Number Seven, who was bleeding pretty badly from the two gunshot wounds he had received in the escape from the Iraqi truck convoy. Kyle recognized Number Seven from a previous mission and hoped that the soldier could hold on until they could get him proper medical treatment. The other three surviving members of Kyle's squad talked among themselves just beyond Number Seven. They seemed in reasonably good condition considering the situation.

Another noise got Kyle's attention as the two heated Arabic talkers from the far side of the storeroom walked toward the captured Kodiak team. The pair stopped at Kyle's feet. The heated talk became an argument for thirty seconds when the Kodiak on the end turned toward Kyle and sputtered softly, "Captain, they want—"

The Iraqi rebel in the rust-covered overalls turned swiftly, pulled his assault rifle from his shoulder, and loosed a clip at Number Six's face almost from point blank range. In response, the rest of the Kodiaks instantly rolled from the line of fire. The two rebels near the door countered that move and rushed over to cover the bound American captives.

Kyle rolled over on his right side and within just a few feet, saw the remains of what had been his sniper expert, Number Six. He turned a gaze at the two rebels who seemed to be in charge and screamed at them with no concern for his own safety.

"What the fuck was that for, he didn't do anything!"

The rebel in the green pants turned and spoke. "My leader did not want you soldiers talking." The English was slow, but more than understandable.

With anger still filling him, Kyle spit out, "God damnit! Why didn't you just tell us?"

"Please," came the reply. "It would not do you well to yell at me, I am trying to convince our unit commander that it would be to our advantage to keep you alive; although, I have lost my first argument with him." He pointed with his sidearm toward the remains of Number Six. He added, "And for that I am truly sorry."

Kyle opened his mouth to speak, but he wasn't exactly sure what he wanted to say, or for that matter, how to say it. His throat had suddenly gone dry to the point where he could barely swallow. Was this some type of Muslim mind game? *If I answer the wrong way, this guy could end my life on a whim.* After another moment, he hoarsely shot back. "What is this, some Arabic version of good cop-bad cop?"

The Islamic rebel had a puzzled look on his face. "I don't understand."
Just then, a sound emitted from a portable radio unit on a nearby table
by one of the rebels. The leader walked over to the table and flipped a lever
on the small console. Several words in Arabic poured out. The leader turned
the sound down a few decibels and snapped his fingers. Two of the three rifle
bearing guards strode over to Kodiak Number Four. They switched their
weapons to one hand and picked up the American. The whole time the Arabic
cameraman captured the scene on film.

"What the hell is going on?" Kyle struggled to get to his feet.

The third rifle-holding rebel kicked him in the chest and knocked him
back to his position on his side. Meanwhile, the two rebels that carried Number
Four pulled him to the center of the room and forced him to his knees.

The leader walked over to a tall cabinet, opened the door, and withdrew a
long, sword-like blade from it. He admired the weapon as he walked toward
the kneeling Kodiak. The only sound for the next few seconds was the leader's
footsteps and the electronic hum of the digital camera.

Number Four squirmed back and forth as he tried to see what was going
on. He then suddenly felt the steel blade come to a rest under his chin. His
body instantly froze except for an involuntary cough that erupted from deep
in his chest.

Kyle figured it had been just over an hour since they were captured. He
had hoped to stall for time because he knew the implants in their necks would
continue to send signals to Washington. The location of the chips should
show that they were easily within striking distance of the American front just
two miles to the west. Then he thought of Number Six just a few feet away
and Number Four right in front of him and knew he was wrong.

"Can't you stop this?" Kyle turned and screamed at the English-speaking
rebel who looked up from his watch.

"I can't." The two words were slow in coming out but sounded apologetic.
It was almost as if this rebel was emotionally shaken by the actions of his
fellow insurgents.

Kyle struggled to get to his feet, but was kicked in his side. He landed on
the tiled floor as a rifle barrel instantly struck him in his left ear.

He heard Number Four cough again. Kyle screamed at the leader, "I'm the
Captain! I'm the one in charge! Take me! Do me instead!" He then glanced
once again at the English-speaking rebel, who had now moved a few steps
back and turned his head away from the impending execution. The rebel's
eyes were closed, and he seemed to be whispering something in Arabic to
himself.

The cameraman walked around the table to get the best angle, knelt and pointed the camera right in Number Four's face.

Between coughs, Number Four looked at Kyle and pleaded for an answer with his eyes.

"Do what you have to." Kyle lowered his head as anger filled his entire being. "Nobody will blame you for anything." He closed his eyes. There was nothing he could do to prevent what was about to happen.

"My name is Joe Vander." Number Four spoke the words for no one but himself, not knowing who would ever see the film but stopped and coughed once more. He quickly continued. "I'm from Chicago. I love my parents and my country. God is my shepherd, I shall not . . . ."

The leader gripped the blade tightly, leaned forward and hunched his shoulder for more leverage.

Joe Vander's prayers were replaced with a wet, ripping sound and his own soul-wrenching screams.

*   *   *

"It's been over an hour since the capture, Sir. We have their implant echoes on screen and we should have the heat imaging pictures any second now since the Monocle is due . . . ." The technician, PFC Bleeker, paused in mid-sentence as green and yellow-colored shapes suddenly filled the monitor screen. "In fact here it is. The Monocle is right overhead at this point."

General Tabler had raced from the control room to personally alert the President to the mission situation, but had been able to quickly get himself back to the monitoring station. He knew that the Monocle would be overhead within a certain window of time and had checked his watch on the way back from the White House. He had just made it.

"What's this now?" Tabler pointed to the left side of the screen.

Bleeker's reply was simple and to the point. "The stationary images seem to be our guys. They must be tied up or being forced into a stationary position, probably at gunpoint by the images moving around. Those are probably their captors. We can also differentiate them from us by the radar echoes that our guys give off. Here, I'll show you."

He reached over to his partner's console, tapped a few commands on the keyboard, then reached over and did the same on his own keyboard. Suddenly the radar pings and small white visual dots emanating from the personal chip implants had merged with the green and yellow hues and shapes of the heat imaging.

"You see, Sir, for the next nine minutes or so, as long as the Monocle's heat imaging radar, or any other similar device is beaming down from overhead, we'll have each of our guys with an image and a small white echo dot. After the Monocle moves on with the Earth's orbit, we'll still have the radar echo and the dot."

"I see, good wor—" Tabler's congratulations were cut short as one of the two green and yellow ambulatory images approached the stationary images. A brief circle of yellow erupted from it transferring itself to the green and yellow image at the end of the line of several non-moving images.

"What the hell was that?" Tabler's tone was immediate and sharp.

Bleeker turned his face toward his right shoulder, exhaled briefly and answered. "That image pattern is consistent with gunfire, Sir."

"Just give me one of our thermo-nuclear devices and I'll have that whole sandy-assed country glazed over like one big fucking sheet of glass." Tabler made such a tight fist that his own knuckles cracked under the pressure.

Just then the image next to the origin of gunfire image moved closer to the line of Kodiak images.

"Is this one going to take a shot at our guys?" Tabler was extremely agitated. "Well, he had better watch his ass. It won't be too long now; we've got another division moving up through the Iraqi front to take the complex. If only our guys can hold on." Another knuckle cracked.

Suddenly the screen became a collection of discolored block-like shapes overlapping one another in a blur of digital disruption, replacing the white, green and yellow shaped data on the monitor.

The tech decided to offer an explanation before he heard any more of Tabler's knuckles crack. "It's probably atmospheric conditions interrupting our transmission, Sir, this is originating from the other side of the world you know. It might even be sunspot activity or a minor solar flare."

"Yes, I understand," bellowed Tabler, but he really didn't. "But can't you boost the signal?"

"The program automatically tries that, Sir, and obviously it still isn't helping. But possibly if it was solar interference the original wavelength designation might have been knocked around a bit. Let me see if I can do something along those lines."

"Put the words in English, soldier!" If Tabler hadn't been wearing such tight fitting shoes, the monitoring room might have been privy to hearing the knuckles on his toes crack as well.

"I'm going to traverse the wavelength scale, up and down like tuning an old radio."

The joints in Tabler's hands eased up. "Please continue."

"The original wavelength was six-twenty-two, and I'm moving downward through six-twenty one, six-twenty, still getting nothing, Sir." Bleeker continued to move the mouse as he clicked different points on the screen.

Tabler continued to gaze at the distorted images and nodded in silent agreement.

"I'm going to try the other direction, Sir." Bleeker stated the obvious as his fingers began punching other buttons. "Six-twenty-two again, and nothing, six-twenty three, six twenty four—"

A single white dot appeared on the screen. "We have them, Sir—wait a minute, there's only one echo." He fingered the button again and all of the white dot echoes, along with the heat imaging returned as the wavelength hit six-twenty-two once more. "Now we have them, Sir."

"Something's changed though." Tabler's knuckles went through their exercises again which led any nearby listener to the conclusion that only a bone graft could save his joints. "Some of the positioning has changed. What's that big green blob in the middle there?" He pointed with a finger that had actually stiffened into a crooked line of flesh from all of the contortions of the last few minutes.

Bleeker squinted at the screen as he pointed. "The heat images are overlapping, Sir, but see the single, white echo dot. One of our guys must be in the middle of two or three rebels. Maybe they're beating him."

Tabler grabbed his crooked finger with his other hand and popped it back into place with a loud crack. "They'll pay by God."

As the two men continued to peer at the screen, a small portion of green detached itself from the larger blob. The white dot stayed with the smaller portion that moved itself away from the larger area of green.

"Now where did that thing come from?" Tabler shouted with true, innocent misunderstanding. "It looks like it's about the size of a football compared to that big area." His face contorted into rage as an ugly thought crept into his mind.

PFC Bleeker tried to answer, but he was choked on the words. He swallowed hard, composed himself and answered with a short, single sentence. "Yes, or about the exact size of a human head."

Chapter 5

MONDAY 08:45 EST—WASHINGTON, D.C.

Sumner bent over the wash basin and took one last handful of water. He splashed it into his face and then grabbed a nearby towel. As he straightened, rivulets of clear water ran off his chin into the enamel bowl. A few of the drops hit the nozzle and bounced outward in a picturesque spray that resembled a tiny display of liquid fireworks. His original post-graduate plans had included teaching government history classes at a small town college. The lecture that he had just finished was, unfortunately, not to a number of college students, but to a room full of reporters who demanded answers.

"You're going to have to give them more; the press isn't moving from the room and CNN is going to be talking about the damn thing all day," said John Babare, Sumner's press secretary. Babare stood in the center of the Oval Office as Sumner reemerged from the washroom. He held a sheaf of papers in one hand while he adjusted the horn-rim glasses that continually slid down his thin nose with the other. The glasses wouldn't stay, so he removed them altogether and exposed his entire thinning hairline and pasty white face to more detailed scrutiny.

"They've got all they're going to get." Sumner patted his face dry and threw the hand towel onto the corner of his desk as he sat down in a nearby chair. "The whole world has seen the clip since it was broadcast on the Internet last night. And if that's not enough, every morning news show has made it the top story."

"But—" Babare began another plea.

"But nothing," started up Sumner once more. "I may be new to this office and have the tag as the laid back, mellow President, but by God I'm not going to let our people die over there at the hands of a small band of murdering rebels." Sumner pointed his finger into space. "But I am going to look into a couple of different ways of saving them without the press or the conservatives climbing up my ass with World War III as the ultimate end resort." He sat back for a moment and tried to gather his thoughts. *It's only Monday—I was right yesterday. It is going to be a long week.*

Babare turned and headed for the door. "I understand, Sir. I'll give them enough spin to appease them for a few hours. But you'll need to come out later today and make another statement."

Sumner waved his hand at the secretary. "Yes, yes," he replied annoyed. As he turned in his chair to try and lean back into a more comfortable position, the buzzer on his phone rang. He picked it up.

"Mr. President, Mr. Davis is on the line."

"Put him through." *Please let him have good news*, thought Sumner.

A moment of silence elapsed before a voice erupted in Sumner's left ear. "Mr. President, I have disturbing news. My contacts believe the organization holding our soldiers is a splinter group by the name of JET. It's the abbreviation for Jihad End Times. This isn't a group known for negotiations, so it doesn't sound promising."

"Is there any chance for a deal, any hope at all for opening a line of communication with them?" Sumner's tone was unemotional. He could negotiate with world leaders because he could offer them something they wanted in return. Was there nothing he could use to leverage *this* situation?

"Well . . . ." Davis stretched out the word. "To them, this is about their ability to appease their god, and the rewards in the afterlife that one can receive for killing a perceived enemy of their religion."

"God damnit!" Sumner cut off Davis before he could say more. "Whatever happened to guns and money for hostages in *this* life?" Sumner paused and thought about what he'd just said. It almost felt like the ghost of Ronald Reagan had entered the room.

"There's more, Sir," added Davis. "They want us to get out of Iraq."

Sumner exploded. "If those bastards had been watching my campaign trail last year, they should know that's what I want as well."

"And also, we've received additional information via the web." Davis was to the point as he continued. "There's going to be another execution within the next few hours."

"That doesn't give us much of a time table to work with." Sumner was firm. "It looks like we're going to need to get creative to save the lives of our soldiers." He paused for a second before he continued. "So unless through some miracle, I get assurances of no more beheadings, we've got to work fast on another military option."

"Yes, Sir," was the only response before the line went dead.

No sooner had Sumner placed the phone in its cradle, than it buzzed again. He picked it up and heard the familiar voice of his personal operator. "You have another call, Sir. This one is from General Tabler, on line one."

"Put him through." Sumner paused and waited for Tabler's voice to come over the line.

"Sir," began Tabler. "Our main body of troops is still tied up to the west of the complex and it doesn't look like they'll be breaking out soon. It's a rather large rebel force. Those bastards are better fighters than we've been giving them credit for." His voice seemed to show a fair amount of concern, almost as if he'd underestimated the entire situation to some degree.

"Probably because we personally trained most of them over the last four years," exclaimed Sumner. "I've made some inroads on my end of things here, but we still need to exert military force to try and deal from a position of strength. We also need to take care of this situation fast, within the next hour or so." There was a way out of this situation; he just needed to think outside the box, or this case, *the oval.*

Tabler exhaled into the phone and paused before he spoke again. "But, Sir, we don't have any available troops within a hundred miles of the trapped commandoes. If we did, we could trap the complex in a pincer movement from the east." Tabler paused for a moment. "Unfortunately, Sir, all of our cards are already on the table."

Tabler's last statement caused Sumner to sit up in his chair. "The Double Joker!"

"What? Excuse me, Sir, I don't understand." Tabler sounded honestly puzzled.

"I think I just found some troops, or at least a small division." Sumner's mood became more positive. He'd searched for a solution though diplomacy, but Tabler had actually come up with the perfect answer. *This is definitely thinking outside the oval, but it could actually work!* He added, "Once I get a handle on it."

"I still don't understand, Sir?" Tabler's reply ended with a grunt.

"Yes, you do," replied Sumner. "A handle, or in this case, Major Bobby Handle."

* * *

MONDAY 16:45 BST—NORTHERN IRAQ, 22 MILES EAST OF BUNKER

A few tanks, armored half-tracks and fifty soldiers covered in body armor slowly approached the village. The rural community comprised of adobe huts and steel pre-fabricated storage warehouses looked like nothing more than an elaborate camp ground misplaced in the middle of the desert.

A soldier watched the military unit advance to a point two hundred yards from the village. He was perched on top of a large boulder about a half mile away, on the other side of the tiny collection of buildings. He peered through his binoculars as he spoke into his walkie-talkie.

"Go ahead and slowly open fire. Don't give them any concentrated bursts, just some shots here and there. We want to give them the illusion that we're attacking, not that we're about to overrun them. I want to see if any rats leave the nest."

As he put the walkie-talkie down, he saw his men open fire, which was answered by return fire from the village. This act made the soldier reach once again for the button on his communication field device.

"Stop where you are. There's hell of a lot more of them than there are you, so why are they gearing up for a full-scale battle. I think they're hid—"

He was interrupted as three trucks raced down a sandy road that led out of the opposite side of the village away from the attacking troops.

The soldier continued his orders over the walkie-talkie. "Yep, here they come, right toward me. Everybody just dig in and hold your position. I don't want anybody hurt."

He lowered the binoculars and winced in pain as the attached leather strap rubbed against the back of his neck. "How many years is it going to take me to remember the dammed sun-block." Major Robert "Bobby" Handle had been in the service exactly thirty-three of his fifty years on Earth. He had seen every type of action imaginable, but he somehow always seemed to forget to take care of himself. He'd already gone mostly gray, or as he liked to tell people, "One gray hair for each near death experience," but overall, he felt good. *I've got a hell of a tan, and running around this desert has helped me stay at the optimal two hundred pound weight for my six foot height.*

His first assignment was in 1974, as both the American and Korean forces decided on a course of action that concerned a tree. The tall woody plant had blocked the view of both their respective checkpoints along the thirty-ninth parallel. The countries had decided that a small detail of six to ten men from both the American and Korean side would tear down the tree to give both sides a better field of view. The Americans dubbed it Operation Paul Bunyan.

The American troops had already taken out their shovels, axes, and spades when the Korean forces jumped them. A hand-to-hand fight ensued, and the Americans were attacked with some of the very tools they had brought to aid them in the stripping and removal of the bushy tree.

By the time the U.S. checkpoint, a few hundred yards away, had sent reserves from behind its walls, the Koreans had fled, leaving one American officer dead and several others wounded. In the melee, Bobby had taken a pitchfork to his left shoulder, which required three months of rehab to get back in shape. Later, Korean generals and officials denied the incident ever occurred. The U.S. eventually chopped down the tree and left only a stump and a plaque that honored the dead and the wounded.

After his recovery, Bobby had spent months honing his abilities in the martial arts. The event had changed his perspective on military life. *Things just didn't happen to other people.* So from that day forward, he always wanted to be in a position of *confidence,* as he liked to call it.

Bobby straightened, clipped his communication device onto his belt, and slid down the side of the large boulder. A moment later, he landed onto an armored transport, complete with a standing fifty-caliber machine gun turret.

He turned his head and barked an order to two soldiers stationed up in the rocks behind him. "Drop a couple of RPGs right in front of the lead car, just enough to make it swerve and go off into the sand. I want to use it to block the road for the other two cars. But if you hit it, don't worry, it's the one in the middle we want."

The car in the middle held a man who was wanted by U.S. forces since the *Desert Storm* operation, Ticar al-Udadise. Years earlier, a set of playing cards had been issued with different Iraqi faces on them; Saddam Hussein's being the most important one. After most of the playing cards had been accounted for, one face remained with its own special designation known only to the highest ranking officers. Ticar's card—the "Double Joker." "DJ," as he was known, survived through many a troubled regime over the years and was almost considered a regime himself, because he had supplied a needy service to multiple men in power. The service was experimentation.

Over the last fifteen years, DJ had performed medical oddities, for they could not be called treatments under any definition, on women, children, infants, animals, and captured soldiers. One of his specialties was the study of animal organs as a substitute for human ones. Normally that would have been thought of as a noble cause to benefit mankind as organ donors were always in need, but DJ took an extreme path as he collected his results. Several of his "hospitals" were discovered by invading troops to have the head and torsos of children and the bottom parts of goats grafted together half and half in a pain-wracked, hideous form of centaur. For this reason, DJ was mainly referred to as the "Middle-East Mengale."

"Let's go, Joe," Bobby shouted down to the driver. The armored vehicle roared to life and literally leapt across the sand as it headed to intersect the convoy's path.

Within seconds, shells burst in front of the first truck and caused it to skid and finally turn over onto its side. The other two trucks quickly came to a halt as they attempted to maneuver around the obstacle.

Now I've got you, thought Bobby. He opened fire on the rear truck with the fifty-caliber machine gun. Bullets racked over the windshield of the truck. He swiveled the gun mount toward the rear of the truck and let off three long bursts. Nothing moved.

In the driver's seat, Lieutenant Joe Manelli turned the wheel as Bobby braced himself. Their armored transport rammed the middle truck in the convoy and pinned it between their bumper and the first disabled truck.

Instantly, four renegade troops burst from the rear of the truck and fired their hand held weapons. Bobby returned fire as he held the trigger down on his gun to litter the desert floor with the four rebels.

He then drew his sidearm and vaulted off the top of the armored car to land in the soft desert sand. The side passenger door opened, and a rebel emerged brandishing his weapon. Bobby put a bullet in the rebel's side, and when the man twisted backwards from the impact, he put another slug into his head.

Just then he heard the driver's door open, and a spray of machine gun fire washed over his armored car. He knelt to one knee and spotted a pair of legs perched beside the front wheel. He fired two shots under the truck and heard screams as the soldier fell to the ground, clutching his knees.

"You okay, Joe?" Bobby shouted while the rebel writhed in pain.

"All good down here." The answer came from inside the armored car.

"Just checking," Bobby shouted back as he placed another shot in the man's chest to silence the cries of pain.

A rustling sound from the rear of the truck caught Bobby's attention. He made his way toward the back when he ran full tilt into a well-dressed, middle-aged man. The man wore a business suit, expensive shoes, and spectacles on his face. He was holding an Uzi machine gun.

"Hello, DJ," commented Bobby dryly.

Before DJ could bring up his weapon, Bobby grabbed the doctor's gun-hand around the wrist and squeezed until he heard a crack. He still held onto his sidearm with his other hand as he forced his forearm up into DJ's throat, cutting off the mad doctor's air supply and screams.

Bobby pulled hard on the wrist while he forced DJ's head back up against the truck. He could hear the evil doctor's shoulder tear, but without an oxygen supply to feed the larynx, the open mouth of the doctor emitted no sound.

Bobby turned the doctor's wrist again until he heard a few more bones crack.

DJ glanced down at his hand that was now broken in at least three places. He dropped the Uzi into the sand, as his eyes begged Bobby to either let him breathe or shout out in pain.

Bobby understood the look of his vanquished foe and replied simply. "I don't want to hear you scream, because I'm not interested in your problems."

He pulled his forearm back and brought his pistol butt down on DJ's head. As the doctor slumped to the desert floor, Bobby let a roundhouse kick fly into the side of the doctor's face.

Look at that, thought Bobby, *DJ was out before his head hit the sand.*

He put away his weapon and pulled a playing card from his pocket. On the face of the card was the visage of DJ. He placed the card against the truck, pulled out a knife and tacked the card to the side of the truck. "That should leave a message."

Just then his walkie-talkie made a sound. He answered it. The voice on the other end was a familiar one.

"Hello, Bobby, this is the President. I know that you're already in the middle of an important operation, but I need your help."

Bobby looked down at DJ and noticed a fleck of blood on his own boots. He tucked his foot under the unconscious doctor and pulled it out quickly to remove the spot with DJ's shirt. "No problem, Sir, just getting my shoes shined."

"I need a job done ASAP."

"Happy to be of service, Sir, what can I do for you?"

Chapter 6

A rough hand tugged on Kyle's collar and jerked him up to a sitting position. He was then shoved back up against the wall between Laurel and the wounded Number Seven. He turned his head toward Laurel as the rebel with the digital movie camera came right up into his face. The eye of the camera, added to the small but bright light atop the device, made him feel instantly uncomfortable. He felt even more uncomfortable because he knew that the wireless, digital camera was connected to a computer in the corner of the room. As he looked at the equipment, he realized that the stage was set for another Internet horror.

The guard with the rifle that had followed the cameraman throughout the room broke off his pursuit and moved in toward Laurel. He slowly rubbed his knee across Laurel's shoulder as he grunted from behind his face-covering scarf.

Kyle looked around. He noted that there were four Kodiaks left. Beside himself, there was Laurel, Number Five, and the wounded, barely conscious Number Seven. All were bound hand and foot. On the Iraqi side of the ledger, there was the cameraman and what seemed like his own personal guard, the two guards who constantly watched the door, and the rebel who had decapitated Number Six. Finally, there was the English speaking rebel who had just answered some Arabic commands over the walkie-talkie he had placed atop a small table.

Kyle didn't like two-to-one odds, with his side being tied up, so he turned back to Laurel and shot a questioning look in her direction.

She squinted at him through the tight grimace on her face as she tried to ignore the advances of the Iraqi guard. The guard grunted again through his scarf as he bent down to place his covered face closer to Laurel's. She involuntarily let out a shudder as she realized her defense, comprised of chiefly body language, wouldn't work or protect her if things went further. She looked into Kyle's face and gave an almost non-existent nod.

Kyle understood the meaning and carefully gauged the time to make his move. The guard had already made Laurel extremely nervous, but if he decided to rape her, Kyle would somehow have to step in. He surveyed the room again and took note of where all of the rebels were stationed. He considered rolling back to his right, making a mental note of kicking out with both legs into the side of her head and breaking her neck. He also thought of reaching out and getting Laurel's head between the outstretched lines of his bound hands and snapping her neck in a deadly headlock.

Kyle slowly turned his head back to look into Laurel's face. He parted his lips slightly and spoke softly through clenched teeth as he tried his best to look no more animated than a ventriloquist.

"Say the word." His parted lips closed together again.

Laurel's eyes squinted together and then relaxed into their normal shape in a parody of a head nod as the growling guard placed his crotch into her face.

The cameraman spoke something short in Arabic and motioned to her before he walked over to take more footage of Number Six's remains. As soon as he had moved away from her, the guard pointed his rifle downward as he tugged at his zipper with his free hand.

Kyle very slowly turned his shoulders toward Laurel as he mentally prepared himself to mercifully take the life of one of his own team.

* * *

MONDAY 18:41—NORTHERN IRAQ, 10 MILES EAST OF BUNKER

"We sent Double Joker home on another bus and should be at our new target within fifteen minutes. Arrange for an air strike all around the compound. I want them to hear a lot of noise inside the complex. I want dust raised outside of it, along with any possible guards or recon resistance being cut down as much as possible." Bobby sat in the front seat of the Hummer beside his friend, PFC Joe Manelli, while he talked into the dashboard microphone. He held it with his right hand while his left clamped the headset against his ear.

Bobby shook his head several times. "Yeah . . . that's right" and finally, "Okay." Just then a large bump in the road interrupted the conversation and caused them to momentarily leave their seats before they bounced back down to their previous positions.

"I'm still here." Bobby shouted into the microphone over the roar of the Hummer engine as well as the small armada that followed behind him. "So give me five straight minutes of bombing, then halt for sixty seconds and resume bombing. The enemy will think it's a natural lull in the strafing, not knowing we're going in during that lapse. The noise from the second bombing will cover us going down the corridors to the captive room." As he spoke, Bobby reviewed the latest images from the Monocle that were delivered to his palm pilot. The images showed a detailed layout of the building, which even included the enemy guard positions and numbers.

Joe reached over with one hand and gave a thumbs-up sign to congratulate Bobby on his strategy. He then gripped the wheel with both hands as their vehicle traversed another small bump.

"But remember," finished Bobby, "this is a nuclear complex." He emphasized the word *nuclear* by raising his voice in volume so that there could be no mistake as to what he said. "I don't want a single brick touched on that building. But I wouldn't mind several *pricks* getting knocked over on the outside." He grinned at Joe. "Over and out."

*   *   *

General Tabler nodded from his seat in the back of the Monocle tracking room. He held his phone tightly as Sumner updated him on the situation. He nodded again and then asked, "Where did your political avenues lead you, Sir?"

"Davis was able to track down some info and it turned into a dead end." President Sumner made the curt reply.

"Are there any other avenues that we might pursue?" Tabler continued to crack his knuckles nervously as he spoke. He really didn't care about other options, but the anti-war stance that Sumner usually kept made him difficult to work with. He asked not out of courtesy, but out of necessity.

"Well, we're working on other possible scenarios, but further military action is beginning to look like our only answer." Sumner spat the words through the phone as if they were distasteful to him. "Leamon Davis is helping with the first angle. He's already called in a few favors and received a reply from the other side. Although his part might be too little too late."

Tabler sat in silence as he continued to listen to his Commander-in-Chief. *Good, a military option is the best option,* he thought. *These people only understand force.*

"I'm beginning to think our best chance to help those soldiers may lie with another force of men about twenty miles outside the hostage site. I've ordered them to take the complex using military means." Sumner sounded confident as the Commander-in-Chief for the first time since the mission had started.

"Is that wise, Sir? We know the rebels have already killed two of our Kodiaks at hostage site ground zero." Tabler couldn't resist playing devil's advocate against Sumner's suggestion to use a military option. *Yet another President who thinks that Bobby Handle is the ultimate silver bullet who can solve all of the world's problems.*

"Well, Tabler, to tell the truth, I agree with you," came back Sumner. "But since the earlier mission of ours went to hell, what have we got to lose?" His confidence seemed to grow with each statement.

"Yes, Sir." Tabler's voice appeared energetic over the phone, but his face melded into a study in puzzlement. After a few seconds, he quickly regained his thoughts and offered up a suggestion to the President. "Well, we can't let Major Handle take on every radical and renegade by himself, can we Mr. President? You did say earlier that he was *already* in the middle of another operation."

"Yes." Sumner's one word response sounded almost as if he'd asked a question.

"Then I'm going to make some calls and try to get our men some extra air support to push through that rebel front to the west of the complex. I know it won't come in time to initiate the formal rescue, but maybe we can get there in time to relieve Major Handle's forces and to help in the occupation of that area and the complex." Tabler cracked his knuckles on his hand that held the phone when he quickly stopped, not sure if the President could hear the cracks over the line.

"Good idea, Tabler," the President said with gusto.

"Oh, Mr. President, is that thrust by Major Handle currently under way?" Tabler's voice was tinged with apprehension as he cracked a knuckle on his other hand.

"Yes, General, I called him about an hour ago. Why do you ask?" Sumner probably wasn't as concerned as he made it sound.

"Because, Sir, if I'm going to get those troops of ours some more air support to bust through that front in time to help Major Handle, I'd better sign off and get things in motion. Time is being wasted, Sir."

"Fine, General," agreed Sumner. "Make it happen. I need to get off the phone and figure out how I'm going to keep the reporters at bay for another few hours."

Tabler hung up his phone and shook his head in the process.

"God indeed looks out for fools and liberal presidents who are in over their heads." Tabler was still shaking his head when he noticed the other people in the tracking room staring at him.

"Is there anything wrong, Sir?" One of the techs, still tracking the personal imaging chip from the Kodiaks called out from his post in front of his screen.

"We're going after the bastards who beheaded that soldier of ours, that's all. And we're going after them in a big way. I just got permission from the President to request additional air support to help our western front line troops make a hard push toward that site we're tracking. I'm going to make the call as soon as I get back to my office." Tabler turned toward the door that led out of the tracking room.

"Then God bless the President, General." One tech thrust his fist into the air.

"God bless our troops, too." Another nearby tech chimed in also.

"After the day we've had," said Tabler over his shoulder as he was almost out of earshot, "I hope God blesses somebody over there."

*   *   *

"No, no, no," shouted the English speaking Muslim as he grabbed the shoulder of the guard that hovered over Laurel. The guard spun around and a short heated exchange erupted between the two men. A few moments later, the guard walked away as the Iraqi rebel who halted the guard's sexual advances took a few steps toward Kyle and knelt down on one knee.

"I am sorry." His speech was still stilted and being brought forth slowly to help its user with its execution. He continued to speak through his mask. "I did not want all of this to happen. I was not even supposed to be here."

"Then why are you with this group?" Kyle shot forth the question.

The eyes behind the mask gazed almost blankly as the mind behind them seemed to process the words. "I don't like Americans taking over my country with their ways." The mask tilted forward as the man stared at the floor.

"That doesn't answer his question." Laurel was the one who remarked this time.

"War is one thing." He got that part out rather quickly. "But murder is not in any of our holy writings." His speech slowed again as he translated his thoughts into English.

"So what are you doing here?" Number Five finally risked talking to someone who had not directly spoken to him.

"I don't want to be here. But I must support my country." He had turned slightly to face Number Five directly. He added, "Yet, I don't want people hurt and my leader is a violent person." He nodded his head in the direction of the man still standing over the remains of Number Six, polishing his sword blade.

As he turned back toward Kyle, his eyes rested on the wounded Number Seven, who was fading in and out of a sleep state due to loss of blood. He spoke again. "This man needs help."

"We all need help . . . ." Kyle's words faded as he didn't know how to address the man before him.

A dark hand went up to pull back the mask, but before he could finish the motion, the walkie-talkie on his belt crackled to life. He diverted the direction of his hand and grabbed the device from his belt, pressed a button and spoke a few commands of Arabic into it. He snapped it back onto his belt and pulled the mask from his face.

It was a handsome face, with a lighter complexion than most Arabs. He had a neatly trimmed beard that surrounded a nose that was at once regal but without being prominent. The features seemed to fit well with the clear, intelligent eyes the group had already seen peering over the scarf he wore to protect his identity.

"My name is Ahlmed Mahkeem." His voice too, sounded more distinct without the muffled effect of the scarf. "Let me see if I can arrange medical things." He pointed at Number Seven's prostrate form.

He stood up and walked toward the leader. Moments after Mahkeem had asked him something, the leader of the rebel cell group waved his arms over his head as he brandished the blade in a dangerous manner. As Mahkeem's voice rose in volume to match his leader, the blade handler raced over to the wall where the captives were and grabbed Laurel by the arm. He yanked her up from her sitting position and dragged her to the center of the room where the last Kodiak had been beheaded. He attempted to say something else when everyone in the room froze as the sound of bombs exploded from right outside the complex.

Just then Mahkeem's device clipped to his belt made static filled sounds as an Arabic word came through the speaker. A few seconds later, the same sound repeated itself. Mahkeem reached for the device and then ignored it as he paid more attention to his leader.

An even louder sound of explosions came from outside, and without warning the blade handler threw Laurel down onto her knees and positioned his sword for yet another execution.

Another explosion sounded from outside the walls that caused everyone to freeze momentarily. In that split second, Number Five leaned forward and got enough momentum to stand up. He balanced for a second before he threw himself toward the leader.

Kyle saw what Number Five was doing. He quickly rolled to his right and dove toward the leader's legs.

He instantly heard three gunshots erupt which blocked out the sounds of the explosions from outside. His rolling dive had almost put him in a position to grab the leader's legs, but before he could touch them, the dead body of Number Five collapsed across his outstretched arms.

The cameraman appeared and spat on the dead body. The leader, too, looked down from where he towered over Kyle and spit. Then the lights from the movie camera turned on bright again as the recording device was pointed right at Laurel's face. The leader looked up to make sure the camera was on, and then positioned the sword under her chin.

Another explosion was heard from outside as well as the crackling from Mahkeem's belt communication, followed by the one word shouting out one more time. The leader steadied his blade and shouted, "Allah!"

Kyle heard the screams of Laurel become muted as the rest of the rebels shouted the name of their god in unison. Then suddenly, the leader of the rebels was silenced as a bullet removed his lower jaw and part of his larynx. He collapsed into a heap with no more than a gurgling gasp.

Kyle craned his neck in the other direction to see Mahkeem calmly firing a pistol in the direction of his rifle wielding guards. One died before he knew what was going on. A second had turned in Mahkeem's direction, but was cut down from the stream of bullets that erupted from the hand gun. The third guard actually got off a couple of shots, but they harmlessly hit the bunker wall.

The cameraman heard the first shot and moved away from his tripod-mounted camera as he tugged at his sidearm. Kyle, still partially trapped under Number Five's body, was lying right in front of the cameraman. He quickly brought both of his knees up to his chest and then kicked out straight into the legs of the cameraman. The rebel tilted forward as he lost his balance. Kyle bunched his knees again and lashed out this time directly under the cameraman's chin. The insurgent's head snapped back with such a crack that it drowned out one of the explosions from outside the building.

Within moments, Mahkeem had already pulled Laurel up from the floor and cut her bonds. Then together, the two of them pulled Kyle out from under the dead bodies, cut his bonds, and helped him to his feet.

Kyle quickly knelt back down and took Number Five's pulse. There was none. He scrambled on all fours over to where Number Seven lay. Kyle exhaled with relief as he found a pulse there. He would need to temporarily field dress Seven's wounds until they could find a way out of the nuclear complex.

He paused long enough to look at Laurel to make sure she was relatively safe and then asked Mahkeem one question. "Why?"

Mahkeem dropped the pistol onto the ground and held up both hands to the sky. "This is not war. This is not holy. This is only terror and evil. I did not know. I want no more."

Kyle paused and listened. The sounds of the explosions stopped as suddenly as they had started. After another second, he returned to tending to the unconscious Number Seven. He needed to save his soldier first. *I'm not going to lose another one.*

He continued to examine Seven when he heard the sound of scuffling feet.

Kyle glanced up at Laurel and Mahkeem as four men burst through the door.

Three of the four remained in a crouch, while the gray-haired, tall leader straightened to his full height and spoke. "Captain Kyle Bradly? I'm Major Handle of the special tactics unit." His pistol was pointed at Mahkeem the entire time he spoke.

"Yeah, I'm Bradly," replied Kyle gratefully. He then added, "But I'd put away your weapons, this man here is . . ." He couldn't think of a term or phrase to describe what had just happened.

He turned to look at Laurel as she finished his statement. "A man that just saved my life."

Chapter 7

"Thank you, Bobby. I knew that you were the right man for this mission. I'm just glad you were in the right place at the right time." President Sumner exalted into the inter-continental phone connection.

Sumner and Tabler had just returned to the Oval Office with Leamon Davis from an endless marathon of meetings that dealt with the public web-cast of the covert mission. Sumner had pulled Davis into the post-mortem not only because of the role he played, but also for some bipartisan support. Tabler and Davis remained silent as the conversation continued.

"Yes, I heard through other channels that the survivors of the mission were freed a little while ago, but it's good to hear it from you personally." Sumner paused as Bobby filled him in on the final moments of the rescue operation. The smile on his face seemed frozen until the reality of the situation crept back into his thoughts—*nine dead men, and no uranium.*

"I need you to do one more favor for me. Look into this situation and find out what the hell happened. The news networks are replaying and analyzing the web-cast like highlights from the goddamn Super-Bowl. I want to find out exactly what went wrong. I need a thorough report on the rebel from the video. The media is treating this guy like he's some kind of hero."

"I'm about to talk to Captain Bradly, Sir. I should have more information within the hour." Bobby's voice came through the phone so clearly that it sounded like he was in the next room.

"I'm looking forward to your report." The President lowered the phone into its cradle and turned to the men in his office.

Before he could say a word, General Tabler began. "I can't believe that the legendary Major Handle was upstaged by some rebel who found his conscience in the eleventh hour." Tabler smiled slightly as he continued, "I must admit, that was an interesting conversation coming from a man who was tagged, The Pleasant President, last year, don't you think?"

"Wasn't he also the President of Peace?" Leamon Davis sat in a chair just a few feet away from where Tabler stood at a state of almost rigid attention.

"So was Lincoln," shot back Sumner, "but he had to kick a little Southern butt first to bring this country back together." He looked down at his watch. It wasn't even noon yet, and he was already exhausted.

"That was a civil war though, Sir." Tabler gently cleared his throat before he made the statement as if that act alone might soften the controversial words to his commander.

"All right, then." Sumner waved a hand in Tabler's direction. "Kennedy signed an order to remove our troops from Vietnam in his attempt to achieve peace, but the year before he wasn't afraid to stare down the Russians outside Cuba over those missiles." He moved closer to where Tabler stood and held out his hand as if to say "stop," before he continued. "And don't tell me you don't remember that, General, because I think you were a low-ranking officer in the Army at the time."

"He's got you there, General." Davis smiled at the high-ranking officer before he turned to his President. "You've made your point, Sir, and there's nothing wrong with a little fact finding."

"I don't like that good men and women are put in a position to die by my order, here at home or anywhere else in the world." Sumner looked down at the floor momentarily and thought of the mission gone haywire. "Major Handle may not have been the on-screen hero the media's latched on to, but if he can tie up any loose ends for my own edification . . . ." He paused as he thought of the individual dead Kodiaks. "Well, let's just say it won't bring back the dead soldiers or help me sleep any better at night, but I'll at least know exactly *why* I can't sleep at night."

"As someone who's been in that position before, Sir, I totally agree with you." Tabler rocked back and forth on his heels, the light from the overhead lamp glaring on and off of the medals pinned to his chest with each motion. "Our tech teams already work twenty-four by seven to guarantee the safety of this country. The last thing we need is some nuclear situation blowing up in our faces while we're withdrawing our troops."

"I appreciate that, but getting back to this mission, the outcome is still unbelievable." Sumner shook his head. "The insurgents got taken out by one of their own," he paused for a moment, "and they basically televised the entire event to the world. I couldn't have written a better ending."

"The action by this rebel is highly unprecedented," replied Tabler. "I've never seen an insurgent waiver in his beliefs for even a second, let alone take out an entire cell just to stop an execution of an American female soldier."

Davis added, "Based on what I've learned from my contacts over the last day, this event isn't going to sit well with the JET organization. This reformed rebel of sorts has defiled them in front of their enemy. We should probably be on a national terror alert just in case JET tries to redeem its reputation."

"I totally agree with you, Sir." Tabler still stood at attention. "The terror alert has already been elevated and Homeland Security has doubled the on-duty personnel at all high-risk sites."

"What about the material that the Monocle was originally tracking?" Sumner pushed his glasses up a bit on his nose as he continued, "Do we have an update?"

"Nothing yet, Sir. But our intelligence teams are on it," replied Tabler. "We're also planning to ask our reformed rebel that very same question." Tabler thought for a moment about the strange twist of events that had just transpired. "You know, based on the large number of insurgents in Iraq, we really didn't have good odds that the one guy ready to switch sides would be in a position to help us."

Davis looked at Tabler and then back at Sumner. "I don't even want to think about the odds we just beat. About five years ago there were approximately 18,000 insurgents in Iraq." He gestured with his hands like a visiting lecturer who wanted to look more authoritative. "That number has almost doubled since then." His face wrinkled into a look of disgust before he relaxed and just shook his head.

"So that means around 35,000 to 40,000 of the Iraqi population wants to kick us out." Sumner still didn't register the direction Davis was headed, but he had a strong feeling he was about to find out.

"But it also means that an overwhelming majority supports the world's newest democracy." He had made his point.

"Including . . ." the General followed Davis' lead. " . . . the rebel who just became America's poster boy for friendship and harmony." Tabler was almost sincere, but his tone was laced with just enough sarcasm that it looked like he'd just suppressed a smirk.

"Let's not get carried away with anything yet," chided Sumner. "We don't know anything about this character. He could have done what he did to save his own skin." He wasn't surprised by Davis' point of view, nor did he agree with it. *Typical right-wing attitude*, thought Sumner.

"His motivation is still our number one question." Tabler walked over and looked out the window of the Oval Office. "By the time Handle arrived, this guy had already become a one-man rescue team." He looked liked he was still thoroughly gratified that Handle wasn't the hero of the hour.

"I'll have Major Handle check him out," said Sumner. Tabler may have held rank on Bobby, but Handle was someone who he could unconditionally trust to get things done.

"You know, Sir," said Davis. "This rebel may have given you an opportunity to put a positive spin on this entire situation. Let's face it, the media is already helping you. The networks aren't talking about hostage executions, they're talking about how the life of our female soldier was saved. In fact, the Entertainment Network has already put a romantic spin on the entire situation, if you can believe it."

"Wouldn't he be branded an 'Uncle Tom' by his own people?" Tabler rocked back and forth again.

"Technically, considering that region of the world, I think he'd be branded an 'Uncle Ahkmed' by his people." Davis turned to Tabler for some sort of reaction to his attempted pun, but Tabler kept a straight face.

"But not by the majority of his own country." Sumner's face lit up. He now knew exactly how to spin this entire situation. "And he certainly *could* be viewed as a hero by most of the American public." Maybe there was something to Davis' earlier love us/hate us Iraqi statistics. *Exit the Commander-in-Chief, enter the diplomat, I'm ready to do battle.*

"That makes my job easier . . . less warfare and more politics." Tabler nodded in the direction of Sumner. "It also makes my job a lot safer."

"I'll look into it," said Sumner as Davis stood up and headed for the door.

Davis' hand was on the knob when Sumner spoke once more. "You know Leamon, with solid feedback like this, you'd make a good addition to my cabinet."

Davis stopped, turned, and divided his gaze between Tabler and Sumner. "No, thank you, Sir, I like my work in the House." Davis smiled as he finished. "And besides, positive feedback or not, remember we're on opposite sides of the fence. Don't forget, I'm a Republican."

*   *   *

MONDAY 19:30—NORTHERN IRAQ, JUST OUTSIDE BUNKER

"Sorry about the interruption." Bobby gave the phone back to the communications officer with one hand while he adjusted the brim of his sandy colored baseball cap with the other. "But the President of the United States is always a call I feel I should take."

As he turned toward Kyle and Laurel, both of them had blank stares on their faces. He remained still and looked at the two of them for a moment or two. He sensed the bewilderment of the pair before him.

"No, really," his face became more animated. "That was our President. He personally asked me to look after the both of you."

Laurel exhaled sharply. "Thank God. I guess it pays to have friends in high places."

"You can thank God if you want," said Bobby, "but my team was a few minutes late. If you're really feeling grateful, you should thank Allah, because I think that's who your new rebel buddy prays to, and he's the one who saved you." Bobby pointed to Mahkeem, who was still in the back of the troop-transport truck parked just outside the bunker. He had been placed under guard from the moment Bobby's team arrived.

"Too bad he didn't find his religious stature a couple of hours earlier." Kyle shook his head from side to side. He looked grateful and disgusted at the same time.

"I guess in this country we'll take the good where we can find it." Bobby sounded like he was going to start to preach, but only added another few sentences. "I've been in this country more than a few times over the last couple of years and the populace is somewhat divided on our occupation. I'm just glad things are turning out as well as they are."

"Hell, the mission didn't even turn out at all." Kyle shook his head from side to side.

"Why don't the three of us talk about that while we go for a drive? We've only got a few more minutes of daylight." Bobby pointed to a nearby Humvee and walked over to the driver's side. Kyle and Laurel followed him to the vehicle and entered from the other side.

In less than ninety seconds, the vehicle had made its way across the two hundred yards of sand to the scene of the Kodiak firefight. Bobby pulled the Humvee onto the side of the road and killed the motor. The sun had just set on the desert, bathing the sky in a spectacular array of colors. As the colors faded into darkness, the soldiers reflected on the mission.

"Anybody know how it started?" Bobby got out and walked toward the center of the small battlefield. The body recovery team had already done their work, but massive amounts of shell casings littered the ground and large patches of sand were still colored red with blood.

Kyle responded, "Number Seven was the only survivor from the second team, and by the time he reached us, he was already in a partial state of shock from his wounds and loss of blood."

"They put up a hell of a fight." Bobby turned his head and fixed his gaze upon the three still smoldering Iraqi trucks parked on the far side of the road.

"I'm sure Big Brother taped all of their comments." Laurel tilted her head forward to shield her face from the sun.

"I'll listen to those when we get back to the States." Bobby kicked his boot at an unusually high pile of spent casings. "Hopefully, Number Seven will pull through, and I can get his first-hand account."

"They got a lot more shots in than we did." Kyle's voice sounded grim as he spoke.

"But there were different circumstances, from what little I gathered." Bobby sounded almost apologetic for the Kodiak leader.

"Exactly." Kyle's tone had shifted to a mix of sarcasm and disbelief. "There was no one to shoot at when we got into the building, and we were instantly ambushed on the way out."

"And damn little to do in-between." Laurel added in a clipped tone.

"What do you mean by that?" Bobby stated the question in earnest. "Did something take the mission down while the team was inside?"

"The mission objective disappeared." Laurel snapped her fingers to emphasize the point. "One minute we had fissionable material, the next—it's lead shielded and gone."

"Yeah, Major." Kyle chimed in, taking over the story from his fellow Kodiak. "It vanished through an underground transport dock. It happened right under our noses, or in this case, right under our feet."

Laurel took up the story once again. "The rebels couldn't have timed it better. Everyone else was already gone. The building was abandoned, and we showed up just as our target was being loaded up and driven off through the back door."

"Considering that the rebel front was crumbling only two miles away, maybe whoever was running this complex figured it was time to save the ingredients for an atomic weapon." Bobby turned back toward the vehicle and climbed in. "Anybody want to talk to the hero of the hour? He might hold a clue into why things went snafu."

The Kodiak duo piled in as Bobby retraced his route back to the complex. He pulled up next to the truck that held Mahkeem and parked. As he jumped out he had already formed some questions for the reformed rebel, but he was immediately interrupted by the communication officer with a phone.

"Sir, the President would like to speak with you again."

Bobby took the phone and placed it to his ear. "Yes, Sir?" It was a question and a salutation all at once. He nodded a few times as he listened, but he wasn't quite sure what to make of Sumner's request. "I understand." After Sumner had finished, Bobby ended the conversation with a terse, "I'll be in touch." He handed the phone back to the officer and walked over to the open end of the truck.

He pulled a small notebook from his pocket, thumbed through some pages and spoke to Laurel's savior. "Mr. Ahlmed Mahkeem, I believe. I hope I pronounced it right?"

"Yes," answered the Iraqi rebel with a concerned nod.

"Have you ever seen the Statue of Liberty?" Bobby let loose with a tiny smirk as he asked the question.

"No." Mahkeem formed the word in an utter state of confusion, not being able to fathom the meaning of the inquiry.

Bobby let an honest grin escape from the tiny smirk. "Would you like to?"

Chapter 8

The Army transport plane had been in the air for several hours. Bobby had used most of that time to talk casually with Kyle and Laurel. He considered most of the time spent as nothing more than a chance to get to know them. He then used another hour to gather information on the mission. As they walked him through the details of the past twenty-four hours, Bobby took notes on everything, but he was especially interested in their interactions with Mahkeem.

After an hour, Bobby left them to get some rest, but he decided to check on the condition of Number Seven first. Army medical personnel in the rear of the plane cared for the wounded soldier in the small airborne hospital. Bobby approached the person who seemed to be the lead doctor.

"How's he doing?"

"Considering he has two bullet holes in him and he's lost a lot of blood, I'd say he's in pretty good shape." The doctor's optimism seemed genuine.

A corner of Bobby's mouth turned slightly upward in an approximation of a smile when he spoke. "Well, it doesn't hurt when the Army sends one of its bigger planes to pick us up after they've gone to the trouble of transforming it into a flying hotel. We've got first class up front, complete with meals and comfortable seats. Amenities for our new friend in the middle, and a portable hospital in the back." Bobby pointed and gestured to the different areas as he named them.

"That has more to do with you than anything else, Major," began the doctor. "I had heard the President ordered all of this for you and your guests. We were going to keep the patient in one of our military hospitals in the Middle East, but once he stabilized—"

"Someone thought it might be safe to send him home?" Bobby questioned the doctors' theory. He always agreed that it was preferable to send an injured man home if at all possible.

"Let's just say that when someone does something to help out our Commander-in-Chief, he likes them to travel in comfort."

"You have that right." Bobby thought about the way the doctor referred to the President. Sumner would have cringed if he'd heard somebody refer to him as the Commander-in-Chief. Bobby had worked for more Presidents than he cared to remember, but Sumner was by far the most anti-war President of the bunch.

"By the way, Doctor, is the patient able to speak yet?" Bobby peered past the doctor in the direction of the wounded Kodiak.

"Certainly. He's stable, and we've got some blood back in him, making his prognosis excellent. Just try to keep the conversation short, he's still weak." The doctor spoke softly and motioned to the bed just beyond where they were talking.

"Understandable." Bobby turned from the medical man and approached the Kodiak. He picked up the patient's chart and looked it over briefly. The soldier noticed Bobby and turned his head toward him.

Bobby put on a friendly face as he walked to the side of the bed. "Your chart says that you're getting better." He paused while he searched the chart for the soldiers' name. "Lt. Robert Sinden. That's a coincidence, since my first name is Robert also. But my friends call me Bobby." Bobby stuck out a hand toward the soldier's wrist that wasn't pierced by needles and tubes.

Sinden grasped Bobby's hand with his free one and squeezed as hard as his current energy level would allow. "Major Bobby Handle?" The Kodiak twisted in his bed slightly to allow himself a better view of Bobby

"Yes, why do you ask?"

"Major Bobby Handle always seems to be the man of the hour, from every hot spot, skirmish, and undeclared war since Vietnam ended. Say, how *did* you find out about that plot to kill the first President Bush? That's become a Kodiak training staple that most of us think of as more legendary than factual." Sinden's eyes seemed to light up as he talked.

Bobby put a finger up to his lips. The motion seemed to accent the still friendly face that the high-ranking soldier had adopted.

"Shhh, no one's supposed to know about that one, at least not anyone in the general public." The words were stated in a loud whisper.

"Well, it certainly is a pleasure to meet such an important man." Sinden hit the button on the bed's remote to raise him into more of a seated position.

"We're all important, Lieutenant." The friendliness drained out of Bobby's face as he thought of all the battles and dirty jobs he had been involved with over the years. "And we've all been chosen to perform important tasks."

The wounded Kodiak nodded his head in agreement even though he wasn't sure if he was. "I can see your point."

Bobby continued with a blank look. "Now before I have you use up all of your strength, I've got to ask you a few questions."

"Go ahead." Sinden said in earnest. Just the mere presence of Bobby seemed to energize him.

"I've been to the location of your firefight. There's a hell of a lot of spent shell casings and some smoldering trucks that'll never be used again except as maybe scrap. How did it go down?"

The Kodiak answered in a strict military fashion. "Our mission objective was to provide support for Team One who was invading the complex to look for hot material. We were to arrive separately at the complex in order to avoid detection or ambush. Two hundred yards to the east of the complex, a rebel convoy came across our position. We scattered and hit the sand, blending in with the landscape as best we could."

Bobby was impressed with Sinden's ability to calmly report the mission in such detail while still weak and in pain.

"It turned out that the convoy only stopped so that one of its people could jump out and take a leak against this huge boulder by the side of the road." Sinden looked down at his own crotch as he spoke, probably thinking about his catheter.

"I saw the rock. It was fairly close to your position. Could he have heard you?" Bobby was matter-of-fact in his tone.

"No way. The coinciding minutes on our throat mike tapes should show that there was total silence."

"So in all of Iraq," began Bobby again, "you think it was this specific boulder that this rebel decided to hose down?"

"Coincidences can happen." Sinden's face was starting to look drawn.

"I agree." Bobby thought for a moment. "Coincidences *can* happen, but when you study them closer, you'll always find that a number of factors removed most of the elements of chance."

Sinden looked puzzled as well as drawn and tired during a moment of silence.

Bobby continued. "I think Einstein was the one who stated that mathematically speaking, there were no true coincidences."

"You think something's wrong?" Sinden's voice seemed a trifle weaker. His increased energy from the excitement of Bobby's presence had now almost worn off entirely.

"No, nothing seems out of place. The President just asked me to bring up some hard questions, so I'm asking. After all, it's not like I haven't hosed down a few rocks out there in the desert myself." The friendly face took up residence once more as Bobby gave the Kodiak a quick salute and turned away.

He looked in the direction of Ahlmed Mahkeem. He wanted to talk to him next, but saw the three men in dark suits with him, all of whom were engaged in intense conversation. He wasn't sure what kind of information they might get out of the Islamic rebel who had helped the Kodiaks, but he knew he could wait until they had finished.

Bobby requested a soda from one of the army personnel stationed aboard the plane. When the private returned, Bobby thanked him, took a sip, and leaned back against the seat until the back of his neck rested on the top of the seat cushion.

His mind drifted back to all the other times he had been left to wait. Bobby knew the "Hurry up and Wait" mentality was a common source of humor that the enlisted men had toward the rules and regulations of their armed forces. He closed his eyes and thought back to the many other times he had been engaged in what he referred to as the "art of waiting."

He remembered waiting on the curb for the moving van to come and pick up his family's belongings. His father had just gotten a job in a new school system to teach band and music. His father switched jobs a number of times throughout Bobby's childhood, but that always meant waiting once more to pack and unpack his toys and possessions, not to mention the wait to make new friends in yet another city.

After he graduated from high school he joined the Army, the first few years of which flew by quickly. Basic training led to promotions, which led to assignments and more action. He didn't fear his military missions, but he did have a strong fear of inactivity. He never wanted to be in a position where he might settle down, and his military life seemed to be just the answer. As soon as he'd gotten comfortable in a location, he was always ripped away into another part of the world.

Bobby dozed lightly as he remembered yet more waiting. There was the wait for his flight to land in Duluth, Minnesota, after he'd received the news of his mother's death. He remembered it was flight number seventeen that he was traveling on. He could always remember numbers and facts, but sometimes struggled with people's names.

Later in his life, he waited for missions more often than he was actually assigned to one. The Army had recognized his ability to solve problems and beat tough odds, so they saved him for special assignments. By the time he had reached the rank of top Lieutenant, Bobby had already become a troubleshooter for one President after another, a career that was well over twenty years in the making.

Bobby eventually waited out the pain of his mother's death. The deep heartache went away, replaced by a constant, wistful nostalgia, but the passing of his father was another matter entirely. He'd died too recently for the feelings to be buried or filed away. Bobby had a pervading sense of waiting in that instance, too. He waited for the cab to get him to the hospital in time once he'd been notified of his father's impending demise.

Bobby remembered as he bound through the hospital doors after he paid the cabby for driving him through the heavy mid-day traffic. His thoughts raced back to the helplessness he felt as he couldn't wait to get up those stairs to his father's room.

Bobby's found out later from one of the nurses that his father, too, had been waiting. He'd been waiting as he held on for dear life until the son that made him so proud could be with him. In his mind Bobby saw the door to his father's room burst open in front of him as he saw the old man with the oxygen mask turn toward him.

A slight smile of recognition washed over the haggard face a moment before a painful gurgle erupted in the man's throat. The fragile head leaned back onto the hospital pillow and was still.

The picture in Bobby's mind grew dim, as he knew that he would never have to wait for anything again, nothing that affected him personally anyway. There was nothing left to wait for that could hurt him anymore, and it was his choice not to marry or have children. He would never force anyone to ever have to wait for him either. Of course he had been involved with a number of women over the years, but most of those relationships amounted to nothing more than a one-night stand.

Sure, he'd still have to wait for an assignment from his commanding officer, or even the President, but that kind of wait allowed him to prepare for the ensuing missions that always seemed to arise. Of course, there was usually danger associated with the kind of tasks that he had been given over the years, but he had been well trained. Preparation was always the key to minimizing risk. Being prepared had kept him alive over the last two decades of service. To him there was no *real* waiting anymore, only time to prepare.

Although the transport plane was cool inside, Bobby opened his eyes as he felt a bead of perspiration trickle down from the corner of his left eye. He sat up, leaned forward and took a huge gulp from the can of soda.

"Major!" The sound of his rank designation being hailed made Bobby quickly turn.

"Major!" The three men stopped beside Bobby as he rose from his chair and gave them his undivided attention.

"Are you done with him?" was the only form of greeting Bobby gave the trio.

"Yes, Sir," stated the man in the middle. "He's not giving us much other than he was horrified by the beheading and that's why he changed sides in the middle of the situation."

The man on the right broke in. "He told us that his primary job was to set up the computer for the web-cast. We also got a report from the CIA identifying him as a Baghdad University student who is fairly intelligent. He joined this JET group after he saw a threat by Western influence to his country. He hasn't been on any of our 'keep watch' files, because he's a fairly new player. He's moderate and not half as extreme as the others in the past that we've been able to question."

"I would agree that a moderate wouldn't have the same stomach for beheadings that some of the fanatics do, so that makes some sense." Bobby had learned over time that levels of faith varied in all religions. He'd encountered Islamic followers that rarely even prayed, let alone blow themselves up for religious reasons. He put his left hand on his hip and turned to directly face the threesome.

"Agreed," stated the only one of the three who had not spoken yet. "But even though we're using kid gloves on him, somehow I don't get the idea that he trusts us."

"Hell," snorted Bobby softly, so that only the trio could hear him, "I *know* we don't trust him, so I guess things are even." He glanced over at Mahkeem. *What did the rebel want? Why take a chance just to save a female American soldier? Weren't women considered just above property in his culture?*

"He's all yours." The original member of the trio spoke this time, breaking Bobby out of his thoughts.

He only nodded as he made his way past the three men toward Mahkeem. He sat down beside him, which made the rebel turn quickly in his seat.

"I'm Major Handle." Bobby didn't bother to extend his hand. "I want to thank you for saving the lives of my fellow soldiers."

"I only did what I felt was right." Mahkeem seemed agitated and instantly became aggressive in his mood toward Bobby. "Questions, questions, questions."

"We've got questions, but believe me, the President himself believes in you. That's why you're going to Washington." Bobby was as polite as he could be.

"I saved your soldiers, and now I am your prisoner. I betrayed my own people, who will now consider me an infidel. They will now try to kill me." Mahkeem almost pleaded as he talked.

"That's something that we'll also look into." Bobby spoke slowly. He wasn't sure how good Mahkeem's English was.

Mahkeem leaned even further in his seat toward Bobby before he spoke again. "I can tell that you are a good man. You show me respect, unlike the others who were questioning me." He motioned to the three men in suits. "Because of that, there is one more thing that I must tell you."

A quizzical look spread across Bobby's face. "I don't understand what you're trying to say." He gestured for Mahkeem to continue.

"I know the next . . ." Mahkeem paused and thought about the next word.

"important . . ." was the only word he could muster.

"person . . ." Bobby was getting very interested now.

" . . . to be killed."

Chapter 9

"That is the situation up to this moment."

The close-up on the beautiful, thirty-something female news anchor crowded Sumner's television screen. Her sandy-blonde hair waved gently around the sides of her head with each word that she spoke. As he continued to watch, Sumner had a feeling that he was about to get slammed. Even so, her perky nose, delicate chin, and beaming smile could have had her in the lead in any beauty contest. When the camera panned back to reveal her stunning figure, her fierce, intelligence-filled, blue eyes still demanded his attention. *Or was it the fact that she was getting ready to talk about him?*

"My opinion is that President Sumner must act now to rectify the heinous acts seen within the last twenty-four hours live over the Internet. Last year one of his campaign slogans was, 'Peace with Power.' And with the bill he signed upon taking office, Americans know how dedicated he is to peace. But with the tragic events of the last day, we now must see how he wields that power. And finally, the question that many Americans are asking—When will the identity of the Iraqi rebel who saved the lives of our soldiers be revealed?" The newswoman's face was stern as she spoke her customary tag line. "This is Jennifer Rayburn for the Washington desk."

Sumner fingered the *off* button on the television remote with one hand as he tried to button his shirt with his other. He finally had to place the remote control unit beside the television so he could devote both hands to the task of dressing himself. *Davis was right, the media can't get enough of the Iraqi rebel.*

"Looks like the media is having a field day with this one." As he spoke, the top button finally popped off and bounced under his bed. He lifted the comforter and looked quickly to see if he could find it but gave up after a halfhearted search that lasted all of five seconds. He shrugged his shoulders and took off his shirt. "You know, times like these make me wish I had never met that girl back at Boston College." Sumner heard a gentle laugh.

"But from what you've told me, meeting her was the best thing that ever happened to you." The response from the adjoining bathroom was offered up in a female melodic voice that was as soft and sweet. In fact, Sumner had many times complimented the First Lady on her speaking voice.

"I know." Sumner used his debate tone to continue the mock argument with his wife of twenty-two years. "Hey, I wanted to be a history professor, and she made politics seem so damned interesting that I changed my career direction." He picked out a different shirt from the rack in his closet and continued his dissertation. "Ah, yes, Cynthia Hawthorne and her double major in poly-sci."

"Don't you think it might have been Cynthia Hawthorne by herself without the political science that turned your head?" Cynthia popped her head into the room and raised one eyebrow to form a quizzical look.

With a smirk in his voice, Sumner capitulated. "That might have had something to do with my career change."

"Don't tell the thirty-two percent of the populace that didn't vote for you about that. They'll burn the poor girl in effigy." Cynthia walked out of the bathroom, her combed hair and make-up showed off a still-fresh, girl-next-door type look even though she was in her late forties.

"She has nothing to fear." Sumner smiled at Cynthia. "The sixty-eight percent of the people that did vote for me will protect her." His further thoughts on the matter were cut short by a tight hug and warm kiss that showed that the First Lady still was quite passionate about her husband after two decades of marriage.

The couple's lips parted and Sumner looked directly into his wife's green eyes. "Besides, if the people who voted me in couldn't protect her, the Secret Service would. After all, that's their job, isn't it, Cindy?"

She playfully pushed him away. "Yes, and they're doing a wonderful job of it." She walked over to the bed and sat down. Her eyes twinkled at her husband's face as she patted the space on the bed next to her. "The airtight security they've placed around you gives me peace of mind, and allows you the freedom to spend some worry-free time with me."

"But what about your breakfast with the American Literary Society? I don't want to mess up your hair." Sumner formed the words as an inquisitive statement more than an outright question.

"Well I guess we've found something that even the Secret Service can't protect—but I'm willing to risk it," she answered in a playful tone. "Besides, you're already half-way there."

Sumner's quizzical look was the only answer he gave his wife.

"You're already half undressed." Her gentle persuasion continued. She moved in closer so that her face was only a few inches from his.

"I guess you're right," started Sumner. "Between campaigning on the road last year, then—"

The phone by the bed rang. Cynthia took a step back and crossed her arms. As usual, their moment had been interrupted.

Sumner never bothered to finish his sentence, but instead held up a hand to his wife, quickly walked over to the bedside, and picked up the receiver.

"Hello," he said tersely.

A few seconds of silence passed in the bedroom. Cynthia walked over next to Sumner and took a peek at the caller ID on the phone. The unit displayed an unlisted cell number.

"Bobby, what have you got for me?" Sumner felt relieved as he recognized Bobby's voice through the earpiece. There was never any bullshit with Handle—just the facts.

There was a long pause as Sumner listened to Bobby's description of the recent conversation with Mahkeem. As Bobby continued, Sumner's eyebrows scrunched together into a frown-like gash.

He stared back at Cynthia, who searched his face for a clue to the conversation. Sumner was well aware that she knew when Bobby called, something serious had just transpired. *Again, she's right.*

"I'll contact the Prime Minister." Sumner hung up the phone and quickly dialed another number.

*   *   *

TUESDAY 14:25 GMT—LONDON, ENGLAND

The slight, cool breeze wafted across the downtown London rooftop and lifted the bangs from the forehead of British Commando Captain Bartlett Hobbs Junior. He hadn't used the "junior" part of his name once his World War II veteran father had passed away some years back. Even so, some of the old-timers at headquarters would remind him that he was not the original, highly decorated by the Queen, Bart Hobbs. So sometimes the "junior" part was still brought into play even though he had just passed his fortieth birthday.

Hobbs walked quickly along the top of the building and peered constantly over the edge. Other Commandos prowled the rooftops on both sides. Only an hour before, his commander had received a priority call from their American counterparts that alerted them to a possible attempt on the life of Britain's Defense Minister. The message also conveyed the method of murder . . . a sniper rifle from a nearby, high-rise building.

Three such buildings matched the criteria. Hobbs had placed himself atop the middle of the nearest structure where the Defense Minister, Kent Sinclair, would exit.

Sinclair had just finished a closed "Parliament only" speech that concerned Western and Middle Eastern cooperation in the world. After the completion of the meeting, he was to head directly to Heathrow airport to confer with his counterpart in America on the same subject. Hobbs' primary objective was to make sure that he made it to his flight . . . alive.

Hobbs adjusted his headset to position his mike closer to his lips. "Is everyone in place?"

His earpiece buzzed with the replies.

He stood on the edge of the building and attached the metal snap to his belt that was situated right below his Kevlar body armor that covered him from shoulder to waist. He turned to see the rope line secured around the base of the roof's chimney. He turned back to peer over the edge toward the street below when he heard the loud "crack" of a rifle blast.

The Defense Minister's entourage had barely exited the building across the street when the weapon was fired. Hobbs saw the man in the middle of the group clutch his chest and stagger backwards to the pavement. A voice from one of the spotters hidden along the street below rang out in his earpiece.

"It's your building, Captain. There's a slightly cracked window two over from the middle and three floors down from the top."

"I'm on it," was Hobbs' only reply.

He turned to his left and ran ten paces along the edge of the building before he threw himself over the side and out into space. Seconds later, he squeezed hard on a clamp with his left hand in order to slow his descent down the side of the building.

The fast action of the clamp brought him to a jarring halt, made somewhat smoother by the hard, rubber, bungee-type harness he wore over his protective vest. As quickly as he stopped, gravity took over and pulled him toward the building face. He twisted in mid-air and pushed his legs out from his body to cushion the impending impact.

He saw the crack in the window where the shooter must have taken aim. *Smart,* Hobbs thought to himself. *The window still looks closed from the ground, but it's open enough that he didn't have to shoot through the glass, which would have alerted the police on the street.*

Thank God for eagle-eyed spotters. Hobbs' pendulum motion pushed him through the glass window. He slapped his right hand across his chest to hit the release catch on his harness, which fell away from him as he tumbled across the hotel room floor.

As he came to a kneeling position on his right knee, he was surprised to see two shooters in the room. One held the rifle while the other opened the weapon's case. Hobbs could instantly see that he had the upper hand. The pair looked surprised if not totally shocked to see a British Commando kneeling before them, pistol in hand, mere moments after they had pulled the trigger ending a man's life.

"Drop the weapon, get on the floor!" Hobbs shout was loud in volume, but still clear enough for both of the snipers to understand.

The man on the left held a rifle case. He peered hard through a slit-like part in his long, stringy, blonde hair. His pale, white face instantly flushed with anger. The man on the right held the rifle. He was a bald, chunky man who had no look of emotion partially because of the wide wrap-around sunglasses strapped to his head like goggles.

Hobbs was about to shout his command again when the bald sharpshooter turned, with rifle in hand. At the same time, the longhaired man dropped the case and clawed for a gun butt secured in his belt.

Hobbs took care of the most immediate threat and shot in the direction of the rifleman. He hit him in the left side, and the bullet traveled upward into the man's lung area. The rifle, though, was still turning toward him. He looked at the size and weight of the perpetrator and realized that one bullet was not going to be enough. He also knew that his own body armor wasn't meant to fend off a high-powered rifle slug at close range.

Hobbs pulled the trigger two more times. One bullet hit the chunky sniper in the side, another in the neck. The rifle stopped twisting toward him as the fat man went down.

Unfortunately, the extra shots had allowed the longhaired member of the sniper team to pull his weapon from his belt. Hobbs knew he wouldn't have time to bark an order to the hit man. Instead, as soon as the third of his shots entered the fat man, he fired in the direction of the blonde gunman. The bullets hit the second gunman in the right shoulder, just below the throat, and the left shoulder. Before he died, the man was only able to get off one shot of his own, which sped harmlessly over Bart's left shoulder.

A moment or two of silence and Hobbs heard a voice in his left ear.

"Stone the crows! Are you all right up there?" A moment or two of silence before the voice added more. "Don't answer back if you're the sniper."

Hobbs closed his eyes and tried to relax in attempt to slow his pulse. "Arthur, if I were a sniper, I wouldn't be answering anyway, you twit, I'd be running like hell to escape the clutches of that crack squad of yours on the street." Hobbs breathed a sigh. Arthur Beamon, along with Jockey Miller, were the two members of his commando squad who had been with him the longest . . . eight years.

"How's our 'victim' doing down on the street? I hope our precautions saved him." Hobbs let a concerned streak creep into his speech.

"I'm nobody's victim, if you please. The extra layer of Kevlar, not to mention the thin sheet of steel I placed between the two, has more than proved adequate." Jockey's voice seemed indignant that someone should actually hint that he might have been injured taking the place of the Defense Minister—the type of job for which he always volunteered.

"That's good." Hobbs made his way toward the doorway in search of a lift to the street. "I'd hate to deprive you of your fun." He reached the end of the hall and decided on the stairs instead. As he descended two at a time, he said into his headset, "Now that our friends in the colonies have helped us save one of our own, all we have to do to return the favor is . . . ."

*   *   *

Somewhere over the Atlantic Ocean, Bobby slipped his cell phone back into his pocket. He turned toward Mahkeem, who had saved both British and American lives, and spoke plainly. "Mr. Mahkeem, I'd like to ask you a question?"

Mahkeem put down the fig cookie in his hand and turned to Bobby. "Yes, please feel free."

"Since the function that the British Defense Minister was leaving was a private government affair, how did your organization know where to place the gunmen?"

Chapter 10

"We go to a live feed in ten seconds, folks," shouted the line producer of the WKDC news network. He held up splayed fingers on both hands as one finger after another curled back into his palm in a crude form of countdown.

Jennifer Rayburn was seated behind her news anchor desk, the one she shared with veteran reporter, Baxter Jameson. Just a few years earlier, when the three major networks had retired their top national anchors within months of one another, she remembered that she had been touted as the next big "voice and face of news." She had felt that she was more than ready for the challenge, but the powers behind the scenes wanted the beautiful and knowledgeable television reporter to gain some experience behind a more worldwide hot seat. As it turned out, none of the major cities, such as New York, Los Angeles, Chicago or Miami appealed to her as did the Washington, D.C. desk. From there she could still cover and comment on events from around the world. Stationed at the nation's capital, she had quick and easier access to Presidential briefings and conferences.

During the first year, her handsome and more experienced co-anchor, Baxter, had taken her under his wing to show her how to hold down the anchor desk in a major news city. She had quickly taken to her new post, complete with a style that mixed commentary along with the news, rather than after it. This different style, sanctioned by the producers, showed important people within the industry that she was no "Barbie" doll reading from a teleprompter, but an adept woman who had made the show her own. Now, Rayburn and Jameson, as they were billed, were no longer viewed as the novice and the teacher, but as the woman who was going places and the older, big brother.

"Live in five," the line producer counted down aloud for everyone on the news set to hear.

Jennifer arranged a sheaf of papers in front of her as Jameson adjusted his glasses. She always felt a slight rush just before the camera light went on. *God, I love this job.*

"We are live in three, two, one." The line producer continued the verbal subtraction for the news crew.

Jameson glanced at the monitor that spelled out the words in bold type, SPECIAL REPORT, before he turned his gaze back to the front teleprompter.

"Go!" The man with the headphones yelled as he pointed his finger toward the two anchors.

"This is Jennifer Rayburn, along with Baxter Jameson, with a live report concerning a situation that has unfolded within the last hour from London, England." She kept her face stern and grim to convey that the newsflash was indeed an important story.

Jameson took over for the next few seconds. "Information has been released concerning an assassination attempt on England's Defense Minister Sinclair. The attempt was thwarted within the last hour by British Commandoes."

The verbal tag team match continued as Jennifer then took up the story from Jameson. "A pair of snipers was killed in a firefight after missing their target, British Defense Minister Sinclair. Sinclair had just exited from a speech he had given to select members of Parliament."

Jameson read the next line. "It was also disclosed that information gathered to help the commandoes in their capture of the snipers came from a source in Iraq."

Jennifer then went into her commentary. "If this inside information is true, then can we speculate that this source in Iraq might not even be in that country anymore? Could the source of that life-saving information now be flying over the Atlantic Ocean as we speak, headed for our shores?" She paused to let her words sink into the minds of the viewers. "If this *is* the case, then there are now two grateful nations that can count saved lives due to the bravery of a reformed Iraqi rebel. Could this be the dawn of a new age when West and Middle East can put aside their differences? Can people from two different sides of the world join over the common ground of humanity?"

As she finished her commentary, Jameson cut back in. "This has been the latest news report of unfolding events. As we get more information, we'll be back to let you know." He paused. "This is Baxter Jameson."

"And this is Jennifer Rayburn."

The red light mounted on the television camera turned to black and the line producer shouted, "We're off the air!"

Jennifer bolted from her seat and turned to her colleague who was still seated. "I'm getting a mobile crew and heading out to the airport. Are you coming?"

"Somebody has to stay here and look important for the camera if anything else breaks on this story."

"That's true." Jennifer agreed without any argument.

"Why run out to the airport?" Jameson inquired as he turned in his chair to face her. "You're big enough in the industry. Let the story come to you."

Jennifer walked away as she answered loudly over her shoulder. "I like to dot my *i*'s as well as cross my *t*'s to go along with the 'truths' in my commentaries."

She saw Jameson nod in agreement as she climbed the stairs that led to the parking lot level of the building. She was on her way to another big story and another of her *truths*.

Jameson stood up from behind the anchor set. "There goes our Lois Lane."

Jennifer knew he couldn't see her expression, but she smiled at the reference. *Too bad there isn't a Superman in this story,* she thought as she exited the building.

*　　*　　*

The technician worked continuously at the computer workstation. Every few minutes he'd pull a silver disc from the machine, label it, and then replace it with a blank one.

"Are you almost done?" Tabler asked impatiently. He knew he'd already made him nervous, but he really didn't care.

"Yes, General." He turned in his seat to give Tabler a salute of respect. "As soon as Major Handle arrives, he'll have his own personal copies to review of everything that went down on the mission."

"Excellent," stated Tabler. "I think this Mahkeem is the real thing. And if that's the case, who knows, we might have more allies over in that hellhole than we think."

Tabler exchanged salutes with the technician and then walked away. As he exited the room, he added a casual, "Carry on," to his departure.

*　　*　　*

"I thought your organization preferred to kill enemies through self-sacrifice to gain rewards in the afterlife. I didn't think you practiced sharp-shooting with rifles." Bobby was matter-of-fact in his conversation.

Mahkeem, who sat next to Bobby, was just as unemotional in his response. "Americans are now too much involved in placing all of my people in categories. I think you call it racial identification?"

"Racial profiling." Bobby understood where Mahkeem was going with the discussion.

"Yes, so rather than be stopped or captured before any of our missions are completed, we hire other professionals that do not ask questions to do the tasks for us."

"Holy crap, you outsource terror." Bobby's face turned to disgust as he thought of the true horror that something like that idea encompassed.

Mahkeem's face seemed puzzled as if he couldn't understand the term. He turned his palms upward toward Bobby in a gesture of confusion.

"You hire others to do your killing for you. You rent terrorism." Bobby almost spit out the sentence.

Mahkeem looked lost in thought for a few moments. His head nodded slowly in some sort of partial agreement with Bobby's last statement. "You Americans are too good now at what you do. There is mistrust from your country toward every dark-skinned man with a beard. So I have heard this is the new way for us to be effective. When we hire Europeans for certain tasks, they prefer weapons over bombs and self-sacrifice." Mahkeem showed no joy or complacency as he told Bobby the type of plans that the terrorists used.

"That still doesn't answer my other question. The meeting in England was private, so how did your people know about it?" Bobby forced the issue.

"I can only guess that leaders higher than my cell commanders would have knowledge of that type of information. My role was only to encrypt and deliver information through the Internet. That is all I know."

"If you were the one encrypting and transmitting the information, you had to be aware of the details." Bobby didn't try to hide his tactics as he attempted to get answers.

"I have not been a member for long, but I do know that all of the details of any mission are not sent together. I only transmitted what I have already told you." Mahkeem continued, "Remember, I joined because I was educated and did not understand why the Western ideas were taking over my country. But as I saw violent murders and beheadings take the place of idealistic resistance, I changed my thoughts. There is no place in my holy writings where this type of action is acceptable. Is it in yours?"

"No." Bobby never thought of himself as a deeply religious person, but he'd seen enough killing in the name of religion for multiple life times.

"I can help you with things . . . more information, if it will help to save Iraqi lives." Mahkeem's eyes pleaded for a second chance.

"Maybe you can tell me and my leaders more about you and your leaders. That might help." Bobby kept his tone non-committal.

"I will try."

"Good." Bobby paused a moment and thought about the timely information that Mahkeem had supplied. "You know you saved a person's life in Iraq and you saved a person's life in England. Now you might even get to save a third person's life in America if you keep telling the truth."

"Whose life would that be?" Mahkeem now looked confused again.

Bobby peered past Mahkeem's shoulder and through the glass window. Framed perfectly in his field of vision, he spotted the bright glow of sunlight reflecting off of the Washington Monument in downtown Washington, D.C. He leaned back in his seat and buckled his safety belt before he turned to face Mahkeem.

"Yours."

Chapter 11

The door of the plane slid open and a rush of Army personnel led by Bobby burst forth down the stairs that led to the tarmac at Andrews Air Force Base.

He knew that the Pentagon, as well as the CIA, wanted a chance to speak with Mahkeem as soon as the plane touched down, so a direct flight to Washington had been ordered. Andrews was the airport of choice due to its close proximity to the Pentagon. The base had played host to military leaders, prime ministers and even kings and queens for well over a half century, but was probably best known as *The Gateway to the Nation's Capital*, the home of Air Force One. In addition to the Air Force, the base also acted as the home for more than sixty other organizations including the Army, Navy, Air National Guard, and Marine Corps. Many people actually considered the base to be a city within itself due to the incredible number of people that worked and lived there.

As the unloading passengers reached the base of the stairs, twenty invited reporters from the White House Press Corp instantly besieged the group.

An older reporter that Bobby thought he recognized from CNN was the first to ask a question. "How do you feel now that you're back on American soil?"

Another reporter yelled from behind the CNN reporter. "Were you tortured?"

"Do you know the extent of the injuries to the wounded soldier?"

"Were you sexually assaulted?"

Bobby couldn't tell where the questions were coming from—just that they were coming too fast, and the time wasn't right. He had told both Kyle and Laurel that the White House would try to spin their situation so they'd need to be prepared for the media's response. As they walked, the two Kodiak soldiers looked shocked by the aggressive reporters. They had worked on covert missions, so neither of them had ever received any public acknowledgement for their service. *I warned them,* thought Bobby, *not that it seemed to help.*

Kyle and Laurel walked in front of Mahkeem along with a host of other security guards. They took Bobby's advice and ducked their heads as they quickly continued toward their waiting transportation. Bobby acted as a buffer between the plane's passengers and the press as he fired back terse answers to questions about what had transpired over the last three days.

"Was the Iraqi rebel from the Internet the one who supplied the information that saved Britain's Minister of Defense?" The CNN reporter led the pack of reporters.

Bobby replied, "Yes. The man who saved our soldiers did supply vital information on the British attack."

"Do you trust him?" A blonde reporter with a New York Times badge pushed her way past the CNN reporter to get closer to Bobby.

"I can say this," retorted Bobby as he stopped to face the reporters, "Ahlmed Mahkeem's actions have saved four lives over the past two days, and I'm proud to have him on our side." He paused for a moment before he added, "We've had a long flight. No more questions." Bobby threw his hand up and took a few steps backwards before he turned and walked back to the waiting transportation.

As the wave of reporters dispersed, he heard a familiar female voice hail him. "Major Robert Handle!"

He slowed down as he turned in her direction. He instantly identified the face, not as one recognizable to an entire television demographic, but as one with which he was personally familiar—Washington news anchor, and national news correspondent, Jennifer Rayburn.

"Ms. Rayburn." Bobby pulled her further away from the other members of the press. "Just because we had a few drinks in Baghdad last year, doesn't mean you're going to get an exclusive."

"It was more than just a few drinks, Major Handle." The beautiful television anchor stared into Bobby's eyes. "I can think of at least one dinner that we shared before we retired to my own private spa where we—"

"How could I forget?" Bobby spoke in a deadpan voice, as if the experience was neither enjoyable nor disappointing. "The Al-Hamra hotel is still a favorite hangout for journalists in the Baghdad Green Zone." His face was as motionless as his voice was flat. *Why did she have to be here? No emotions,* he told himself, *just keep this business.*

"The atmosphere was almost surreal in its effect." She smiled as if to draw Bobby deeper into the conversation. "You would think that you were in one of the finer hotels in London, New York, or Paris."

"Except for the AK-47 tracer bullets that keep flying across the night sky, reminding you that you're still in a war zone." Bobby almost surprised himself with his reply. Jennifer looked really good, but he didn't have time to revisit what happened last year. *Although, he was going to be in town for a few days . . . .*

Jennifer shook her head from side to side with exasperation. "You really know how to destroy a mood, don't you?"

Bobby turned away. "Look, I can't stop to talk. I've got a guest of the nation to escort to safety." He kept an emotionless face. "If you need a sound bite for your show, you'll have to contact the White House Press Secretary."

"Oh, I've done better than that, Major." Jennifer's face almost beamed with the knowledge that she thought she had the upper hand in the discussion. She held up a sheet of paper faxed directly from the White House. Bobby took a quick look and recognized the electronic signature affixed to the bottom.

"That's his handwriting all right." Bobby still hadn't moved as much as an eyebrow. *This isn't good,* he thought, *I don't want to be alone with this woman, although . . . .*

"I believe he's also your Commander-in-Chief." Jennifer looked as if she were suppressing her smile from becoming too *I told you so.*

Bobby pulled a slip of paper from his back pocket and a stub of a pencil from his front pocket. He hastily scribbled a few notations for Jennifer.

"We're staying at the Royalview Suites for a couple of days while Mahkeem makes his rounds with the CIA and the Pentagon. This is the room number. The other two numbers are the rooms where the two freed soldiers will be staying. I'll leave word so that you'll have limited access to our floor." He paused long enough to let his eyes narrow to a slit. "I want you and only you to show up. But give us about forty-five minutes to get settled in first."

"Actually, I've already got a room about two floors down from yours. I checked in earlier today." Jennifer's smile was even more visible as she finished. "I'll also need my cameraman."

Bobby finally looked pissed. "Bring a digital camera and a recorder. You can do a split screen voice-over." He gave a quick wave and jogged back to the waiting transportation before she could utter another sound. The mission had just gotten very interesting. *Too interesting.*

After they'd piled into two vans, the vehicles, heavy with Army personnel, made their way across the tarmac and through the nearby fenced gate. People stood on both sides of the airport entrance. Some of them held signs and placards. A few were derogatory, but most were supportive, complimentary of the new Iraqi hero.

Bobby let out a long, slow breath as he mentally reviewed his previous encounters with the American media, especially the one with Jennifer Rayburn. "It seems like the media has come out full force for this. I guess I'm not surprised based on the amount of airtime that the web-cast has been given." He peered through the window to his right to get a good cross-reference of most of the hand made signs.

"Will I be safe?" Mahkeem looked puzzled as he searched Bobby's face for a clue.

"You will be as long as I'm around." Laurel put her two cents in. "You saved my life."

Kyle came into the conversation next. Besides the debriefing comments, he hadn't said much since the end of the mission, and the very act of speaking made Bobby turn back in his direction.

"Who knows, Mr. Mahkeem?" Kyle used an upbeat tone, but it still sounded as if his mind was someplace else. "With the proper training, we might even make you an undercover Kodiak."

*   *   *

President Sumner threw down the sheaf of papers he had just perused and looked up at General Tabler and John Babare. He leaned forward as he kept one hand on the chair's armrest while his other toyed with a pen located on the desktop.

"The polls are in, gentlemen," started Sumner. "After the media ran the story about the foiled sniper attempt in England, and that our Mr. Mahkeem was the one to supply the information, I have a feeling he might be able to successfully run for Time Magazine's *Man of the Year*."

"Mahkeem has definitely made my job easier," said Babare. "He's basically changed the entire tone of this situation overnight." As Press Secretary, Babare had faced many challenges over the last year, but none of them had even come close to the media attention of the last few days.

"Yes," agreed Sumner. "But now we need to focus on how to take advantage of our reformed rebel's fifteen minutes of fame. We finally have an Iraqi that most movie-going Americans can relate to."

"He could very easily be a public relations gem for our country to see that both nations can work together." Tabler had finally joined the conversation. "But only if their insurgents start seeing some light!"

Babare leaned forward and raised an eyebrow. "What about an on-camera meet-and-greet at the White House? Britain has already extended a similar invitation for Mr. Mahkeem to meet with the Prime Minister. We could—"

Before the Press Secretary could finish, Tabler interjected, "A medal would actually make a lot of sense in this situation, sir. Let's give the press a perfect photo-op and at the same time send a message of our appreciation."

After a few moments of contemplation, the President nodded. "I agree. A medal ceremony at the White House with an extended list of press core members in attendance would be the best way to maximize Mahkeem's quick rise to fame." He then continued, "It would also give me a chance to add proper closure to this event, and continue with my campaign promise to keep pulling our troops out." Sumner paused for another few seconds before adding, "And who knows, maybe this entire ordeal will actually raise my approval rating. It never hurts to add a percentage point or two."

"Good idea, Mr. President, although I believe your current approval rating is already quite high." Tabler was enthusiastic in his praise.

"Calm down, General, flattery won't get you promoted, you know. You're already as high up as you can go in rank." Sumner displayed a campaign smile as Tabler laughingly agreed in a perfunctory fashion. *Amazing what a difference a day can make*, thought Sumner. *Maybe I wrote this week off too soon.* As he continued to think about his stressful week, he finally understood how FDR did it—the World War II President must have savored the victories, no matter how small.

Babare still smiled from Sumner's last comment. "Mr. President, shall I inform your speech writers that you have a new ceremonial speech to deliver?"

*   *   *

"A driver will be at your disposal." Bobby stated dryly to Kyle. "If you need anything else, call for room service. The media's got all of us under a microscope right now, so let me know if you need to leave the building for any reason."

Bobby turned his back and headed for the door to Kyle's suite. When he opened it, he found Laurel in the hallway.

Kyle shot out a quick, "Thank you, sir," as Bobby closed the door behind him.

Outside in the hallway, Bobby switched his attention to Laurel. "At ease, soldier."

Laurel quickly fell in step behind Bobby as they made their way down the hall to the next suite. When they reached the entrance, he stopped and turned to Laurel. "You probably heard my instructions to Captain Bradly. The same goes for you. Try to get some rest. Things are going to be a little crazy for the next few days. There are going to be interviews and most likely a press op with the President. After that, you'll just have to play it by ear."

"Yes, sir," Laurel saluted.

Bobby waved off the salute. "I'm going to check on our reformed rebel." He turned and walked further on down the hall.

After he'd passed a few more rooms, he came to a halt before two armed guards stationed on either side of a door. "Why don't the two of you go get something to eat, I'll baby-sit our guest. Besides, we're going to be interviewed shortly, and the floor is totally locked down."

The men nodded in appreciation and promised not to be gone long as they headed for the elevator. Bobby inhaled a deep breath before he opened the door and entered into the new and temporary home of Mr. Ahlmed Mahkeem.

*   *   *

Agent Belfore pressed the elevator *up* button a second time as he waited in the Royalview lobby with Jennifer. Belfore had already explained that he was one of five CIA agents assigned to secure access to the hotel's upper floors. After another few moments the bell rang to signal the arrival of their vertical transportation. The polished metal doors opened smoothly, and Jennifer stepped in with her CIA escort.

Belfore inserted his cardkey into the reader on the right side of the elevator control panel. With the card still inserted, he punched in a quick series of numbers on a small numeric keypad adjacent to the reader. After he'd typed in the final number, the button assigned to the seventeenth floor lit up.

"So our new friend gets an entire floor to himself?" Jennifer already knew the standard security protocol, but couldn't resist a conversation with her emotionless companion. She had encountered a number of agents of whom she was convinced weren't trained by the CIA, but built by them in some remote robotic lab.

Belfore pressed the button for the seventeenth floor and turned to Jennifer. "Standard operating procedure for any important guest of the American government. Floors seventeen through twenty-one are locked down with key access only. The elevators in this bay are the only ones that are programmed to access these floors."

As Belfore finished the statement, Jennifer could have sworn she had just listened to a prerecorded message played back at a slightly increased speed.

Belfore tried to speak again, but he was interrupted as the elevator doors suddenly reopened to reveal a second CIA agent. He stood next to three men, one of which held a large television camera.

"Agent Belfore, would you mind taking these three up with you? They'll also be interviewing our guests for their network." The second agent reached in and held the elevator door open

"Not a problem." Belfore stepped toward the back of the elevator.

Jennifer thought to herself—*Was Belfore his name, or was he model number, BEL-4?*

She moved to the side of the elevator to allow the three men room enough to enter. She noticed almost immediately that the cameraman's camera had a large *Bridges TV* logo on the side of it. She also noticed that he'd checked her out about three times since they'd entered the elevator.

"The first U.S. Muslim lifestyle network in English." Jennifer once again initiated a conversation as the elevator doors closed for the second time. "Your network has done well. I personally feel that you've achieved your goal to be more objective than your competitors."

The man who was most likely the lead reporter turned to her. "Thank you. You are very kind. I am a very big fan of yours, Ms. Rayburn. I enjoy your commentaries and agree with much that you have to say."

Jennifer nodded her head and smiled. "I'm just trying to keep things interesting."

As she studied her cable competition a bit closer, she noticed that the men were all neatly dressed and clean-shaven. The lead reporter sported a white knit shirt and wore way too much cologne. His two-man support crew, which consisted of a cameraman and probably some type of production assistant, wore blue T-shirts with the network's logo on the back. The cameraman was much taller than the other two men, and at first glance, she almost didn't notice that all three were of Arabic descent.

"That camera's a bit outdated, don't you think?" Jennifer referred to the somewhat large size of their camera. The cameraman stared back at her chest until she finally crossed her arms.

"Although we are successful, we have a much tighter budget than that of a major network," replied the Arabic lead reporter as the elevator came to a stop.

"Floor seventeen." Belfore pressed the button to keep the doors open.

Jennifer exited the elevator and headed in the direction of Laurel's room while the Bridges' crew headed straight for Mahkeem's. She wanted to speak to the Kodiak members first so that she could get a feel for what they had experienced before Mahkeem had saved them. As she walked, she shook her head and quietly spoke to herself. *Don't bring a cameraman, he tells me, just you and you alone. Well, Bobby, what about Team Bridges over there with Mr. Pervert camera-guy?*

*   *   *

Mahkeem rose from his chair as Bobby strode into the living area of the large suite.

"Please, there's no need to stand." He motioned for Mahkeem to sit back down. "Be comfortable, you're free to do most anything. We'll let you stay here and enjoy yourself. To the American public, you're a hero." He tried to sound relaxed and upbeat so that Mahkeem would feel safe and appreciated.

"I only followed my inner moral instincts." Mahkeem seemed earnest as he spoke.

"My President is grateful for your convictions and your actions. The fact that you were caught on tape saving an American soldier has got everyone in this country talking. That's why he'd like to have you interviewed on television by Jennifer Rayburn. She'll give you a chance to tell your story to the entire country."

"My English should be good enough. The more I use the language, the quicker the words are coming back to me. I took many classes in Baghdad that were actually taught in English."

"Good," replied Bobby. "By the way, are you hungry, we can get—" Bobby was cut off by a knock on the suite door.

Bobby nodded his head. "That's probably her now." He turned toward the door. "Come on in, it's open."

The door slowly opened to reveal three men. Two of them wore blue T-shirts, while the third was dressed in a white shirt. Each man held a long sharp dagger. As one, the trio took steps toward Bobby.

Chapter 12

Joe Manelli took one last drag before he flicked his cigarette into the sand. The cooler night breeze carried the butt across the desert until the hot ember disappeared from view. He and Bobby had been paired together on several missions over the years and he knew they were good friends. Bobby had always said that one could measure a friendship by the number of shared life and death experiences—which meant they must have been really close. When the President called for Bobby to personally look into the hostage situation, including the aftermath, it came as no surprise that he would be asked to stay behind to look for anything out of the ordinary.

The Kodiak troops were safe, but the uranium was still missing. Joe spent the entire day in search of a clue that could lead them to the missing material. He had already been to the nuclear facility and found it strange that although it was a suitable complex for minor atomic testing, it gave the illusion that it was more of a barren laboratory than a working one. He had taken several digital photos of the complex and sent them back to Washington for further analysis.

Joe had finished his work at the bunker a half-hour ago. He now stood at the site of the firefight that had involved the second strike team. Between the two sides of fighting, he was amazed at the amount of cartridges spent. He shook his head as he thought, *If the Texans would of had this much ammo at the Alamo, they could have held out for a year instead of only two weeks.*

"Hey, Joe!" The loud shout broke his thoughts. He looked up and saw PFC Mark Lexton wave to him from inside the wreckage of one of the Iraqi trucks that had been destroyed in the fight.

As Joe walked over to what used to be the side of the truck, Lexton propped up a blackened piece of equipment that was the size of a computer laptop upon the passenger side window.

"What's that?" Joe was honestly curious.

"You're not going to believe this." Lexton tilted the device to its side. He peered into the bottom of it, turned it around, and stared into the other side. "I think it's one of our tracking devices."

"What do you mean?" Joe crossed his arms and gently bit his lip. He knew of at least a half dozen different tracking devices and GPS locators that were used to navigate through the desert.

Lexton stared back. "It's one of those portable devices that keep track of soldiers through the chip implants in their neck and shoulders." He sounded almost mechanical, as if he almost didn't believe his own statement.

"Where the hell did they get technology like that?" Joe uncrossed his arms. The cool desert seemed to grow ten degrees hotter as his jaw dropped open. He hadn't found a clue to the whereabouts of the uranium, but as far as national security was concerned, this discovery ranked a close number two.

"They got it from us. They either bought it or stole it." Lexton held the tracker up to give Joe a better look.

"Are you fuckin' with me?" Joe shook his head in disbelief as he grabbed the unit to inspect it himself.

"No, I'm not, look right there." Mark pointed to a place on the charred device. "The goddamn thing has an American serial number on it."

Joe let out a sigh of exasperation. "Oh shit, Bobby's going to want to hear about this."

*   *   *

"Do you want to interview us separately or together?" Laurel opened the door to let Jennifer enter. Laurel had been on countless high-risk, high-profile missions, but she looked surprisingly nervous in front of Jennifer.

Kyle stood next to Laurel in the doorway to the room and motioned for Jennifer to enter.

"Together is fine," replied Jennifer. "I'll try to make this as painless as possible. You both look like you could still use some rest." She could tell from their tired faces that they probably didn't feel like an interview after the last three days.

"No problem," replied Laurel. "So what do you think of Mahkeem? Was he nervous during his interview?"

Jennifer stepped into the room. "I don't know. I haven't met with him yet. I wanted to start with the two of you. Besides, the television crew from the Bridges Muslim network is with him right now."

Kyle gave Jennifer an inquisitive look. "You're the only interview scheduled for today. I'm positive that Major Handle said you had an exclusive, compliments of the White House."

Jennifer shrugged her shoulders. "Well, they had CIA clearance, so somebody with some serious clout got them in." She went to close the door to the room when a dull thud, followed by what sounded like a wrestling match echoed down the hallway from the direction of Mahkeem's room.

Jennifer stepped back into the hallway. Her eyes darted first toward Kyle, and then back down the hallway. A number of grizzly thoughts flashed through her mind as the sounds of a struggle echoed through the floor. "That doesn't sound like an interview."

*   *   *

As the three men came at Bobby, he retreated a few steps and scanned from left to right with his eyes to keep the trio in full view. All three men were expressionless, but the two in blue T-shirts seemed to get their cues from the one in white. He also noticed that as the men advanced on him, they eyed Mahkeem intently.

"Ahlmed!" Bobby commanded. "Lock yourself in the bathroom now!"

No sooner had he shouted the words, than the tall assassin in blue broke ranks from the other two and headed for Mahkeem. As he did, the other two made straight ahead thrusts with their weapons aimed directly at Bobby's chest.

Bobby lunged to his right to elude the pair of blades. He threw an elbow into the tall assassin who tried to race by him toward Mahkeem. He caught him high on the shoulder and upset his center of gravity enough that the assassin tumbled to the floor.

Bobby's momentum carried him past the fallen knife wielder, but he was able to stop himself as he grabbed onto the corner of the heavy love seat. With both hands, he quickly spun around and faced the remaining attackers who continued to rush toward him.

The shorter assassin suddenly halted and reared his right shoulder back as he balanced his dagger in his palm.

Bobby dove for the man and shouted, "Get down, Mahkeem," even as he plowed through the space that separated them. He hit the assassin and knocked the dagger from his hand. The blade spun and fluttered as it sailed toward Mahkeem.

A split-second later, Bobby heard a yelp of pain from behind him. As they landed in a heap in the middle of the suite, he dared a quick glance over his shoulder. He had knocked the dagger off of its deadly trajectory enough to save Mahkeem's life, but the blade had still cut through part of the ex-rebel's right arm and his chest. Mahkeem's shirt was already damp with blood when Bobby turned back to the assassins. He hoped it was a minor wound, and he was relieved to see Mahkeem stagger into the bathroom and close the door behind him.

That brief distraction gave the assassin dressed in white time to turn around and brandish his dagger in Bobby's direction. More so, it gave the tall man who he had knocked to the floor time to get up and advance on him.

Bobby flung himself off of the blade thrower, rolled to his left and bounced up to a full standing position. As he looked at the trio, he cursed himself, because he had left his pistol belt back in the transport plane. The blade thrower jumped to his feet. The three of them crept closer as Bobby stood his ground and squeezed his hands into tight fists.

The short assassin in blue stopped and spoke in Arabic to the tall one. He shifted the dagger to one hand while he made a slicing motion with the other. The large attacker on the far right then turned toward the bathroom where Mahkeem had barricaded himself.

At that instant, Bobby hurled himself at the man who gave the order and got his body under his raised dagger. He slammed the assassin into the wall, and then with his left hand, shoved the man's wrist with the dagger into the wall as well.

The assassin's fingers opened from the pain, and the blade slipped from his grasp. As it did, Bobby spun around so his back would be toward his adversary. He then drove his elbow deep into the man's gut, and as the groan of anguish trumpeted from behind him, he clutched the falling dagger in mid-air and hurled it underhanded at the tall assassin who was still headed toward the bathroom. The blade caught him high in the side of the neck. Without a sound, he collapsed to the floor.

The assassin in the white shirt stood almost transfixed in his amazement for what had transpired in a few seconds. He and his fellow intruders had the upper hand on their mission, but now one of their numbers was dead and another on the ground, temporarily incapacitated.

Two down, one to go, thought Bobby.

The last remaining assassin in white charged straight at Bobby's midsection, dagger point first. Bobby sidestepped the thrust like a matador as the eighteen-inch blade went by him and imbedded itself into the plaster wall. Bobby then countered with a strong roundhouse knee kick to the man's lower groin. The attacker fell to his knees with a high-pitched scream.

Although Bobby thought that his last action would have stopped the assassin, he was surprised to see him grab for a knife hidden in his belt. He squinted hard as he noticed the position of his attacker's head to the imbedded sword. He also knew there weren't a lot of options.

Bobby grabbed the side of his opponent's head and forced it toward the lip of the dagger blade. Using his hip as leverage against the dagger, he forced the man's head over the top of the blade's edge and pushed down. The attacker screamed in a desperate sound that Bobby had never imagined he'd hear in his life. That's when he realized he was wrong. He remembered the recent execution displayed over the live Internet feed. Using the assassin's hair as a grip, he began exerting downward pressure with his arm and shoulder. His elbow rocked steadily back and forth as the screams turned to wet gurgles.

Bobby suddenly felt overwhelmed by a wave of emotion. "I thought your kind liked beheadings."

He let go of the bloodied head when he heard the man behind him moan again. He turned to his left and looked down. His last opponent was also slowly pulling a long knife from his belt, but his groan of pain had given his intentions away.

Bobby balanced himself on his right foot as he raised his left in readiness for a deadly strike. With his foot now hovered over the last living assassin, the man's eyes grew wide as fear overtook his facial features. The knife still lay across the assassin's stomach as he shifted his weight in preparation to make a move against Bobby.

The assassin screamed and pulled the knife upward toward Bobby's lower stomach.

"Not today!" Bobby shouted back as his left foot came down hard on the intruder's hand to force the blade back into the man's own stomach.

Bobby looked down at his ever-reddening pants. They had become sodden with the arterial spray from the half-decapitated man on his right. He turned to his left and looked at the man he had just killed, the blade sticking out of his mid-section.

"I didn't think you guys had the stomach for this kind of fighting."

Chapter 13

The door to the suite swung violently open as Kyle, Laurel, and Jennifer burst into the room. The trio quickly made their way across the large foyer to the corner near the bathroom.

"Major!" Kyle was almost at his side when Bobby warned him back with a sideways flinging motion of his right arm. Kyle and both of his female companions halted in their tracks.

Bobby reached down to his left and quickly tore a strip of cloth from the assassin's shirt. He twisted the cloth and tied a makeshift knot around the kneeling man's ruptured neck. As he tightened the cloth, the blood flow slowed to a trickle.

"Don't worry, I'm okay. I just didn't want any of you to take a plasma shower." Bobby continued to tighten the knot.

Kyle turned to Jennifer. "Do you want to wait in the hall?" His facial expression showed that he was either shocked or impressed by her non-reaction to the gory scene.

She casually looked back at him. "Don't worry about me, I've seen worse than this. Ask Major Handle."

Bobby looked back in Jennifer's direction and shook his head. This wasn't the way he'd pictured getting reacquainted with her.

"Where'd this pack come from?" Laurel asked.

"I'm not sure," responded Bobby. "Mahkeem said he felt he was in danger by turning his back on his country and helping us. Looks like he was right."

Jennifer kept her eyes focused on Bobby, but occasionally glanced at the dead assassins. "I rode up with these guys in the elevator. They said they were from the Bridges Television Network. But if they weren't reporters, how did they find out where Mahkeem was?" Jennifer asked the questions as if she were already on the air in front of millions of television viewers.

"I think it's pretty obvious, Jen, but in a way, it has to do with your profession."

"I don't follow." Jennifer ignored the fact that Bobby used a more intimate form of address and waited for his answer.

"A live Internet feed showing a beheading is a lot like a national broadcast. Regardless of what else is being televised on cable channels elsewhere, you're going to get a majority audience. And if that audience happens to include a radical Islamic cell with certain sympathies, someone might want to kill our newfound hero. For all we know, this cell may even have a direct connection to Mahkeem's splinter group."

"But so quickly, I mean all of you just returned from the airport. They also had to have clearance to get to this floor." Jennifer still played the anchorwoman.

"The sleeper cells are becoming incredibly resourceful. They're attempting to integrate themselves into every part of our society. The media attention surrounding this incident gave them an opening, and they took it. Our country has a ton of nationalities within it. Remember it's the great melting pot. So in this case, part of it has boiled over."

"How'd they know where? The CIA has kept your location on a need to know basis." Jennifer could have been cutting a promotional piece for the eleven o'clock news.

"I'm just making an educated guess off the top of my head, but I think they were just following the money." Bobby walked toward the bathroom and knocked on the door. "It's all right to come out now, Mr. Mahkeem, you're safe."

"Following the money?" Jennifer repeated Bobby's statement, as the other two stood mute and looked curious.

"You're a well-known media personality. They probably saw you with me at the airport. They figured it might be worth it to keep an eye on you in case you got a chance to do an interview with me or Mahkeem."

Now even Jennifer was silent.

"They followed you straight here." Bobby didn't smile in any form of smug satisfaction. He turned his head as Mahkeem exited the bathroom with his hands pressed tightly against his upper chest.

Mahkeem looked around the room as he joined the others. "I have betrayed my people. This will probably not be the last attempt on my life."

"Well, we're going to do our best to make sure there isn't a second attempt." Bobby moved closer to Mahkeem. "Let me see that if you don't mind." He gently pulled the Iraqi's hand away to see blood seeping from a slight wound.

Kyle stepped into the hallway for a moment while Bobby attended to Mahkeem. A moment later, he returned with the large television camera that the assassins had carried. The lens of the camera had been removed to reveal a long, narrow cylinder that ran the length of the camera.

"I'm guessing this is how they got those daggers past the security screening downstairs." Kyle pointed to the cylinder. "Not to critique these guys, but I would've packed something with a little more heat than three daggers into this camera. What about—"

"*No way* they would have gotten a gun past that security check," Laurel interrupted. "The CIA was using a K-10 filament scanner. It's the next generation electronic equipment duster. The K-10 not only picks up chemical residue, but can also identify any number of explosive compounds, gunpowder included."

"And that's why you're a Kodiak number two hazmat specialist, and I'm a Kodiak number one. Remember, you handle that crap, and I don't," Kyle reflected.

"You should see the specs for the K-11, it may even be able to detect C-4." Laurel turned to Bobby. "But what I really want to know is what happened to the guards that were posted, sir?" She took another quick look around the floor and surveyed the carnage that Bobby had wrought single-handedly.

Bobby shook his head and let a look of disgust cross his face for a moment. "That was my fault. I let the guards go grab a bite to eat." The look of disgust was replaced for a fleeting second with one of sheepishness. "I won't make that mistake again." He knew better, but he'd felt distracted since his reunion with Jennifer. *Get over it*, he said to himself, *you can't afford to be sloppy . . . not now.*

*   *   *

Ahlmed Mahkeem sat on the stainless steel table and took a deep breath. He repeated the act and looked straight ahead before he turned his attention toward the pleasant and kindly voice.

"One more deep breath, please." The Iraqi doctor moved the stethoscope across Mahkeem's ribs to his back and then pressed it.

The doctor removed the device and clipped it around his neck. He picked up a nearby bandage and applied it to the raw spot on Mahkeem's chest. After he taped the gauze patch in place, the physician, Dr. Husas Samaan, used his latex-covered fingers to trace a small round spot on his patient's side.

"And where did you get this burn mark?" Dr. Samaan stroked his neatly trimmed mustache as he asked the question.

Mahkeem, finally breathing with normal regularity, answered. "I was holding a portable missile launcher pressed against my side. The heat from the launcher caused that mark as it went off."

Dr. Samaan applied some cream to the spot and quietly replied. "That sounds about right."

Mahkeem thought about how many questions he'd answered in the last twenty-four hours. He'd saved multiple lives and he was almost killed, yet most of the Americans still looked at him with mistrust. *Did Samaan feel the same way?*

"Your English is very good." Mahkeem was honestly being complimentary.

Samaan reached over and typed a few notes into his computer. "Is that why you made the request of Major Handle to be seen by an Iraqi doctor?"

"No, that was in case my English was faulty," said Mahkeem.

"Actually," started the doctor, "for someone who probably didn't get a lot of chances to practice the language you're doing quite well." He hit another button on the computer and then turned back toward Mahkeem.

"Do you like it here?" Mahkeem's voice sounded innocent and childlike as he asked. "In this country, I mean."

"I would have to say yes." Dr. Samaan paused for a moment before he continued. "I am more of a traditionalist Muslim. My wife and I still believe in the old ways, but this country has many freedoms that ours did not at the time I left."

Mahkeem leaned forward. "But they are sending soldiers to end our way of thinking."

"I think it only appears that way." Samaan exhaled the statement with a slight nod. "I think their original reason for invading might have been reasonable to them, but then another after another surfaced until the U.S. soldiers were always there. Some of our people didn't want to appear to be occupied, even though we've always seemed to be on the brink of our own civil war. At least the current President wants to withdraw forces from our country." Dr. Samaan handed Mahkeem his shirt.

"But it's been so long." Mahkeem took the shirt and carefully put it on.

"These things take time," said Dr. Samaan. He took another few steps before he added almost to himself, "I guess that's why insurgents are born and civil wars break out; no one has the patience for peaceful change anymore."

"Will I be all right, Doctor?" Mahkeem pointed to the area on his chest that had been cut open by the dagger.

"Oh, yes," assured Dr. Samaan, "just a few butterfly strips to keep the cut closed. Try not to lift anything heavy for a few days with that arm; the muscles in your shoulder tugging through your upper chest might re-open the wound. After that you should be fine."

"Thank you, Doctor," Mahkeem smiled as he lowered himself off of the examining table.

"Congratulations on your fine deeds, my friend. You have bridged the gap between the two lands by displaying courage in the face of terror." Samaan placed the end of his stethoscope into his front pocket.

"Thank you again, I will certainly try to honor your traditional beliefs." Mahkeem walked out of the room and through the exit door where multiple guards waited to transport him back to his hotel room.

No sooner had Mahkeem left the office, than Dr. Samaan picked up the telephone. He waited while the connecting signal rang. A moment later, someone answered.

"Yes, sir, my patient has just left. You asked to be contacted if I found anything unusual. There was just one thing on his x-ray and another small item, possibly nothing, on his side that I examined. The wound itself was superficial and will heal quickly."

Samaan nodded his head a few times, verbally agreed with the party on the other end of the connection, bid farewell and hung up the phone. He then sat in his office and typed up more notes on Mahkeem into the patient files on his computer. After he'd finished, he stared at his report and thought about what he'd found. After another few moments, he moved the cursor into the middle of the report and added a final statement.

*   *   *

While Mahkeem was with the doctor, Kyle and Laurel had gone down to the hotel lobby for dinner. Meanwhile, Bobby had checked into his own room and had taken advantage of the respite to shower off the blood and change clothes. After he'd toweled himself dry, he put on his army semi-dress uniform, and exited into his own spacious foyer. As he looked around for his black leather shoes, he spotted Jennifer sitting in a high backed chair.

"You never give up, do you?" He continued to look for his shoes while he tried to ignore the fact that they were alone.

"I come for a simple interview with an old friend and wind up finding you swimming in blood." Jennifer threw out the comment like an old duelist throwing down a gauntlet.

"Acquaintance." Bobby was stoic in his response. *Stay focused*, he thought.

"What do you mean?" Jennifer seemed to have missed Bobby's direction.

"Just that we're more like . . . old acquaintances, not friends." Bobby's reply was still deadpan.

"I thought after that night at the Al-Hamra, well . . . ." She let the thought dangle in mid-air.

Jennifer had been sent to Baghdad to cover the finalization of three new amendments to the Iraqi Constitution, an assignment she requested due to its magnitude. Bobby was already within the city gathering intelligence on recent insurgent activity in the Green Zone when he was asked to personally ensure the security of the rather important U.S. media figure. The Green Zone, located on the West Bank of the Tigris River, housed the core of Saddam's empire. The area was now home to the U.S. Embassy, the Iraqi Parliament and most of the Iraqi government offices. Bobby had escorted Jen on dozens of trips from the Al-Hamra hotel to the U.S. Embassy as she covered the various government events taking place. The trips had become routine when one of them almost turned fatal.

Jennifer and Bobby had just exited their armored transport in front of the embassy when a man in a heavy coat appeared from behind a parked car. The man approached them at a rapid pace when he suddenly plunged his hand into the coat's pocket. Bobby realized instantly that this man was a suicide bomber. He pushed Jennifer back into the vehicle as he reached for his gun. He got off a single shot that hit the Islamic bomber in the neck, but it was too late. He dove into the vehicle as the bomb exploded. The blast did significant damage to the front end of the armored Humvee, but his quick action had left both of them unharmed. Jennifer had been severely shaken up by the incident and returned immediately to the Al-Hamra. She asked Bobby to stay for dinner to help her get her mind off the attack. He agreed and neither of them left her room until the next morning.

"I think we can both agree that the night at the Al-Hamra was clearly a mistake. We just needed a quick escape from everything that was happening at the time." Bobby talked with little or no emotion as he stared out the window at the downtown Washington skyline. He was afraid that if he made eye contact, she would see past his façade.

"If you think that night was a mistake, Major Handle, you'd better tell me that it will always be your *favorite* mistake." Her eyes stared into Bobby's as he turned his head from the window. Her tone of voice was a bit harder now.

Okay, Bobby thought to himself, *we've made eye contact—now hold it together.*

She moved closer, grabbed him by his shirt, and buttoned the top button for him.

*　　*　　*

The voice on the phone was hushed. "The traitor is still alive. He did not die in the attack."

The voice on the other end spoke firmly. "He will. Our country must be spared the repercussions of his actions."

The first voice stated plainly, "The doctor has relayed his findings. As you expected, we have a problem."

"Unfortunate," came back the second voice. "But he will still be rewarded."

*　　*　　*

Bobby stared into Jennifer's eyes and waited for her to make the next move. He thought that she may have been carrying a slight grudge against him due to the way he had left things in Iraq, but things seemed to be going okay so far.

"I've got clearance from the President, so I don't need your permission to get an interview, but I do need to ask you a few things before we get started." Jennifer's grip tightened on Bobby's shirt as she changed the subject back to the interview.

"No problem, but are you going to let go of my top shirt button first?" asked Bobby politely.

Jennifer's grip tightened slightly in response.

This is probably a bad sign, thought Bobby. The confrontation that he wanted to avoid was now about to take place.

"Sure. Right after you tell me what the hell happened last year. You took me into the Green Zone for the amendment's finalization and then you vanished." Jennifer extended her grip to include Bobby's collar which made it more difficult for him to reply.

"Intelligence contacted me with a tip on the cell activity we were tracking in the Green Zone. And as I remember it, we were able to take out the entire cell the next day." Bobby's voice was stifled from the pressure on his neck.

Jennifer continued her interrogation. "I understand things happen, but no call, no letter, not even an e-mail? How about a simple good-bye?"

Bobby attempted to breathe in. *God, she smells good.*

"I never had a chance to get your e-mail address, things just happened way too fast," he stated defensively.

"Hold it," said Jennifer in a clearly annoyed tone. "You're trying to tell me that you can track down a bunch of evil insurgents from hell using millions of dollars in technology that was probably built with my tax money, but you couldn't figure out how to contact me?" She narrowed her eyes before adding, "Wrong answer. Would you care to try again?"

Bobby shook his head in agreement as Jennifer exhaled in frustration. A moment later, she finally released him from her grip.

"Okay, I see your point. Maybe we can talk when this is over." Bobby was finally able to breathe again as he fixed his collar. "I'm sorry, Jen, this is just a really bad time."

"When have we ever actually had the time?" exhaled Jennifer as the anger in her voice faded. "And speaking of time, how long has it been since you've had any to yourself? You look terrible."

"You saw the guys in Mahkeem's room didn't you? Let's see what you look like after getting attacked by three assassins trying to skewer *you* with daggers."

Jennifer gave Bobby a look that caused him to drop the sarcastic tone as he added with a touch of sincerity, "Maybe when this is over, we can get together."

She picked up her purse and walked toward the door. "The only reason I like you is because I think you're the most genuine person I've ever met."

"Thanks, but you do know that I kill people for a living." Bobby replied in a very matter-of-fact tone.

"And in doing so you've saved countless lives, including mine. That's why I'm going to let you slide on the lack of a good-bye *this* time." Her answer was in a much more light-hearted tone.

"I do whatever the President tells me to." Bobby ran off his comments like a litany of excuses.

"That's the advantage of being the President, I guess." Jennifer's features took on more of a quizzical tone. "You've captured enough criminals from the *Iraqi Most Wanted Deck* to have a royal flush two times over. You're a highly respected man, but you never stop for a second to help yourself."

"And?" Bobby gave her an uneasy smirk.

"What do you see when you look at yourself in the mirror every morning?" Jennifer emphasized the word *you* when she asked the question.

Bobby thought a moment on his life and all of the missions, Presidential and otherwise, that he had performed. All that he could feel was that he was still waiting, but waiting for God knows who or what.

"What was the question again?" His face eased itself into a blank.

"What do you see when you look in the mirror each morning?" The emphasis was still on the same word the second time around.

Bobby had the true answer ready for her now.

"Nothing."

*   *   *

Dr. Samaan walked toward his chauffeured limousine. He usually drove his Porsche when the weather was this perfect, but tonight was a special night. Tonight his wife would be joining him to celebrate their twenty-third wedding anniversary. They were to be driven to a symphony concert after a quick meal at one of her favorite restaurants.

As Dr. Samaan entered the rear driver's side door, he nodded a quick hello to his driver, Musann Kekk, who held the door open for him. After Dr. Samaan was seated, Kekk closed the door firmly and climbed into the front of the vehicle.

Kekk ran a small limousine service that specifically catered to the Washington elite. Dr. Samaan preferred Kekk's service for special occasions due to the limo driver's attention to every detail, which is why he had reserved this particular date more than six months before.

"Good to see you again, Kekk." Dr. Samaan nodded to the back of his driver's head. He then reached for a glass of chilled white wine from the fully stocked bar as he gave salutations to his wonderful and faithful wife, Emira.

Dr. Samaan, for a split second, became troubled when he thought that through the rearview mirror, Kekk didn't seem to be himself. A second later, he instantly put the thought out of his mind as he stared lovingly at his wife's eyes, which were surrounded by the traditional garb of black headdress. A black veil covered all of her lower face.

His thoughts became troubled again when he saw his wife's right hand. She held a device with her thumb hovering over the plunger—but that wasn't his wife's hand.

Dr. Samaan saw his wife move her left hand up to her face and remove the veil.

When did my wife grow a mustache?

He heard the scream of "Allah" echo through the limo just before it exploded.

Chapter 14

Laurel sat in a plush chair in Kyle's suite as he poured himself a drink by the well-stocked bar. He drained the glass with a single gulp and exhaled through pursed lips. "Smooth. Want one?" He held up a bottle of Crown Royal Whiskey.

"No, straight scotch, no water . . . but throw in some ice." Laurel leaned back into the chair and looked totally exhausted. "In fact make it a double and I'll just sip it until it knocks me out."

Kyle fixed Laurel's drink, made himself another, and then joined her with the two full glasses. As he sat down, he still couldn't believe that Laurel was alive because of the actions of an insurgent. *Why did Mahkeem do what he did?* Kyle thought about the mission again. *Maybe the mission wasn't actually over yet.*

He handed Laurel her drink and took a sip of his own. "You know, Laurel, right before the gladiator games began down the hall, I got a call from the White House Press Secretary."

"So did I." Laurel shook her glass back and forth to chill the scotch quicker. "Was your call about the medal?"

"Yeah, I'm getting a medal for the failed mission." Kyle took a small sip of his drink. "Oh, hell, the way it was explained to me over the phone, you'd think our team had just solved the entire Iraqi insurgency problem."

"The White House guy with the funny name, Barber, Baby, or something like that . . . ." Laurel hung on to her drink with one hand while flinging her free one out into space, extending it as far as her arm would let her as if she were trying to snatch the correct name and pronunciation from mid-air.

"Babare, I think." Kyle cut in.

"Babare, yeah, you're right, that's it." Laurel was silent for a couple of moments to make sure they were correct. "To him it's not a *real* fight, just a paper one. We almost lost our entire team, but the White House thinks if we can turn this into something good for the American public to smile about, that's the way to go."

"Shit," started Kyle, "it wasn't even a fight. There wasn't one goddamned enemy we could pull the trigger on. Things just fell apart before we could take anyone down." He tipped his glass back and took another gulp along with a few chips of ice. He chewed the ice as he spoke through the corner of his mouth. "And that fissionable crap is still out there, probably buried in the desert somewhere until they can figure out how to use it against us." He swallowed the last of the ice and wiped his mouth with the side of this thumb.

"At least Team Two didn't go down without a fight, according to what Number Seven said." Laurel sounded as if she were trying to be consoling as she spoke.

Kyle thought about Team Two. *My Team Two.* He may not have been involved in the firefight directly, but he still felt responsible for each man who was lost.

He shook his head in disbelief. "And then they'll show us on television, pin medals on us, and allow the American people to feel good about something . . . just because one of the rebels changed sides and fucked over his own cell. What a bunch of bullshit."

"You mean about Mahkeem saving my life?" Laurel seemed somewhat irate at the thought.

"No," answered Kyle, "I meant the spin the politicians place on it."

*   *   *

After he'd changed clothes and walked Jennifer to her room, Bobby called for a car to take him to the Pentagon. The ride over, which could have taken up to forty-five minutes during rush hour, only took a quarter hour due to the time of day. As they drove, he could see the sunset just beyond the trees that lined the Potomac River. Bobby silently laughed to himself thinking about the unobstructed view he typically had when the sun set in the middle of the desert. The car pulled up to the front of the visitor's entrance at the Pentagon, and he exited the vehicle. As he walked to the building, the lampposts on the surrounding streets came to life to signal the end of another day.

After he entered the building, he showed his special pass with the Presidential seal, and was taken directly to the room where Private Bleeker sat before an array of computer monitors. As Bobby walked in, he gave a quick salute to Bleeker, waved off a return acknowledgement, and motioned for the Private to sit down as he took his own seat next to him.

"What have you got for me . . ." Bobby paused long enough to lean forward in his chair to catch the technician's name, and then leaned back in his chair. " . . . uh, Private Bleeker?"

"Well, sir," said the eager, young Private. "We've taken the four different media sources and combined them into one timeline for you. As you can see, the screen is divided into four quadrants. In the upper left, you have the images from the Monocle. Since the satellite is only in position for a short time period, you'll only see information in this quadrant about every ninety-minutes or so. The lower left contains both Internet web-casts. We added them into the overall timeline as they actually appeared, so again, this quadrant is going to be empty most of the time. The upper right corner will be the only part of the display that will always have information for you. This is because it contains the echo imaging from the chips. The chips, of course, were transmitting information through the entire mission. The quadrant in the lower right of the screen is where you'll see the audio wave representation from the throat mikes. You'll see this window go blank right after the mikes were taken and destroyed by the captors." Bleeker took a short breath as he continued, "And finally, this small window floating on top of the other four displays is your timeline controller. You can see that it's got your basic controls to play, pause, fast-forward or rewind the videos as you need to. They're all in perfect sync, which took us a while to get right, but you shouldn't have any trouble replaying any portion using the on-screen controller."

"Can I take a copy of this with me?" Bobby pointed to the display.

"We're actually using your copy." Bleeker seemed proud that he'd already taken care of Bobby's first request. "That way we'll both be sure there are no problems with your disc."

"Good, this looks easy enough." Bobby smiled because he knew that the tech team had come through again.

Bleeker snapped his finger, "Oh, and one last thing."

"What's that?"

"You'll also be able to adjust the audio by using the advanced equalizer." Bleeker clicked on another button using the mouse and caused a graphical representation of an equalizer to appear on the screen.

"Excellent." Bobby saw Bleeker crack a bit of a smile. He could tell that Bleeker had put in a lot of hours on the project. He also liked the fact that he'd taken ownership of the data.

"So let's go over what our technology team has put together," said Bleeker. "We've already confirmed the five motionless chips, signifying the ambushed Team Two by the Iraqi convoy. Then there's the escaped and wounded second squad team leader, the dead lookout, crushed by the falling chopper outside and the remains of Team One inside the complex being held captive. Altogether, all twelve members of the two six person teams are accounted for."

"Yes, Bleeker, I'm familiar with the devices, I've had one implanted in my shoulder as well." Bobby tried not to allow his voice to appear bored with the eager technician's directions. His mind drifted back to Jennifer for a second. Maybe things would . . . . *Concentrate*, he told himself.

"Now here come the video images the rebels were transmitting." Bleeker tapped the mouse with his finger as if to emphasize his words. "That even includes the attempted and . . . successful beheading."

"I know," was the only reply that Bobby gave.

Bobby then turned all of his attention toward the screen as he watched one quadrant at a time for several minutes each. His eyes continued to move from quadrant to quadrant for almost ten minutes. He then repeated the process several times before he asked Bleeker a question.

"Can you tell me, Private, why is there a change on the view with the personal implants? There seems to be some form of interference on a small section of the recording." Bobby hardly moved his frame, but did turn his head slightly in the technician's direction as he asked the question.

"That's exactly what it is, sir." Bleeker shot back the immediate reply. "It seems that we had a moment of sunspot activity which knocked out our radar echoes from all of the Kodiaks. General Tabler had me search up and down the adjoining frequencies to make sure the signal hadn't slipped to another setting."

"Can that type of thing happen?" Bobby turned in his seat and gave Bleeker his undivided attention.

"Generally, no. But the General was here beside me and this was the mission he initiated, so he got a touch irate and asked me to surf the channels, hoping not to lose the locations of the Kodiaks."

"Yes," agreed Bobby, "but why the single echo on this other frequency?"

"I've had some other techs look at that, sir. That echo is in the exact same position as one of the other Kodiaks that we've already accounted for. Since I was searching the other frequencies, I thought that maybe this echo just flip-flopped over to another heading temporarily." Bleeker hit a couple of buttons on the keyboard and overlaid the single echo with the heat signatures from the Monocle. The distortion had caused each of the images to move slightly upward in a northwestern direction. The single echo was in the center of one of the relocated signatures.

"But now we're back to the fact that this generally does not happen."

"We are, sir," agreed Bleeker. "It generally does not happen."

"But can it?" Bobby pressed the issue.

"Only because we see it on screen I'd have to say it must be able to."

"Have you checked the equipment?" Bobby was becoming impatient, but still exuded a friendly demeanor.

"Yes, as well as the fact that there was some solar flare-up activity at the exact same time as these images were being captured." A trickle of sweat ran down Bleeker's cheek as he ran his index finger between the collar of his shirt and his neck. Bobby's abrupt line of questions must have taken Bleeker by surprise.

"That settles it then." Bobby turned wholly back to the other two screens. "All twelve echoes have been accounted for, with the twelfth one showing up twice."

"Exactly," chimed in Bleeker.

Bobby gazed at the monitor that displayed the images from the Iraqi movie camera. He sat and looked long and hard as he scrutinized every corner of the picture. After several more minutes he turned to Bleeker. "Right before our new friend saves the day, there's a noise coming over the camera microphone. Can you isolate the background sound from the foreground parts?"

"That wouldn't be a problem, sir." Bleeker tapped a few commands into the keyboard to adjust the equalization settings. Just as quickly, he turned some on-screen volume dials back and forth with his mouse to adjust the noise level of both the foreground and background. He finished by clicking on some switches that were connected to a few sound filters.

Bobby then heard Kyle pleading loudly with Mahkeem, yet the conversation was but a whisper in the background as he heard a guttural voice, mixed with radio static urging something that sounded like the words, "hello, hello," or possibly "yellow, yellow." They repeated a few more times before Bobby heard Mahkeem's gunshots, mixed to a lower pitch into the background as he saved the lives of the remaining Kodiaks.

Bobby thought about the voice and the words being transmitted through the speaker. He thought a moment and watched some of the other media sources again. He tapped the edge of the console as he became lost in thought.

Suddenly the door to Bobby's right, about thirty feet away, burst open as a tall Pentagon official strode down the aisle at a rapid pace.

"Major Handle," started the official, "there's someone here to see you. A couple of CIA agents came in with a woman from the D.C.P.D. Based on her tone of voice and attitude with the folks out front, it sounds like something important is going down."

"Okay," nodded Bobby, "lead the way."

As he got up to leave, Bleeker popped the disc out of the computer, slid it into a thin plastic case and handed it to him.

After a brief walk, Bobby had arrived back at the Pentagon's reception area. A nicely dressed, full-figured woman stood near the reception desk. As she looked around the room, she tapped her fingers together in a nervous, yet fairly syncopated rhythm. The two agents who probably came in with her sat in a couple of chairs just beyond the desk.

Bobby slowly walked over to the woman and looked her up and down. She was indeed a full-bodied woman who was probably just a few years younger than he was. Her blouse was form fitting with the top half a trifle tighter than the bottom half in a description that could only be called *buxom*. Her smart looking blazer that matched her shoes filled out the rest of the very chic ensemble. Her eyes were a piercing green, and she had a small, perky nose. The thick straight light brown hair, which seemed in constant danger of falling down over her left eye in a Lana Turner peek-a-boo fashion, stopped at her shoulders.

"I'm Major Handle. I understand that you need to speak with me."

The woman held up a card and flipped it close enough to Bobby's face so that he could read it as she spoke. "I was told that I had to come to you with the news."

"Who told you this and what news?" He was honestly puzzled, but still had to grin at the awkwardness of the situation. As he waited for her to reply, he took the card that she'd stuck in his face.

"The President's staff told me to check in with you and you alone." The woman's voice seemed agitated, but her face didn't betray that fact.

"He does like to pull rank occasionally." Bobby sighed hard and then asked, "And you are . . . ?"

"I'm Police Captain Anne Bethert, from the local D.C. office."

"What can I do for you, Captain?" Bobby made the statement in earnest. Her tired eyes told him that she'd been through a long day and was probably on her way home when she had received the orders to track him down at the Pentagon.

"I believe you have a Mr. Ahlmed Mahkeem in your protective custody?"

Bobby squinted hard as he thought of the ramifications of what the Police Captain was saying. "Yes, I do. He's under the protection of the U.S. Army. We've actually just elevated the security level around him . . . ." He paused slightly as he thought about how to describe his afternoon encounter with the three dagger-wielding assassins. " . . . due to an earlier mishap."

"Yes, I know," answered back Bethert. "I heard from the receptionist that the doctor's office was fairly packed with Army personnel a few hours ago. I believe the CIA also went through the trouble of securing the entire building before the entourage arrived."

"Then what's wrong with Mahkeem?" Bobby didn't like the fact that the local police were involved in a national matter. His faced dropped into a worried look as he prepared himself for the worst.

"There's nothing wrong with Mr. Mahkeem." Bethert plucked the card back from Bobby's hand. "I've been asked to come here and tell you that his doctor has been blown to jelly."

Chapter 15

The two D.C. patrolmen held up the yellow, plastic police tape that surrounded the burned-out husk that used to be Dr. Samaan's limo. Bobby and Police Captain Anne Bethert both bowed their heads slightly as they made their way under the plastic barricade, then straightened as they approached the forensic team examining the bodies among the wreckage.

"The President's staff thought that the entire situation seemed a bit suspicious," began Bethert, "but the very fact that the Doc had seen the insurgent just a few hours before he got atomized . . . ." She let the sentence dangle for a moment. "Well, let's just say that somebody who's been featured on the front page of the newspaper and the nightly news like this ex-rebel, of course he's going to get some Presidential, err, make that preferential treatment."

"Which is why you were asked to call me in, no doubt." Bobby made the statement aloud so that Bethert could hear his words plainly, but he made sure they were void of any malice or sarcasm.

"When the White House asks me for a favor, I tend to listen." Bethert let the side of her mouth curl into a smirk with her reply.

"The same with me," agreed Bobby as they pulled up their saunter just a half-foot short of where the rear driver's side of the Doctor's limousine used to be. Bobby knelt down and saw what was left of Samaan's body as it hung out of the car into the street.

"The door of the limo was blown off by the force of the explosion," said a voice from inside the vehicle. "It looks like the doctor's body may have also slammed into the door. His inertia was then used up, and he was probably flung back into the car where he absorbed the rest of the blast. Hence the mashed, pulpy look of his remains."

Bobby looked across the wreckage of the rear seat to see a shorthaired, bespectacled man of about thirty-five years of age. He wore a white, rubberized apron and latex gloves that were smeared red. The man stepped over a blood-drenched area that may have been part of the backseat as he approached.

"It does look like he hit the door pretty damn hard, now that you mention it." Bobby stuck out his hand. "Major Bobby Handle."

The forensic technician waved Bobby off with a single hand motion. "Yes, I heard you were coming. Sorry, but no handshake for now, I'm covered with evidence." The man gave a grin revealing a mild overbite and a zigzag of different colored braces that ran across his upper teeth. "I'm Gerald B. Orlando, head of D.C. pathology, if you need to know." He stated the sentence in a friendly fashion and smiled widely.

Bobby squinted hard at him, almost too hard.

Gerald looked back at Bobby and tilted his head to the side slightly. "I get that look all of the time. Adult braces are indeed a hell of a thing, you know. It's still as hard to eat peanut butter as it was when you were a kid, but totally knocks the hell out of your sex life."

Bobby stopped his stare and concentrated on understanding Gerald. The words came out of his mouth so fast that it was hard to make out exactly was he was saying. Bobby leaned forward and attempted to understand what Gerald had just said before he spoke again, but Gerald continued to talk as he worked through the gruesome human remains.

"My mom blames the family genes, but my dad blames the thumb sucking. It doesn't really matter who wins the argument at every family gathering though, because I'm the thirty-something that still sleeps with orthodontic head-gear at night." Gerald lifted his hands to his cheeks briefly and extended his thumbs toward his mouth while his little fingers pointed toward his ear in a mock imitation of headgear.

Bobby was about to apologize for his abrupt stare when Gerald reached down and grabbed something from the wreckage. He turned back around and then straightened his arm to dangle a see-through plastic evidence pouch in front of him.

Captain Bethert poked her head into the back of the car. "What do you have there?" She didn't seem to give a second thought to his braces that looked as if Walt Disney manufactured them.

"Tickets to a symphony concert tonight." He paused for a breath and continued, "I've already had it checked out while you were gone. The good doctor and his wife ordered the tickets about six months ago. You know, I like the orchestra, too, but I'm actually more of a classic rock guy myself. I'll take Led Zeppelin to Mozart any day of the week. Although I do like the Night Music thing that Mozart wrote, but I have to be in the right mood."

Bobby listened to Gerald's explanation. *This guy not only loves his job,* thought Bobby, *but he can't stop talking about it.* He continued to listen as he tried to separate the facts from the commentary.

Bethert pointed toward the blood-sodden seat. "I take it that's where the wife was seated?" Her lips parted in a small gesture of revulsion.

"Yes," replied Gerald in a cheerier fashion than accommodated the gruesome scene. "The bomb must have been sitting right below her seat, since her torso, hip area and most of her upper legs were all vaporized. Most of her features were wiped off of her face also. We have her skull in a bag."

"Can we make a dental identification?" Bobby asked the next question.

"Certainly," said Gerald. "Once we find the family dentist it should be no problem at all." He looked down and picked up the doctor's feet and legs that were strewn across the well of the rear, right passenger area.

"What are you doing now?" Bethert raised one eyebrow as she finally let a look of disgust cross her face.

"What's left of the wife's lower legs and feet should be here under her husband's remains and, oh, yes, here they . . . ." The forensic specialist dropped the Doctor's legs back onto the tangle of bloody body parts. He instantly reached behind him to retrieve the plastic bag that contained the wife's skull. He whipped out a small pen light from his outer apron pocket and played the light through the plastic bag and over the bony structure.

"What's wrong, Gerald?" The statement from Bethert sounded less like an order from a commanding officer than it was a genuine question from a fellow co-worker.

"These feet below the Doctor's body don't belong to a woman, and if the follicles on this skull's remaining lip were protruding from an area anywhere else but the face, I'd have to say they were pubic hair." Gerald seemed incredulous at his findings.

Bobby stared at Gerald as he thought about the gender discrepancy of the lower torso that was just uncovered. *If the doctor's wife wasn't in the limo, then . . . .*

"Cut to the chase, Gerald." Bethert's voice was once again in the mode of superior officer.

Gerald scrunched his eyebrows and tilted his head back. "The Doctor's wife has the feet of a man and her upper lip was, before the explosion, sporting a better mustache than my dad used to grow."

Bobby pulled himself from the opening of the rear passenger door and ran toward the squad car.

"Goddamn and double goddamn." He almost spat the words out.

Bethert, close on his heels, opened the driver's door to her police cruiser and hopped in behind the wheel while Bobby jumped into the passenger seat beside her. As she started the engine and pulled the car away from the crime scene, she took a guess aloud. "I know the first 'damn' was because we both know the Doctor's wife may be in terrible danger, but what was the second one for?"

Bobby's firm voice had a touch of exasperation in it. "I really wish I hadn't forgotten my gun aboard the plane."

*   *   *

The phone from the living room was still ringing as Bobby popped open the servant's entrance door with his shoulder. He rolled twice across the floor and came to a halt in the corner next to the hallway that led to the downstairs dining room. He pointed the borrowed gun in several directions before he whispered the single word, "Clear."

Bethert came in and knelt beside him, her gun in her right hand in readiness. She raised her left wrist-communication device to her mouth and contacted the D.C. SWAT team that she had called in on the drive over to the Samaan residence.

Within moments, a loud crash was heard as four officers, clad in helmets and body armor, knocked down the front door and rushed in with their rifles pointed in all directions. Before Bobby could hear the "all clear" signal that most officers shouted when a room was secured, he heard the loud voice of one of the SWAT team exclaim, "Two bodies."

Bobby and Bethert both got to their feet and ran through the hallway, past the dining room and into the spacious living room where they spied the bodies of Mrs. Samaan and the couple's eight year old girl, both with their throats slashed.

*   *   *

Bethert and Bobby stood on the tree lawn of the Doctor's house and sipped hot coffee from two metal tumblers.

"So the limo driver arrives to pick-up Mrs. Samaan, but instead gets forced to drive our terrorist to the doc's office." Bobby looked up to see a few neighbors down the street being questioned by some officers. "Anybody see anything?"

"It's a quiet neighborhood, most folks were at work or fighting D.C. rush-hour traffic when this went down." Bethert took another sip. "I've got to tell you, Major, the limo was one thing, but the scene inside that house makes me sick."

"That's why everyone is going a little overboard with this Mahkeem thing. If one rebel can change, maybe there are more like him that just need a wake-up call. And if we can get enough inside information, we can take organizations like this down for good." With each word, Bobby sounded more tired. They'd lost a little girl today just because her father, Dr Samaan, had helped a man. *Cowards, always going after the defenseless.*

Bethert looked down and noticed a sprinkler head sticking out through the grass. "You mentioned three other assassins at the hotel on the ride over. Do you think this bomber was a member of the same group that attacked you earlier?"

"Same group or another group working in cooperation." Bobby took another sip from the tumbler. The more he thought about the little girl, the angrier he became. Bethert had been right; the scene from the doctor's house was sickening.

"So maybe this bomber was the fourth member of their team, you know, held in reserve. They couldn't kill the new national hero of ours because you got in their way, so they shadowed him and killed everyone that he touched." Bethert shrugged her shoulders and kicked at the sprinkler head.

Bobby shook his head. "Like sending all of us a message that says, sooner or later, the traitor will get his. Is that what you're saying?"

Bethert kicked again at the sprinkler head and with a click, it disappeared back into the thick lawn. "I've seen similar tactics used to intimidate rival gangs right here in D.C. This just happens to be a much bigger gang."

"Yeah." Bobby took another sip—this time a long one.

Chapter 16

After only a few hours of sleep, Bobby found himself wide awake as he stared at his computer screen in his hotel room. Morning had arrived, and the second cup of coffee he'd poured himself in the last thirty minutes was almost gone. He reached over, grabbed the small coffee pot, and refilled his cup. He took a sip as he tapped at the keyboard repeatedly to review the images that Bleeker had loaded onto the disc at the Pentagon.

As Bobby gazed at one picture after another, he mentally consolidated the information on the Kodiak mission and combined it with the results from his own investigation. First, God's Monocle had picked up fissionable material in Iraq. Second, the Kodiak mission to recover the material was compromised. The uranium was being shipped out as Team One arrived. Of course then came the beheadings over a live Internet broadcast which caused the President to call him in on the rescue.

He also knew he arrived too late to save his fellow troops. He had gotten there just in time to see the last, three, living Kodiak team members saved by the quick actions of rebel-turned-rescuer Ahlmed Mahkeem. Mahkeem's actions had marked him as a target to the fanatic factions of his countrymen. Assassins were sent to his hotel room to execute him in similar symbolic fashion. Finally, the Middle-Eastern doctor who had treated him was murdered. Bobby guessed the terrorist threesome had probably followed Jennifer to the hotel. Because of the intense media attention, the assassins had posed as a Bridges Muslim Network news crew. They had a perfectly forged White House authorization to interview Mahkeem that included a legitimate looking signature from the President himself.

A few questions still remained, but the answers seemed obvious enough as Bobby examined them closer. The same people who blew up the doctor, his chauffeur, and killed the Doctor's wife had probably kept the hotel under surveillance to confirm that Mahkeem was killed. When the attempt on the life of the reformed rebel failed, the second bunch of terrorists decided to send a message to those who had helped him. Bethert's theory was that when the doctor had treated Mahkeem, he sided with an infidel and was at that point marked for death. The terrorists then retaliated by bombing the doctor's limo and killing his family. And on top of everything else, Mahkeem had given up top-secret information to prevent another death in Great Britain.

"God damnit, who knew?" Bobby moaned aloud to no one but the empty hotel room.

He looked at the computer screen for a few more minutes and mentally juggled pictures from the Monocle's position, the bodies near the convoy, and the placement of the bodies held hostage inside the abandoned nuclear complex. He stared for almost a full minute before he turned away and finished off the last of his coffee.

As he got up to make another pot, his train of thought was broken suddenly when his phone rang. He put down the cup and clicked the small portable phone to the *on* position. "Handle."

"Hope I didn't wake you up, and that you're having a perfectly wonderful Wednesday morning so far." The cheerful, yet very sarcastic voice on the other end of the line belonged to Bobby's good friend, Joe Manelli, and he recognized it immediately.

"Very funny, Joe. It sounds like we have a good connection, where are you at?" Bobby let his face soften slightly, happy to hear from his friend and partner.

"Back in the Green Zone, trying to chill out at Hussein's old palace," replied Joe. Saddam Hussein's palace in the Green Zone had been converted into a command post during the war. The palace contained a large pool with many amenities, which were still used by the American armed forces. "I just made sure I got a decent line for our call."

"Then what gives, partner?" Bobby was curious now as well as happy to hear his friend's voice.

"I found something in the Iraqi convoy. One of their trucks had a personal chip-tracking device on board. Damn thing is, it was one of ours. No doubt stolen or bought on some black market somewhere." Joe's last sentence sounded as if he was thinking out loud.

"Interesting," replied Bobby slowly, "but based on what I've learned about the chips in our shoulders, the tracking device should have been useless. The chips have a small receiver in them so that they can be programmed with a unique key-code before each mission. The corresponding key-code and digital frequency are then entered into the chip-trackers to activate them, allowing communication to take place with the chips."

"Yeah, but—" Joe tried to break in.

Bobby continued, "The Pentagon is the only organization that can track all active chips regardless of their key-codes, but a pin protected ID card has to be inserted into the console to enable the global tracking mode. I actually got a tour of the area last night. And by the way, you can thank PFC Bleeker for my sudden in-depth knowledge of our personal tracking devices." Bobby took a quick look at his notes. "The Private also told me that we use RSA 128 bit encryption, which is virtually impossible to hack. Whatever that means."

"Well, I've got some news for your friend Bleeker," Joe hesitantly replied. "Our techs opened up the tracking device and found that the internal chips were still in pretty good shape due to the titanium case that protects the electronic components."

"And?" Maybe the last cup of coffee was responsible, but Bobby was now wide awake.

"The bastards hacked the security chip somehow. I don't understand the details, but the insurgents basically had the ability to track all Special Forces activity within one hundred miles of that bunker."

Total silence filled the line for what seemed to be an eternity before Bobby spoke, "Then they knew we were coming. They tracked the Kodiaks like a group of tagged animals. Those soldiers never had a chance."

Joe continued Bobby's thought. "The way I see it, part of the splinter group went to intercept Team Two while another faction went to quickly remove the uranium. A third group then converged on Team One. The tech told me that for every form of security we invent, someone will break it given the proper time and resources."

"They probably traversed the frequencies until something came up, and the next thing you know, it's no more Kodiak team." Bobby stoically reiterated his thoughts with Joe's and extrapolated the concept back to his friend. Bobby remembered the first time he'd been briefed on the new chip technology. The chips were supposed to save lives. A breach of this magnitude had just violated the safety of thousands of soldiers. *How many other black-market tracking devices are out there?*

"At any rate, I hope this helps your investigation." Joe's statement still sounded clear from thousands of miles away.

"Yeah, it does," replied Bobby. "I wonder how many of our other Special Forces missions have been compromised because of this security breach. Thanks for the extra effort and keep out of trouble until I get back."

"Will do, Major," came the somber response in Bobby's ear before the line clicked dead.

He sat in the chair for several minutes and thought how Joe's new information might affect his investigation. Except for a few minor details that nagged at the back of his head, everything seemed to fit and make sense . . . almost.

He turned off the computer and put on a fresh set of officer's dress khakis when his phone went off again.

"Handle!" This time he answered it on the first ring.

"Bethert here." Both words ran together as her voice cracked through the phone.

*　*　*

Mahkeem's eyes were still adjusting to the darkness of the room when the set of four holographic projectors hummed to life. Two CIA agents who were doing their best to make him feel comfortable were seated to the left of him. The agents had met him at the Pentagon security check-in and escorted him through the maze of hallways to the Advanced Reconnaissance Amphitheater, better known to government employees as the ADA. The ADA was home to some of the best three-dimensional imaging technology available in the world. A large blue platform mounted on numerous cylindrical legs filled most of the room. The platform was surrounded by two rows of seats on three sides, the back row a step higher. The fourth side housed a control panel to operate all the equipment within the amphitheater.

As Mahkeem sat down in his chair, he held a bottle of orange juice that had accompanied his earlier breakfast made up of kiwi fruit and flat bread.

A few moments later, the lights faded further, and the holo-projectors placed a three-dimensional model of the Iraqi landscape directly on top of the blue platform.

Mahkeem recognized the terrain instantly as he stared in bewilderment at the miniature scene made of light. The bunker where the Kodiaks were held was visible directly in the center of the model. The holographic image of the building resembled a plastic hotel in a giant sized game of Monopoly.

A short, stocky man with a laser pointer stood behind the control panel to the left of the platform.

"Hello, Mr. Mahkeem, my name is Albert Rhodes. Before we start, I would like to personally thank you for the help that you've provided our country over the last few days."

As Rhodes spoke, a woman entered the room and sat down in the row behind Mahkeem. She reached over and handed Mahkeem a laser pointer similar to the one Albert held. Mahkeem gave her a quick nod and turned his attention back to the speaker.

Rhodes continued in his gravelly voice. "The three dimensional model you're looking at represents a two hundred square mile area of Northern Iraq. We can traverse the model in any direction and zoom in or out as needed by using data previously collected from our earlier PriCam series of satellites." He motioned with his arm to the woman seated behind the reformed rebel. "Amy, would you like to add anything?"

Mahkeem turned to face the tall blonde woman.

Amy leaned forward in her chair. "Mr. Mahkeem, we're here today to save Iraqi civilian lives. And whether you believe us or not, we also want to bring our troops home to their families. As we work through this session, any information you could give us to stop the violence in your home country would be greatly appreciated."

Mahkeem nodded again, stood up, and activated his laser pointer. He pointed the instrument at a spot on the three-dimensional map that was twenty-five miles to the north of the bunker, just outside the small city of Binahaja. As the laser pointer hit the platform, the exact latitude and longitude coordinates were instantly displayed on a screen overhead. "This is where you will want to start." He turned and looked directly into the face of Albert Rhodes. "This is where I was trained."

*   *   *

Forty-five minutes after receiving the call, Bobby was escorted into Doctor Samaan's private office. Police Captain Anne Bethert sat in the doctor's comfortable chair and tapped away at the keyboard attached to his computer.

"Good morning, Major, I thought you'd want to see this." She turned the screen at an angle so that Bobby could see the contents of the file without straining his neck or peering over her shoulder.

"Thank you. Are these the doctor's notes on Mahkeem that I asked for last night?" His tone was all business.

"Yeah, but I was too tired to look at them yesterday, so I had the admin-assistant cut-and-paste the information from Ahlmed's patient record into a local file. I threw the file onto this mini hard drive." Bethert pointed to the small flash-memory hard-drive that protruded from the USB port on the computer. "This little drive makes bringing paperwork home almost too easy. Anyway, I'm glad I made a copy of that file when I did."

"Why?" The tracking chips had been compromised, and now there was another technical problem. *Am I fighting terrorists, or the goddamn technology that we created and gave to the terrorists?*

"The Global/Med-Clinical network had a crash last night, and they lost a ton of recently added information that hadn't been backed up yet, including all of Samaan's patient records from yesterday."

That didn't sound good. Maybe the crash had deeper motives. "Does anyone know you have this information?"

"Just the admin-assistant and me," replied Bethert. "And I told her to keep it that way."

"You may want to reinforce that one more time before you leave today." Bobby turned away from Bethert and peered at the screen that contained the rambling notes from the doctor.

Patient brought in by request of U.S. Army. Patient wanted medical attention administered by a doctor from his own part of the world. Said patient had mild chest wound from dagger thrust. Applied butterfly strips to close the wound and prescribed antibiotics. Noticed puncture wound that had been sutured closed, high on left shoulder. There was also a burn mark on his right rib cage area that patient said was received as result of firing portable rocket launcher and holding it too close to body. I applied salve to burn, but feel wound is newer than patient allows, or is not healing at the proper rate. Want to see patient back in a week to check strips and monitor burn's healing progress.

The bottom of the cyber-page had Samaan's electronic signature affixed to it.

"This doesn't seem to be too ominous, but I wanted you to be the first one to see it when we opened the file." Bethert swiveled her chair toward Bobby and gave him a look like she was trying to read his thoughts.

"Let me have a printout of that will you?" he asked politely. "I think it's time to see the President.

*   *   *

An informal meeting that included many of the President's cabinet members was under way when Bobby walked in an hour later. Not all of the members were there, but most of the important ones were in attendance. He saw Secretary of Defense, George Haftee, on the couch next to Secretary of State, Keeler Wickman. Bobby looked to the other side of the room where he saw a few other top members when General Tabler caught his attention and waved a mild salute in his direction. He was in the process of returning it when Leamon Davis slid past Bobby and excused himself.

"Come on in, Bobby." President Sumner waved Bobby into the room with a circular motion of his arm. "The meeting's just ended."

"Davis looked like he had to be somewhere." Bobby made the observation over his shoulder as the door Davis had pushed himself through closed.

"He had to catch a flight out of here. He's overseeing the re-starting of one of his company's nuclear plants. Standard maintenance, but the plant was delayed in getting back on-line, so he's taking some heat for that."

"That's something I think the owner *should* be watching over." Bobby made the remark without trying to be funny.

"So what have you got for me, Bobby?" Sumner seemed in a decent mood considering everything that had transpired over the last few days.

"I'm pretty much done with the investigation you had assigned to me." Bobby paused before he continued. "Except for maybe a few minor details I have to tie up, I'd say we have a fairly zealous rebel who has turned over a new leaf and is happy to be under our protection."

"Good," replied Sumner. "Because the day after tomorrow we're going to give the American people a little pre-weekend present."

"What's that, Sir?" Bobby hated surprises.

"We're giving Bradly, Crickowski, and Mahkeem all Congressional Medals of Honor, live from the White House. Mahkeem will be receiving the top civilian honor, a

Freedom Medal. The members from the cabinet will be here for it. The Vice-President, Tabler . . . you're invited too, if you'd like."

"No, thanks, Sir, I think I'd rather just finish my final report for you over the next day or two and fly back to the Middle-East." Bobby glanced at Tabler and then back to Sumner.

"Suit yourself, but it's really going to look bad for the rebels over there to see one of their own realizing that maybe the Western world isn't so bad after all." Sumner smiled and grabbed a sheet of paper off of his desk. "Hell, Bobby, Mahkeem has even given some of our Army and CIA top brass some site coordinates for camps over in Iraq that harbor major numbers of insurgents."

"Really, can I take a quick look at that?" Bobby had to restrain himself from grabbing for the list.

"We'll be hitting those sites with air strikes within the next forty-eight hours," Sumner said smugly.

Bobby squinted for a moment before he handed back the paper. A nagging fear tugged at his thoughts. "One of those sights, Sir, site designation 1128. My team and I knocked it out earlier this year. Don't you think that's odd?"

Before Sumner could reply, General Tabler cut in. "If the boat is no longer sinking, Major, the rats have been known to come back aboard ship."

Bobby nodded his head in agreement and let a small smirk appear at the corner of his lip. "I think you're right, General." He saluted Tabler and Sumner before he turned and left the room.

Once he was outside in the hallway, the squint came back to Bobby's face as he thought of designation 1128. He pulled out his cellular phone and dialed a number. Moments later a familiar voice answered.

"PFC Bleeker here."

"Bleeker, it's Handle, I need a favor." He looked up to see if anyone was within earshot.

"Yes, sir, anything to help." Bleeker sounded energetic.

"I need to log some more time with you and your computer equipment." Bobby tried to hide his worry and eagerness in a matter-of-fact tone of voice.

There was a slight pause before Bleeker answered. "Which equipment would that be, sir?"

"I want to look through God's Monocle."

Chapter 17

Bobby sat next to PFC Bleeker for the second time in twenty-four hours. Bleeker had called up more visual data for him—data that had come from the transmissions of God's Monocle.

"Are you getting what you need, Major?" Bleeker asked with his customary honesty.

"Yes, I am, thanks. But it's still not adding up to much." *Something is wrong, I can feel it.*

"Take your time, Sir. There's absolutely no hurry. Private Price and I are here to help in any way we can."

At the mention of Price's name, Bobby turned and noticed him at the far end of the electronic console. He nodded in his direction, and received a quick salute.

Bobby then turned back toward Bleeker. "Can you give me some data from previous orbits of the Monocle?"

"Certainly, sir, I can do that right away." Bleeker rapidly fingered the keyboard in front of him, halting only a few times to twist some knobs at the lower end of the console.

The multi-colored screen instantly sprang to life carrying new images that presented more or less the same picture that had frustrated Bobby when he had first arrived forty-five minutes earlier—a small set of ruins in the desert, occupied only by a few heat images, or men.

"Not many rebels have re-occupied the ruins of position 1128, so I guess the General was right." Bobby let out a sigh before he finished. "Rats can leave a ship or come back to a ship, and neither action can be determined in exact numbers."

"What's wrong, sir?" Bleeker asked.

"Nothing, really." Bobby shook his head. "I received some information from our newest national hero and thought that he might have been mistaken.

He wasn't really, but on the other hand, the Monocle can only pinpoint facts, not intentions or strategy."

Price spoke up in what seemed as if it were a feeble attempt to buoy Bobby's outlook. "You know what they say, Major, six of one, half a dozen of another."

Bobby flashed a knowing smirk as he repeated, "Six of one, half a dozen of another." He nodded with an inner smile as he added, "My father used to say that all of the time."

He stood up and gave a casual salute to both Bleeker and Price before he turned to walk away from the millions of dollars worth of electronic equipment.

"Will that be all, sir?" Bleeker asked.

"Yeah, you guys can go back and work on something else for a while. I just remembered something." Bobby looked at his watch as he quickened his pace.

"What's that?" Price asked the question as Bobby exited the room.

"It's almost noon, I've got a funeral to catch."

*   *   *

"This man died with honor, son. I've listened to the detailed review from the throat microphones; you did a hell of a job just keeping yourself alive out there." Tabler replied quietly after he'd listened to Kyle's apology that pertained to the mission's outcome.

Tabler stood next to Kyle, Laurel, and Bobby. All of them had come to pay their respects at the funeral of Jonathon Tagfree, Kodiak Number Six. Tagfree had grown up in a suburb just outside of Washington, so the close proximity of the funeral had given Laurel and Kyle a chance to pay their respects.

"I still feel like I should have been able to do more, sir," Kyle shook his head.

"Give it time, son. Just give it some time. Trust me, I've been there. You've served your country well." Tabler tried to re-assure him as he placed his hand on Kyle's shoulder and gave him a small nod.

Their conversation was cut short when seven soldiers came forth and pointed their rifles upward. The first shots of the twenty-one gun salute rang out to break the silence of the afternoon. The day was relatively warm with a steady breeze that kept the humidity in check, making it comfortable for the many military men in their dress uniforms.

The combination of the weather and the sound of the guns took General Charles Tabler back to his childhood. He had spent many summers on his uncle's farm along the Merrimack River, just outside of St. Louis, Missouri.

On this land Tabler learned how to shoot a gun, an old Winchester rifle. Nothing could beat a slow summer day of target practice, shooting tin cans out in the field. His father would drop him off at his uncle's place on his way to work each morning. Like Tabler's grandfather, his dad had worked in a large brewery in St. Louis, and as he put it, "If baseball was America's number one pastime, then beer and hotdogs couldn't be that far behind."

Uncle Kevin was a World War II veteran who never seemed to run out of stories about the war or his time in the South Pacific. His commitment to his country along with his tales of the exotic lands where he had served had enticed Tabler to enlist.

In addition to his own military adventures, his uncle was also a Civil War buff. His interest in the battles had led him to become one of the chief organizers of the yearly re-enactment of the Battle of Lexington. The event was a large scale re-enactment of the well-known Civil War battle, so everyone involved had to follow the script exactly as it was written. Tabler took an active part and helped his uncle organize the event. He'd also played the role of one of the soldiers for a couple of years.

Throughout his own years of service, Tabler's ability to follow a script, or the chain of command as it was formally called, had helped him climb that chain rapidly. Many times he'd disagreed with a commanding officer's order, but he had always carried out each task with conviction, regardless of how he personally felt.

"The circular chain must never be broken, or everything will break down as we know it." His uncle had given him this advice right before he left for basic training. "Everyone answers to a higher authority, right up to the President himself. The President then answers to the people of the country, linking the chain in an endless circle."

Tabler had risen through the ranks so that now he only basically answered to two people, the President, and his wife of thirty-plus years. Although his military career had been a long and successful one, he was glad that his three children had chosen other professions. His oldest son was an interpreter for the United Nations in New York, while his two daughters were both primary grade school teachers. They both taught in suburbs of Baltimore, Maryland.

Tabler refocused on the present when the final shots of the salute had been fired. As Taps played, he thought of the mission and of the other Kodiak funeral services that were being held in other parts of the country. He glanced over at the two Kodiaks that stood next to him. He reflected again on his own military career as silence was restored to the afternoon when the last note of Taps had been played. The burial flag was then folded and handed to the family of the fallen Kodiak. As the service came to a close, General Charles Tabler had only one thought—*This soldier did not die without a purpose.*

*   *   *

No sooner had Bobby returned from the funeral, than he heard a soft knock on his hotel room's door. He quickly strode to the door, checked through the peephole, and opened it, knowing a tired expression was affixed to his features.

"I saw you at the funeral, Bobby, but I was doing another segment for the special on Mahkeem and didn't have a chance to come over and talk with you." Jennifer Rayburn, just back from Arlington Cemetery, still looked as fresh and as beautiful as if she had just exited a salon.

"Laurel and Kyle were attending so I just went to give them the support they deserve. Kyle's been beating himself up ever since the mission ended. I didn't really have the time to attend the funeral, but it was the right thing to do." Bobby fought the urge to yawn. "You know, I'm normally complaining about waiting around for something to happen, but this week is killing me. I'm not sure if I'm more physically or mentally exhausted at this point."

"I just wanted to say hi. I've got to finish my interview with Mahkeem. If you remember it was cut short last time." Jennifer smiled and stepped into the room. "No pun intended."

"Huh?" Bobby had only been partially listening to her. "Oh, yeah, the daggers. In fact, I just got off the phone with the President and assured him that everyone was okay and that there would be no chance of a repeat visit from our local chapter of assassins."

Jennifer leaned against the doorframe. "Did you ever get any more details on how the phony news crew got the credentials to get in?"

"Intelligence is still trying to track the documents back to their original source, but it looks like they got a hold of some White House stationary and were able to reproduce whatever they needed." Bobby rubbed his eyes and exhaled. "I took a good look at the forged papers myself, and whoever set them up really knew what they were doing."

"Unbelievable. You were right when you said these guys were getting resourceful." Jennifer paused and looked down at her watch. "I've got to go, let's hope the second interview goes smoother than the first."

"Yeah, take it easy on him, okay?" Bobby held his palms out in front him as if he were telling someone to stop.

"Don't I always?" She smiled again.

Bobby opened the door for her. "Why don't you stop by later. I'll buy you dinner downstairs and then who knows?" He gave her his most innocent look.

"Yeah, like I'm going to make that . . ." Jennifer moved closer to Bobby. "What did you call it? Oh, yeah, like I'm going to make that *mistake* again." She walked out the door and flashed a quick smile at him. "But dinner sounds good. I think I'm in the mood for the most expensive thing on the menu."

Bobby shook his head. "I should've just let the dagger guys finish me off."

*   *   *

"So they recruited you for your language and technical skills?" Jennifer was using a different tone than she typically used during an interview of this nature, but Mahkeem's soft-spoken replies had caused her to ease her approach mid-interview.

"Yes. They knew I was a moderate. My job was to help move information through the networks, not kill others. I was present at the executions because I was told that a portable system needed to be set up. I did not know that the system was going to be used for a web-cast featuring the beheading of soldiers. There was a lot of fighting going on a few miles away, so I was trapped in the bunker with a group of radical cell members." Mahkeem looked directly at Jennifer. "I was handed a gun, and how do you say it in English . . . ." He paused for a moment before finishing, "Told to make myself useful."

"But you *were* trained to use a weapon, and as most of America has seen, use a weapon well." Jennifer glanced down at the small notepad she held on her lap as she waited for his answer.

Mahkeem looked her straight in the eye. "Yes. I learned to fire a gun. But killing others was not my job."

"But I was under the impression that all of the members of your organization were trained to kill your enemies, with the preferred method being that of suicide." Jennifer was almost unnerved by Mahkeem's stare. Kyle and Laurel were nervous when she'd spoken with them, but Mahkeem never even flinched.

"The organization has people lining up to become suicide bombers. It is much harder to find a good technical resource in Northern Iraq than it is to find someone willing to die for his or her religion. The radical members are much more respected in the group for obvious reasons, but still, you do not want your computer people blowing themselves up." Mahkeem seemed to reply with brutal honesty. Even as the questions became more sensitive, he held his ground.

"I guess that makes sense, but based on your beliefs, aren't you missing out on the rewards in the afterlife?" Jennifer regained a harder edge as she moved into some of the tougher questions.

"I feel that I will be rewarded justly for my own beliefs. While it may seem like there is an endless line of people ready to die, you must remember that only a small percentage of Islamic followers believe in such rewards."

"But do *you* believe in those rewards?" Jennifer came to the realization that no question was off-limits. He'd answer anything. As she asked the question, she wondered how he'd answer it.

"If I did, I do not think that I would be sitting here with you today. As I have told Captain Bradly, killing an American is not in the true holy writings that I follow." Mahkeem swallowed hard and reached for the glass of water that was on the table next to him. "I only wish to stop the killing. The organization's members have the same goal, but they go about it differently. They just want America to leave Iraq to the Iraqi people."

Jennifer nodded her head as she listened to the reformed rebel's words. "Well, America would like to see the same thing happen." She reached out to shake Mahkeem's hand. "Thank you for taking the time to sit down and talk with us, Mr. Mahkeem. And in closing, I would just like to personally thank you for giving all of us in America, and Iraq, a little bit of hope."

The red light went out on the camera, and the cameraman broke down the equipment. "Good interview, Jennifer."

"Thanks, Allen. You can take off, we're all set."

Allen continued to pack away his equipment while Jennifer reached for her own glass of water. After the attempt on Mahkeem's life, Jennifer never thought that she would be able to bring a cameraman in to do the interview, but with Bobby's help and her national reputation, it was easier than she had thought.

"So that wasn't too bad, was it?" Jennifer fired one final question at the reformed rebel as she took a small sip from her glass and waited for Mahkeem's response.

He let out a long sigh. "No, I believe that I have already been through much worse."

*   *   *

A phone rang in the dark. Without any form of greeting, a voice stated, "He is still alive."

"This, too, has been looked into. The traitor will not live to enjoy his new found fame."

Chapter 18

"The television special on Mahkeem will run tomorrow night at nine." Jennifer sounded relieved to have gotten the interview finished. "The tabloids have already warped everything surrounding him, so my program should give people a chance to learn the truth about our new friend."

"For everything he's done for this country, I guess he deserves his own special." Bobby tried to appear nonchalant and ignore the irritating unrest that he couldn't shake from the back of his mind. He knew something was wrong, but his inner voice told him to concentrate on dinner and Jennifer. *You need the downtime.*

"You don't act like you're so sure." She stared across the table at him. She looked the exact same as she had a year ago.

"No . . . ," began Bobby, "it's not that; it's just that I keep thinking there might be a second level to this, and so far there isn't. I even told Sumner as much."

"Then, why so apprehensive?" Jennifer took a bite and gazed at him.

"I guess it's just a habit with me." Bobby wanted to be distant as he spoke. He needed to be careful with his words because he didn't want to give the media anything that they didn't need to know. "I've been in the Army thirty years and spent most of my time looking under rocks and checking for secrets for every administration since the end of Reagan's term. As an assistant before that, I ran a few favors for Carter." Bobby took a bite of the well-done steak he had ordered from the hotel restaurant. "So after all these years, I could be getting a touch cynical." He chewed momentarily and then held up a finger to let Jennifer know that he had another thought left to convey. "Plus, I've been thinking about what you said the other day."

Jennifer squinted and tilted her head in a mock form of surprise. "About taking some time off?"

"Yeah, and that I really do owe you an apology." Bobby held up his hands, the fork still clutched in his right one. "I just want you to know that I enjoyed the time we spent together in Baghdad last year, and that my career has gotten in the way of a few relationships, that's all." He tried to imagine what it would have been like to have been in an ongoing relationship with Jennifer. Both of them took their careers seriously, which would allow them plenty of time away from one another, but their current relationship was more like two bookends on either side of a non-committal work oriented year. He stared back for another moment. *Then again, who even knew there would be a second bookend?* There was definitely a spark between them, but as experience had taught him, most explosions start with a small spark. *I want to trust her . . . .*

"Mine, too," she agreed. "Everyone has some type of agenda. It's hard being under the celebrity spotlight when you're trying to start any type of relationship. It just makes things very . . . difficult." She smiled and sipped from the thin glass of white wine at her side. "Apology accepted."

As she placed her glass back onto the table, the tension between them seemed to disappear. Bobby felt like it had only been a day since he'd shared a night with Jennifer. His job had taken him away from her, but now . . . maybe things could be different. *I really want to trust her.*

"At least we made it to the second date." Bobby let a genuine smile escape from somewhere deep inside of him. "I'm honestly going to make an effort to get your e-mail address this time."

"Just in case you forget, it's on my station's website." Jennifer's teeth sparkled as she lowered the glass. She was attractive, but the fact that she didn't act like she knew it made her that much more seductive. "Just make sure that you actually use it." She rose from her chair as she gave a coy smile.

"It's that time already?" Bobby showed respect and stood up.

"I've got a ton of work to do tonight. The rough-cut of the television special is waiting for my approval, minus the actual White House medal ceremony segment. And I still have to write the lead-in piece, which we're supposed to be taping early tomorrow."

Bobby shook his head back and forth. "That's right; I forgot." His head continued to shake, but now in agreement with what Jennifer was saying.

She reached over and kissed him on the cheek. "That's for dinner. Try to get some rest tonight, we've got a big day tomorrow."

Bobby sat back down and watched her walk from the restaurant. A few moments after she was gone, he continued to stare at the space she'd occupied for another thirty seconds. As his minded drifted, he suddenly remembered every detail of the night in Baghdad with her. *Maybe a night in Washington is what we both need.* He thought for another few seconds and remembered her media reputation. *Or maybe not.*

*   *   *

WEDNESDAY 23:10, WASHINGTON, D.C.

A van with the markings of a local food store on its side pulled into the Royalview Hotel's underground parking garage for its standard, Wednesday, late-night delivery. One clean-cut, swarthy-faced deliveryman exited the passenger side with a package and walked toward the service elevator. Moments before, the driver had already okayed the delivery at the entrance gate. The deliveryman pushed the button for the second floor, which housed the hotel's kitchen. As he waited, the driver backed the van into a nearby parking space and killed the engine.

Seconds later, the service elevator stopped at the second floor, but before the doors could open, the deliveryman's right hand quickly fingered the button for the sixteenth floor. All floors above sixteen were locked down and could not be reached without a proper ID badge and code.

Less than twenty seconds later, the door opened to reveal the hallway of the sixteenth floor. He immediately pressed a button to close the elevator doors. After the doors were fully closed, he pressed the elevator *stop* button and looked up to find that the service hatch was locked down with a small padlock.

He quickly reached into his shirt to retrieve a small, narrow device with a number of short metal prongs protruding from one end. He inserted the device into the lock and then pressed a small button on the other end. A few moments later, the open lock fell to the elevator floor with a muted clank. He reached down and pushed the package into the shaft above him.

He pulled himself through the open maintenance door and made his way to the service ladder. The elevator shaft was dimly lit from the light coming from the open elevator hatch. Additional light seeped into the area from the outer elevator doors that belonged to the floors above. He quickly climbed the ladder to reach the seventeenth floor. Once there, he pulled a small release lever next to the heavy metal doors that separated the hotel hallway from the elevator shaft. He pushed apart the doors, and squeezed through to the hallway beyond.

A second later, he pulled the elevator doors closed and walked softly to the corner where the adjacent hallway began. He peered around it, noticed the two guards in front of Mahkeem's room, pulled his head back around into the foyer, and pressed the regular guest elevator button. It opened silently.

He placed the package on the ground temporarily and moved into the elevator. He was only in the elevator for a few moments before he opened the control panel with the same tool that he had used on the padlock a few minutes earlier.

Each hotel floor button had two wires attached to it, a ground wire and a live wire. The live wires all went back to a central circuit board, where they were screwed into small terminals that were marked with the corresponding floor number. The man cut the live wires for all of the floor buttons minus one. He then took a piece of metallic tape and connected the now broken buttons together to form a single circuit. He checked over his work to confirm that all of the elevator buttons would now lead to a single destination. He closed the pane, checked his watch, and then nodded when he realized that he was ahead of schedule. He quickly repeated the operation on the other two elevators. He then checked his watch again. *Two minutes per elevator, not bad.*

He walked to the other side of the foyer and climbed onto a tall, elegant-looking, trash can. He reached up and pushed one of the hanging ceiling panels out of its frame and placed the package as far inside as he could reach.

Finished with his task, he lightly leapt down to the floor and calmly walked to an unlabeled, solid white door. He once again used his lock-picking device to open the door quickly and slip into the small room. After he'd entered, he turned on the light and surveyed the room. He was in the main wiring closet for the floor. There was a cable television hub with individual lines for each room, telephone lines, and an incredible amount of electrical wiring. The electrical wires all led back to a large cabinet that contained separate breakers for the various circuits. He located the circuit that controlled the smoke alarms on the floor and flipped it into the *off* position. He found the special battery backup unit on the smoke alarm circuit that would kick in if the floor lost power for any reason. He verified the connections and then clipped the wires to disable the backup power supply.

Now that he'd completed his final task, he turned off the light, exited the wiring room, and slipped silently through the well-lit, double doors marked *Stairs* at the end of the hallway. Once in the stairwell, the sounds of his shoe leather on the concrete steps became apparent as each little tone became amplified with echoes.

After the door had closed, he took a moment to extract a thin but heavy metal tube from inside his jacket. He untwisted the metal tube until it elongated. He then slipped it through the handles of both doors and bound them together with a roll of duct tape he'd pulled from a side pocket. He then tugged at the door for a moment and nodded before he turned and casually strolled down the seventeen flights of stairs. As he walked, he fingered a plunger type device that was hidden in one of his inner pockets.

*   *   *

Shortly after dinner, Bobby returned to his hotel room to peruse the findings of some of the Pentagon discs that PFC Bleeker had made for him. The monitor screen on his computer showed the same data he had researched for the last two days. He even had the findings from the information that Mahkeem had supplied, including that of site 1128. Bobby thought that by looking into the training site they'd cleaned out, he might jog something in his mind, but he was wrong. It seemed Private Price was right. "Six of one, and half a dozen of another."

A full dozen Kodiak soldiers had been sent over for a mission, Bobby thought to himself. *Three came back alive along with the nine bodies. Twelve echoes altogether from the personal tracking chips back in the States.* He clicked on the on-screen timeline until the echo quadrant of his monitor displayed the lone ping by itself. "And throw in a thirteenth echo for good luck."

Just then someone pounded on the door as one of Mahkeem's guards burst through the entrance to his room. Bobby was about to question why the guard had left his post, when the guard announced sharply, "Major, quick, we've got to evacuate, there's a fire on our floor!"

Chapter 19

"Fire?" Bobby stated the word almost as if it were impossible. Something wasn't right. "But the smoke alarms aren't going off. Corporal Roberts, where is Mahkeem right now?"

"Simpson is back in Mahkeem's room getting him into a body armor vest." Roberts held his light carbine with both hands in front of him as if he were still on guard duty.

"Good," Bobby replied sharply. "Then let's get the hell over there right now. This fire seems too convenient to me." He looked momentarily at his computer and thought of the discs and the information from the Pentagon. After a split second of thought, he knew he could get the same data back from Price or Bleeker. He grabbed his borrowed gun, still on loan from Bethert, and joined Roberts. They raced through an ever-thickening cloud of smoke and down the hallway toward Mahkeem's room.

As they entered the suite, Simpson had just gotten Mahkeem buckled into the Kevlar harness. Bobby turned to his left and barked a command at Roberts. "Get Bradly and Crickowski."

As the guard left the suite, Bobby turned to Simpson. "Is he ready?"

"Yes, sir." Simpson reached down and a grabbed for his gun.

"Mr. Mahkeem, I want you to come with us, but stay behind me. It'll be safer for you." Bobby grabbed him by the shoulder and herded him behind Simpson. As they all piled into the hallway, Roberts, Kyle, and Laurel came to a halt next to them.

Bobby stood in the doorway. "Get to the stairway, with Roberts and Simpson in front, I'll trail behind. Mahkeem, stay behind me; Kodiaks, bring up the rear." All of the participants did as they were told and within a half a minute the group had traversed their way through the darkening smoke and arrived at the metal doorway marked *Stairs*.

The group stopped instantly as Roberts and Simpson flattened against the metal door. They both pushed violently at the release bar that ran straight across the width of the exit with no change—the door wouldn't budge.

"Out of the way." Bobby jumped forward between Roberts and Simpson and kicked out with a powerful snap of his leg. The sound from his boot echoed through the hall, but the result was the same—the door barely moved.

He turned toward the other side of the hallway. "The door's jammed from the other side. Follow me back to the elevator, but be careful. I don't buy this coincidence for a minute—someone's trying to trap us up here." Bobby tugged the borrowed, nine-millimeter glock from his belt and held it in front of him as he talked. After a few seconds, the group reached the elevator and Bobby pushed the button for the next car. Quickly, he backed up and pointed the glock straight at the place where the two doors would open, half expecting there to be danger when they did.

The doors slid open momentarily to reveal nothing more than an empty car. The group moved toward the entranceway, but as they did, Bobby held up a hand. "Hold it!"

He turned his back on the bunch and as smoke continued to filter along the corridor, he raced back to his room. A few seconds later, he returned with a wooden desk chair. Before anyone could question him, he tossed the chair into the open car. The chair echoed as it bounced on the floor of the elevator car.

"Smart thinking, sir, it could have been a bomb." Simpson held his rifle in front of him.

"It still could be." Bobby leapt into the elevator. The resounding thud of his landing made Simpson's face scrunch into a picture of question.

Bobby saw the confused look. "Between the weight of the chair, my own weight, plus the force of my landing, I don't think the car itself is mined. Let's go!"

Everyone piled in quickly as Bobby pushed the lobby button. The doors closed and the car began its descent. All of the passengers huddled together with Mahkeem, Laurel, and Kyle in the rear of the compartment, Bobby off to the right side, and Simpson and Roberts in front.

Bobby slipped out a cell phone as the numbers lit up in reverse order on the elevator panel.

SIXTEEN

FIFTEEN

FOURTEEN

Bobby hit the speed dial button for the connection to General Tabler.

THIRTEEN

TWELVE

He put the cell phone to his ear as soon as he had correctly dialed the number.

ELEVEN

TEN

The ring tone buzzed in his ear.

NINE

EIGHT

SEVEN

"Damnit." Bobby held the phone tightly. "Come on."

SIX

FIVE

FOUR

"Hello, this is the voice mail of General Tabler. At the tone—"

Bobby hung up and thought about his next move.

THREE

TWO

ONE

"When the doors open, everybody head out into the lobby, but for Christ's sake, be careful. This fire is way too convenient for me to swallow." Bobby held his handgun next to his face.

He watched as the display read LOBBY, but the elevator did not stop and continued on its downward descent.

"Oh, shit, now I know somebody's screwing with us." The disgust was plain in Bobby's tone of voice. "Simpson, Roberts, when the doors open, each of you advance two feet and take a side. I'll take the middle. Kodiaks, stay put, watch our guest, and be careful. All of you are national heroes at the moment." Bobby had the borrowed gun still at his face and was thrusting it forward when the final light on the panel made a dinging sound.

BASEMENT

As the door opened, Bobby saw the huge, grey expanse that was the underground parking garage. The doors slid a little more open, and the two guards lunged forward, both of their weapons in a firing position. Bobby jumped between them.

Two men stood a few feet back from either side of the elevator. They were dressed in jeans and loose jackets with scarves wrapped around their faces and heads, leaving only slits for their vision.

Bobby spotted the figure on the right and noticed that the man's hand was poised in readiness upon some form of triggering device. He snapped off a shot that traveled over Roberts' shoulder and struck the unknown person in the left eye. The attacker collapsed instantly without activating any suspected device.

"Down!" Bobby knew there was no time to stop the figure on the left, and he was correct. The blast drove Simpson off of his feet and into the already diving figure of Bobby. They tumbled back into the elevator and slammed into the right wall of the compartment. Bobby, out of the corner of his eye, saw Roberts flung backward as well.

Shouts resounded within the elevator car as debris from the blast ricocheted throughout the tiny space. Luckily, due to the angle in which the bomber had stood, the blast was directed more across the front of the elevator than into it.

"Come on," said Bobby in a woozy fashion. "We're sitting ducks in here. We've got to get out." He pushed Simpson gently off of him, but only the top half of the soldier rolled over. His bottom still lie strewn across Bobby's legs, gushing blood. He kicked the set of legs from his own and struggled to his feet. He stood in the center of the elevator car, painted red from neck to ankles with Simpson's life-giving fluid.

He heard the first bullet strike over his head into the rear of the compartment. He squinted hard and took a deep breath that helped clear his sight and chase the dizziness from his head.

Across the parking garage fifty yards away to the other side, he saw at least six, maybe eight, hooded men with automatic rifles. All of them ran toward the elevator as the first terrorist fired his opening volley.

"Jesus and Allah both," muttered Bobby barely aloud.

Chapter 20

Jennifer leaned back in her chair, stretched out her arms, and looked at her watch. "Three hours down already."

She had returned to her room immediately after dinner to work on the finishing touches of her television special. She'd already downloaded and reviewed the segments that had been completed by the postproduction crew at the station. She had also gone over the content and structure of the program. As she checked each segment, she focused on the order in which they would be broadcast.

The special started out with a lead-in by Jennifer, which was to be filmed the next day in front of the White House. The second segment featured edited versions of the Internet web-casts, each with a brief introduction from Harvard University professor Dan Perry, a renowned expert on international terrorism. The web-casts were then to be followed with a timeline feature, which highlighted the events surrounding the last few days. Finally, an edited version of the medal ceremony, which again, was yet to be filmed, would complete the first half-hour of the special. The second half would start out with a brief background on Laurel Crickowski, followed by her interview. The final segment, the one that most people would be tuning in to see, contained the interview with Mr. Ahlmed Mahkeem. At the end of the interview, Jennifer would make some closing remarks back in front of the White House to finish out the hour-long special report.

She continued to refine the dialogue for the lead-in segment when she suddenly heard her cell phone and quickly reached into her purse to retrieve it. She recognized the number that was displayed on her caller ID and quickly pressed the talk button as she raised the phone to her ear. "Hey, Curtis, what have you got for me?"

"I've got some good news, and I've got some bad news," replied Curtis.

Jennifer sat up in her chair. "You've been the executive producer for enough of my television specials to know that I always like to hear the good news first."

Curtis Pullman was one of the single best producers in the country when it came to putting together a television special based on a current event. He had the ability to hold the audience for the entire presentation by using clever editing techniques to coax the viewers into hanging around for just one more segment.

"Well, Jen, the good news is that your special is not only going to be shown on network television at nine o'clock, but our cable affiliate has picked it up for an encore presentation at ten." Curtis' voice beamed as he spoke.

"That's fantastic, Curt, now let me have the bad news before I get too excited." Jennifer held her breath as she anticipated his reply. *Please don't tell me I have to cut a segment.*

"The bad news, which is also sort of good in a way, is that the network has decided to air the entire special without commercial interruption." There was a moment of silence on the phone before Curt added, "So we've got approximately twelve extra minutes of air-time to fill."

Jennifer exhaled, more time was always a luxury, and at least they wouldn't have to cut anything. "The flow of the special is already pretty tight. What about adding an additional interview or two? Maybe we could focus on the personnel behind the Army's rescue mission?"

"Not a bad idea, but I wanted to run something else by you." He paused and she recognized Curt's tone. He was cooking up something to pull the audience in even deeper.

"Okay, Curt, let me have it." Jennifer tried to stay open-minded. This special was her baby, but a little Curt input never hurt.

"I want to recap your personal encounter with the suicide bomber last year in Iraq. We'll slide in the new segment right before you interview the ex-rebel guy. It'll remind the audience that you've looked death in the face, and can truly appreciate what he's done." Curt sounded excited as he finished his pitch.

Jennifer thought about the idea for a moment. Enough time had passed where the idea didn't actually bother her, but the idea sounded slightly off-topic. "Won't we lose momentum going from Laurel, to me, and then to Mahkeem?"

"Not if we do it as a re-enactment, using actors to play the roles of you, the Army guy who saved you, and the bomber." Curt sounded a bit smug.

Jennifer shook her head. "That'll take too much time to pull together; we've got less than a day before airtime."

"It's already done. We took some stock footage from two other re-enactments we had on file, did a little editing, and presto, we've got Rayburn versus the suicide bomber."

Jennifer was really shaking her head. "Okay, okay, slide it in. But I'd like to view the transitions from the segments leading in and out of the re-enactment."

"Not a problem, I'll get it rendered up and send it to you," said Curt.

Jennifer knew he loved putting together a special. Before she could reply, Curt added, "Although we still have one other small problem. Even with the new segment, I'm guessing that we're still going to come up about a minute short."

Jennifer thought for a moment and then laughed. "Why don't we just fill the time with a quick medal preview, running down a few of the people who have received the congressional freedom award in the last few years? You know, sort of like an Olympic recap of sorts."

"Done," was Curt's only reply.

"Good, because I need to get back to this dialogue I'm working on." Jennifer stared at the sentences she'd written on the computer screen in front of her.

"Okay, Jen, I'll see you tomorrow."

"I'm looking forward to it." She pressed the button on her phone to end the conversation and set it down on her desk.

Time to get serious and finish this thing, she commented to herself as she thought about an extra large café-mocha, with a double shot of espresso, from the gourmet coffee shop down in the lobby.

Jennifer stared at her computer screen for another few seconds before she jumped up and grabbed the card-key to her room. A moment later, she was out the door.

She walked briskly down the hallway, entered the elevator, and pressed the button for the lobby. As the elevator started its descent, she closed her eyes to rest them for a moment and thought. *I definitely need a little kick of something to wake me up.*

* * *

Bobby reached over and tugged the carbine from Simpson's lifeless hand. He tucked his own borrowed hand gun back into his belt, stood up, and snapped off a few shots in the general direction of the advancing terrorists. The figures scattered as each one went to seek refuge from the gunfire.

"I thought these bastards liked committing suicide." Kyle shouted out his concern from the left rear of the elevator car where he and Laurel shielded Mahkeem with their own bodies.

"They weren't taking anyone with them this time, that's the difference." Bobby fired another shot at one of the figures near a pillar. "It doesn't matter how fanatic some people are, you fire a shot at them, and they'll flinch. It's human nature."

"Then cover me and I'll go for Roberts' rifle." Kyle, who had been despondent over the way the mission had turned out in Iraq, looked eager to jump back into battle and prove himself.

Bobby tossed him the carbine he had been using and ordered, "No, you stay glued in front of Mahkeem and cover me through the open door."

"You okay? That bomb blast took you off your feet."

"No, the bomb blast took Simpson off of his feet, and then it was Simpson who actually took me off of my feet." Bobby pulled his pistol from his belt. "I've just got a splitting headache, then again—this entire mission has been one damn headache from the start." He finished and raced through the doorway and turned to his right toward Roberts' body.

Bobby heard Kyle open fire from behind him as he saw a few flashes of rifle fire erupt from the other side of the parking garage in his direction. He fell flat into a pool of blood that used to belong to Roberts. Bobby reached up with his free hand, felt the soldier's neck for a pulse, and found nothing.

Ricocheting bullets landed a yard in front of Bobby's face and skipped over his head, burying themselves in the concrete wall behind him. He looked around and saw the parameters of the garage. It was about two hundred yards wide and fifty to seventy-five feet deep. He looked at the deep end where the terrorists had exited the van one-half of a football field away from the elevator door. They advanced toward them quickly, always stopping to re-position themselves behind one of the many dozen, twelve-foot thick, rounded pillars that made a sturdy foundation for the hotel above.

Bobby crawled forward, through the blood slick, toward the terrorist bomber that he'd shot in the eye. He lie there, arms outstretched, unveiling the explosive device that had been strapped to his stomach. He noticed the plunger in the man's hand and the long wire, coiled many times around the man's arm before it connected to the base of the device on his torso. Bobby thought about Mahkeem's safety for a moment as he unwound the coiled up wire and backed up toward the body of Roberts.

Just then he froze as he heard a sloshing sound from behind him. He spun around onto his side when he saw the terrorist, his automatic rifle pointed at an angle into the elevator compartment, but he hadn't begun to fire yet.

Bobby pulled the trigger on his own weapon and caught the terrorist high in the shoulder. The terrorist spun around, but unfortunately, the recoil of the weapon against Bobby's blood-covered palm caused him to lose the weapon. The gun slipped from his grasp onto the garage floor and skidded away.

As the terrorist recovered from the initial shock of the shoulder wound, he raised his weapon. Bobby knew he only had a moment to address the danger. He quickly dropped the plunger, leapt to his feet, and dove into the hooded figure like a football defensive back might tackle a wide receiver.

He caught the terrorist in the stomach and drove him back into the concrete wall. The terrorist raised his rifle horizontal to the ground and placed it alongside Bobby's lower rib. Bobby grabbed him by the face and pushed with all of his might as he slammed the terrorist's head into the cement block wall. There was a loud clunk as the man's body went limp, followed by the sound of gunfire.

Three slugs from the man's rifle discharged parallel with Bobby's lowest, left rib. They cut through the cloth material of his shirt and burned a quarter-inch groove into the flesh on his side.

The stinging sensation instantly doubled Bobby over to a kneeling position. He fell to the garage floor on one knee as he sharply grunted and gasped for air. Just as suddenly, bullets from another terrorist's rifle raked a pattern across the chest of the rebel who had just shot Bobby. Had Bobby not reacted to his own injury, he would have been cut in half.

Bobby looked up and focused on the still standing dead rebel. He grabbed the weapon from the dead hand, tucked the butt of the rifle under his own right shoulder, and fired the entire clip in the area where the latest burst of enemy gunfire had originated. A moment later, Bobby saw another hooded figure slump forward from behind a pillar and fall dead on the garage floor.

"You still doing okay?" Kyle shouted from inside the car.

"Yeah, keep up the cover fire." Bobby tried to shout in return, but the pain in his side distracted him. Instead, his reply was more of a hoarse cough.

He grabbed the plunger he had dropped, rose to his feet and ran for the elevator opening. Several more shots fired in his direction. Four or five bullets bounced off the concrete floor just behind him, but the last one caught him in the left calf and sent him sprawling into the elevator car face first. He landed with a thud.

"Are you al—" Laurel shouted.

"Everyone, be quiet!" Bobby barked. "Bradly, quit firing and shout out twice, like you're in pain."

With a quizzical look on his face, Kyle complied and once finished, placed his rifle by his side.

"What the hell was that for? They already know you're hit." Laurel looked confused.

"Correct, but they don't know how badly. Now everyone stay quiet and get ready for a nice game of possum."

Chapter 21

"Late tomorrow afternoon, President Sumner will be decorating two Special Forces soldiers as well as awarding the Congressional Medal of Freedom to the Iraqi ex-rebel, Ahlmed Mahkeem. The ceremony will take place live in the White House Rose Garden with an extensive list of radio and television personnel in attendance." The brown-haired, non-descript reporter paused while he held a serious look on his face. "This is Rick Burton for WNN."

"That should make your Presidential approval rating soar." Cynthia Sumner lay in bed next to her husband. She reached over and hit the mute button on the television's remote control.

"I don't care about my rating as much as I want the insurgence to see that America and Iraq can work together." Sumner rolled over to face Cynthia. "Can you turn the volume back up? I thought we were going to watch some more television."

Cynthia shot a very motherly look back toward her husband. "You're the President, you've got a big day ahead of you. I think you need your rest."

"Yes, but you know I always like to catch the Tonight Show to see if I make the monologue or not." Sumner dropped his shoulders slightly and raised one eyebrow as he gave the most convincing look he could muster.

"I still can't believe that you're not bothered by the late night comedians always cracking jokes about you." She pushed herself backward until she rested against the headboard. "And you even laugh at the jokes."

"You know, there is actually a lot of truth to most things said in jest. I think of it as a social commentary that helps me see things from a slightly different point of view." Sumner suddenly looked very serious. "I had to sign nine Presidential certificates for the Kodiak members that died as a result of the failed mission. Those certificates were presented to the families of the fallen soldiers at their funerals throughout the country today. These late-night shows take my mind off of everything that I deal with on a day to day basis and give me a chance just to laugh at myself."

Cynthia reached over and rubbed his shoulder as she leaned into him. "I'm glad you've kept your sense of humor, and I'm also thankful that you've given yourself a number of ways to relax, let go, and just be my husband." Her face softened further. "But at least the late night skits during last year's Presidential race are long gone. Those were terrible. Do you remember the debate skit where they depicted you as a history geek reciting every obscure Presidential historical reference?"

Sumner's expression lightened. "Yeah. The historical references weren't even close to accurate. But I *am* a pretty big fan of the guy who plays me. He's got my mannerisms down perfectly. I sometimes wonder how often he walks around pretending to be me. He might even do a better impersonation of me than I do." Sumner felt a sense of calmness come over him. Just the thought of the late night comedies helped his mental state. No matter what had happened in the world, the late-night talk-show hosts had always been there for him. "And for your information, the network sent me copies of those shows, which I still have on disc if you'd like to watch them sometime."

Cynthia hit the *off* button on the television remote and reached toward the lamp by the side of the bed. She clicked it off and sent the room into total darkness.

"I'll take that as a no," replied Sumner.

"Come on, honey, you've got to really try to get some sleep tonight." Cynthia pulled the sheets over them as she slid down until her head rested on her pillow.

Sumner was tired, but he wasn't ready to fall asleep yet. He thought about arguing with her, but knew he'd lose. "You're probably right." He gave Cynthia a hug before he rolled over and settled his head in against his own pillow.

*   *   *

"Price, would you come and take a look at this?" Bleeker's face felt tortured as he asked, only with the aspect of pain being replaced with unanswered questions.

"What's wrong?" Price rolled his chair up to the console.

"I've been checking the Monocle's progress the last hour or so." Bleeker tapped his fingers on top of the computer mouse nervously.

"Yeah," Price seemed almost disinterested.

"Sector 1128 came up, the one that Major Handle was checking earlier." Bleeker pulled up the site's image on the screen.

"So?" Price still showed that he couldn't have cared less.

Bleeker pointed to the screen, zoomed in on the image, and then pointed again. "It's empty. We saw rebels there just a few hours ago, and now it's empty."

"It doesn't take much to spook those guys out of one of their training camps." Price stared blankly. "So what's the problem?"

Bleeker decided just to spell it out to his partner. "The air strike is due in two hours, and they've got nothing but an empty target."

Price bit his lower lip.

"Also," continued Bleeker. "I was just given a list of the other strike sites so that we could make sure to record them on the Monocle's camera."

"And?" Price's forehead finally showed furrows of worry.

"All of the other sites have been abandoned within the last quarter hour. I even double-checked the Monocle's error log to see if we had some type of heat sensor malfunction, but everything checked out. Do you think we should wait for another pass of the satellite ninety-minutes from now, or should we contact someone?" Bleeker looked to his partner for an answer. Their superior officers were not going to be happy.

"This is way over our heads," said Price. "Let's get a hold of General Tabler right away. He'll know what to do."

*   *   *

IRAQ

Joe Manelli walked down the line of rebel bodies that had been lined up, cleaned off, and readied for transport. He looked at every toe tag of information, if one was available, before he motioned for the rubber body bag to be zipped up by the private beside him.

On the eighth figure, Joe gave a cursory glance at the tag, and then at the face. He nodded for the private to zip up the bag when he suddenly caught sight of something. He immediately thrust out his arm and halted the private in mid-motion.

"What the fuck have we got here?" Joe just got an overwhelming sense of déjà vu. He knelt down, grabbed the dead rebel by the beard and pulled upward. At the level of his collar, he saw a diagonal scar, shaped like a jagged letter Z.

He paused momentarily before he grabbed the dead man's left shoulder and ripped the fabric of his shirt. He continued to rip and peel the shirt back like the layer of an onion until the rebel's shoulder area was totally exposed. Joe stopped when he saw the new growth of pink skin over a recent shoulder wound.

"Anything wrong, sir?" The Private was still in mid-zip when he asked the question.

"Fuck yeah, something's wrong." started Joe, "I've got to make another call to Bobby."

*   *   *

"From my angle it looks like they're about fifteen feet away from the door and all bunched together." Kyle whispered the words through lips that barely parted for fear of the attackers spotting the movement.

"Good." Bobby was face down in the elevator. A combination of blood and sweat dripped from his hair as he remained perfectly still. "Let me know when they're about eight to ten feet away."

Kyle counted the steps of the advancing attackers through the half closed lid of one eye.

Bobby tried to slow his breath. He hoped there was no terrorist among the group that had better than twenty-twenty vision, or else they'd spot his shallow breathing as well as his one half-opened eye.

Kyle counted off another five seconds before he whispered again, "Now!"

Bobby pushed the plunger on the small triggering device in his hand, sending the electronic command through the coiled wire and into the package of explosives wrapped around the dead attacker's waist.

The explosion wasn't that large or devastating, but it was big enough to kill half of the advancing figures and stun the others.

Laurel instantly leapt away from Mahkeem and onto her feet. She grabbed the carbine that Kyle had used and opened fire on a few of the figures that were still moving.

"What the hell was that all about?" Kyle was at Laurel's side as Bobby stiffly rose and joined them.

"I'm tired of being a damn pawn for their cause. I was captured on a mission and almost beheaded on a live Internet feed. Now they're shooting at us because they want to kill the guy that saved me." Laurel was livid as she spoke. She scanned the garage a final time, ready to kill anything that moved.

Before Kyle could respond, Mahkeem appeared next to them. "I believe she is justified. These fanatic factions, who now seek to take my life, cannot understand the Western world. I am sorry that two more of your soldiers died protecting me."

"Yeah, and these terrorists won't be bothering any of us again." Laurel continued to survey the carnage as she spoke.

"Yeah," began Kyle, "but if one of them was still alive, we could have interrogated him and got him to talk."

Bobby shuffled past them with a slight limp. He bent over to pick up his handgun when he felt a sharp pain on his left side. He knew he was going to medical attention, he just hoped he'd be able to get it before something else happened. "I wasn't really in the mood to talk anyway." He straightened up and then turned as he heard an engine roar to life in another part of the garage.

The food van, which had transported the hooded attackers, had come to life. A second later, it raced toward them.

So much for getting medical attention first, thought Bobby.

He turned to the Kodiaks. "Get Mahkeem out of here." Bobby yelled the order so loudly that he caused everyone to jump.

Kyle grabbed Mahkeem and pulled him past the elevator doors until they disappeared behind one of the concrete pillars. Laurel followed behind them, with her gun at the ready.

Bobby grabbed the blood-soaked gun and fired two quick shots into the front right tire. The van instantly wobbled as the punctured tire exploded. He then fired two more shots just above the steering wheel. He struck the driver in the chest to kill him instantly.

The van jerked to the left and tipped. It tumbled over and over across the garage floor as it veered to Bobby's right. The sound of crushing metal and glass echoed throughout the garage as the side-view mirrors and door handles were ripped from the vehicle.

"Keep moving and get the hell out of here!" Bobby raced to get out of the way of the tumbling truck. Mentally, he didn't know which way was the safest to run because the van could change direction at any time. After a split second, he decided to run to his right.

The van was now stuck on its side. A shower of sparks erupted from underneath the vehicle as the metal scraped across the concrete garage floor.

The roof of the van pointed directly at Bobby as the truck continued to slide.

He ran as fast as he could force his legs to move.

Twenty feet and the van still skidded.

Bobby was away from the first elevator door, but was still not out of the deadly swath of the sliding vehicle.

Fifteen feet and the van still skidded.

Bobby, concentrating on the trajectory of the van, lost his footing as he slipped on a patch of blood.

Ten feet and the van still skidded.

Bobby got up quickly but saw that it was no use trying to avoid the van, skidding on its side directly for him.

Five feet away, and although the speed of the van was now slowing slightly, Bobby knew he had no other choice.

He leapt into the air and let the roof of the van catch him in the side. He instantly reached out and grabbed an open side window which was now pointing straight up. Whether he liked it or not, he was going for a ride, hitched to the side of the mangled piece of metal.

The wall was coming up fast behind him as he tried to throw his legs over the top of the van before he was crushed between the vehicle and the second elevator door. Then, from behind him, he heard a dinging sound and chanced a look over his shoulder. The middle elevator's doors were opening.

Bobby changed his tactics and turned his body as he released his hand from the van window. He aimed himself at the widening crack of the second elevator compartment.

Just as the vehicle rammed itself into the outer concrete basement wall, Bobby was flung literally through the air. He threaded his body between the opening doors, and into the compartment. He bounced off the back wall of the elevator and fell to the floor with a grunt.

Jennifer screamed at the sight of her blood-covered friend.

Bobby rolled onto his back and groaned. "Hi, Jen. What's wrong? I thought this was the life that you wanted to be a part of." He rested his head back on the floor of the elevator and closed his eyes for what seemed like an eternity.

*   *   *

Bobby opened his eyes again less than a minute before the trio of Laurel, Kyle, and Mahkeem returned. Kyle reached over and helped Jennifer through the partially blocked entrance of the second elevator. A moment later, Bobby slid down past the van, and onto the concrete floor behind them.

As they walked toward the nearby stairs, Bobby, his limping more pronounced now, still gripped his gun.

"Want to lean on me, Major?" Kyle walked beside Bobby and offered him his shoulder.

"No thanks," said Bobby. "Until we get around some people and I know we're safe, I don't want to relax."

Just then the light above the third elevator door blinked on and resonated with the typical dinging sound. Bobby pulled up his weapon and pointed it straight at where the two doors met. Laurel followed his lead, knelt down, and drew her gun on the soon to be opening doors. She shot a quick look over at Bobby and nodded her head, letting him know that she was ready. At the same time, Kyle quickly grabbed Mahkeem and pulled him behind the van to protect him against the next impending wave of attackers.

As the elevator doors parted, a slightly paunchy, balding, middle-aged man in a robe and slippers, carrying a clear plastic bucket, gasped at the sight of a gun mere inches from his face.

His lips quivered, and he asked in a quaking voice, "Ice?"

Chapter 22

Captain Anne Bethert yawned as she checked her watch. She was headed home after another late night of filling out paperwork when the police scanner picked up a disturbance at the Royalview Hotel. When she heard the whereabouts of the altercation, she had a strong gut feeling that she would probably find Major Handle and his ex-rebel friend right in the middle of it.

Because Bobby Handle was involved, Bethert called in Gerald B. Orlando immediately. Gerald had earlier uncovered a very interesting piece of evidence from the doctor's office that she wanted to personally discuss with Handle.

She had already been inside the hotel and given the crime scene a once over before she had headed back outside to wait for her colleague. Her wait ended as quickly as it started when his car flew into the parking lot.

The more than thirty-year-old car sputtered to a stop a few feet from where she stood. The driver smiled, turned off the single operative headlight, and then forced open the barely functioning door.

"Gerald, I know how much you make. You've *got* to get yourself a new car." Bethert addressed Gerald as he slammed his car door shut to the accompaniment of grinding metal.

"This was my grandfather's car. He used to take me to the zoo in it when I was little. When he passed away, my dad saved it for me. I love this car." Gerald smiled and in the process, showed off his braces in the moonlight. "And besides, you just don't see too many AMC Pacers on the road anymore."

Bethert shook her head. "I think there's probably a good reason for that."

Gerald stared at his car for a few seconds, lost in some type of thought before he turned to face Bethert. "Your call made it sound like a serious battle took place. How many bodies this time, Captain?" He got right to the point as he usually did. "You're going to have to give me the count. Based on the carnage in there, I'm not really sure." She knew Gerald was basically immune to crime scenes after so many years working in his field, but this one was nothing less than a war zone.

Gerald's eyes grew wide as his eyebrows seemed to elevate right into the bottom of his hairline.

"Oh." It was only a single word reply, but it took a good three seconds for him to completely utter it. He then added, "I brought the item from the doctor's office for Major Handle." He proudly held up the evidence bag. "I can't wait to see the look on his face when I tell him about this one."

"Yeah, well, why don't you go on in and have a quick look around. I'll grab a couple of drinks from the lobby." Bethert fished in her pocket for loose change. "What do you want?"

Gerald ran his tongue over the braces attached to his upper front teeth. "Just get me a jumbo cherry soda and a large iced-tea." He scrunched up his nose and thought for another couple of seconds. "And grab an extra cup so I can mix the two of them together easier."

Bethert nodded and turned to walk into the hotel. "And to think that Gerald is still single, amazing."

*　　*　　*

The hotel doctor removed the blood soaked shirt from Bobby's back. He took a wet cloth and gently wiped the blood away from the side of Bobby's body where the gun had gone off.

The Royalview was equipped to provide its guests with services typically not available in most hotels. One such amenity, was that it included a fully equipped medical facility on the first floor with a rotation of on-call doctors and specialists. Bobby had limped into the facility less than a half-hour ago and had less than a fifteen-minute wait before the on-call doctor showed up. *Better service than a hospital*, thought Bobby. *Almost no wait.*

"Well, Major," the doctor began. "I guess the good news is that most of this blood isn't yours, and these wounds aren't going to require any sutures. It looks like the heat from the discharging weapon cauterized the skin, giving you three distinct second-degree burns." He dipped a large cotton cloth into a solution and cleaned the damaged skin. He then applied a topical salve and wrapped Bobby's mid-section in a long cotton bandage.

Bobby continued to wipe the blood from his other arm as the doctor moved on to review the injury to his leg.

"Your lower calf looks like it took quite a shot, you were lucky this was just a ricochet. The bullet didn't penetrate too deeply, but you're going to need to stay off of your feet for a couple of days." The doctor rotated Bobby's leg slowly as he continued to examine the extent of the injury.

"So is there or isn't there a bullet in my leg?" Bobby just wanted to get back to his room and get some rest. *The quicker this is over, the better.*

"There's at least a partial bullet in there all right, but not for much longer. I'm going to need you to lie down and stay still. The pieces are just under your skin on the side of your calf, so I'll only need a few minutes." The doctor unwrapped a number of small sharp instruments and wiped Bobby's leg down with some sort of yellowish solution.

Bobby slid down to lay on his side.

The doctor grabbed a syringe. "I'm going to give you a local. You shouldn't feel a thing."

Yeah, I've already felt enough tonight, thought Bobby. As the doctor continued to prep his leg, Bobby closed his eyes off and on. He stared mindlessly at the light over the table and couldn't help but think about the bright light people said they saw before death. He'd almost drifted off when a familiar face suddenly appeared right over his head. His thoughts about his own mortality drifted away quickly because Washington's favorite pathologist, Gerald B. Orlando, had eclipsed the light.

"How are you feeling, Major?" asked Gerald in earnest. "Looks like I'm going to be here the rest of the night trying to match up heads with body parts." He paused and then took a long sip from a cup that smelled like a mixture of cherry soda and iced-tea.

"I've had better days. What's up, Gerald?" As Bobby spoke, he looked to his left to see that Captain Anne Bethert had also just entered the room.

"Major, this is obviously a bad time to talk." Bethert motioned to Gerald. "Come on, we'll catch him later."

"No, hang on," started Bobby. "As you can see, I'm not going anywhere for a while. Now is probably as good a time as any." He looked down at the doctor who had just dug something out of his leg. "So seriously, did you find something interesting down in the garage?"

"I haven't really gotten started yet." Gerald curled his arm up in an attempt to make a muscle. "I'm still pulling my equipment out of my car and trying to get set up. When I heard you were involved, I brought some extra of everything."

Bobby winced as the doctor tugged on his calf with a sharp metal instrument. *Okay, I felt that.* The local anesthetic had worked, but this pain had come from another part of his leg. In addition to the calf wound, his knee had been badly bruised when the van catapulted him into the elevator.

"Yeah, good thinking, Gerald." Bobby knew how much Gerald loved his job, but he really just wanted him to get the point.

"Gerald and I are going to get to work down in the garage in a few minutes, but we really need to talk to you about Mahkeem's doctor." Bethert stepped forward. "Go ahead and give him a little background about what you found, Gerald."

Gerald moved to the side of the table and pulled out the evidence bag that he had carried in from the parking lot. He placed the bag a few inches from Bobby's nose so that he could see the contents clearly.

Bobby turned to look at Gerald, who once again had his braces displayed through a large grin. He then looked at the contents of the bag again before he turned to Bethert and then back to Gerald. "What the hell is that?"

*   *   *

Laurel and Kyle decided to follow Jennifer back to the twenty-four hour coffee counter in the lobby. Hotel security had already informed them that they would probably be able to return to their rooms within an hour because an actual fire had not been present. The coffee shop had a number of small round tables outside the counter area. Kyle sat with the two women at the table farthest from the counter.

"What the heck was that all about?" Jennifer exchanged glances with both Laurel and Kyle. "I just wanted a quick pick-me-up so I could keep working on my special. After the scene in the basement, I don't think I'm going to be able sleep for the rest of the week."

"You're not putting all of this into the news special, are you?" Kyle felt like his entire world had turned surreal. He'd gone from a Special Forces mission to having coffee with a newswoman who was practically a national celebrity. *Unbelievable.*

"This isn't really like me, but I think that I'm going to pretend that tonight never happened. I've already got enough on my plate as it is." Jennifer took a sip of coffee and stopped to look around the lobby. "So where's Mahkeem?"

This time Laurel spoke up. "The CIA grabbed him right after we came up from the basement. I'm sure he's around here somewhere."

As Laurel finished the answer, a member from the hotel security staff approached the table and sat down with them.

"Hello, I'm James Arthur, hotel security." He shook each of their hands. "I want to apologize for tonight. This has never happened in the history of the Royalview." He swallowed hard and gave Jennifer a nervous look.

"Then what about the dagger guys from Wednesday?" said Jennifer.

Ha, thought Kyle, *talk about being in the crosshairs.*

Arthur, not more than thirty years of age, seemed to suddenly recognize Jennifer.

"Oh, Jennifer Rayburn. You look different on television." Arthur paused while he prepared his defense. "The other event you're referring to was a CIA security breach, our staff at the Royalview was not responsible." His voice cracked slightly as he spoke. "If you'll excuse me now, I have to attend to a few things." He quickly left the table and disappeared through another door in the lobby.

"You always have that effect on men?" Laurel leaned back in her chair and stared across the table at Jennifer.

"Only when they're trying to hide something or they're lying to me," said Jennifer. "And most men are always hiding or lying about something."

Both Laurel and Jennifer turned to look at Kyle as he slurped down a large iced-cappuccino. He tried to pretend that he wasn't paying attention to the conversation, but it wasn't working. He looked up and suddenly wished he'd accompanied Bobby to the doctor's office as the two women stared at him disapprovingly.

"What?" Kyle felt the crosshairs shift, this time, onto him.

*   *   *

"That should just about do it," commented the Royalview's in-house doctor. "You were very lucky, Major. Most of the bullet shattered when it hit the concrete floor. You only had a few small splinters of shrapnel embedded in your calf. Any more than that, and I wouldn't have been able to help you."

"Thank you, doctor, I didn't feel like checking into a hospital tonight," said Bobby. *And if I would have, I'd still be waiting, I'm sure of it.*

The doctor gathered his instruments and stood up. "Just remember to take it easy for a couple of days."

"Got it." Bobby nodded as he lifted himself up off of the table and slid down onto the floor. As he stood up, he was careful to favor his wounded leg that was still partially numb. The doctor gave a quick wave and opened the door to exit the room. The door had almost closed when Bethert and Gerald re-entered.

"Sorry I cut you guys off back there," said Bobby. "But at this point I really don't trust anybody, so I didn't want to discuss the contents of your evidence bag in front of the doctor." He pointed to the bag. "So what did you find, Gerald?"

"Well, sir, I had completed my investigation of the limousine incident and decided to take a quick look around Dr. Samaan's office to see if I had missed anything. I'm not really much of a detective outside of my obvious biological abilities, but my instincts turned out to be right this time."

"Gerald, we appreciate your attention to detail, but could you *please* just get to the point?" Bethert moved her hands in a circular motion to try to prod Gerald along.

Gerald looked at her and seemed to get the message. "So anyway, I found this latex glove with ointment on it. I remembered that the patient file said that the ex-rebel guy was treated for a burn. I thought that this might have been the glove that Dr. Samaan used to apply the treatment, so I grabbed it." He paused and nodded his head, like he was in total approval of what he'd done.

"I'm not really following you, what connection would a latex glove have to the death of the doctor?" Bobby knew some lab basics, but wasn't sure what type of a lead they'd gotten from a glove with ointment.

"I took the glove back to the lab and had the forensic geeks go over it." Gerald smiled. "It's just your everyday latex glove." He paused and raised his hand as he shook one finger in the air. "Except for the fact that it's still, to this very minute, emitting a very low, almost undetectable level of radiation."

"Which means the burn that Mahkeem was treated for didn't come from a missile launcher," added Bobby.

"Exactly!" Gerald excitedly tapped his fingers together. "I did a little research and found that most people are treated for low-level radiation burns when they hit the beach without wearing sun-block." Gerald walked over and sat on the table that Bobby had just been laying on. As he sat, he kicked his legs out like a little kid on a big chair.

Bethert motioned to Gerald until he stopped kicking. She then added, "A sunburn is a mild radiation burn, but your man Mahkeem—"

Gerald interrupted, "Came in contact with something *really* nasty to be able to transfer radiation from his dying skin cells to the ointment on the end of this glove. I would actually like to examine him if we have time." His legs pumped again, now in excitement.

"I don't think so, Gerald," remarked Bobby. "He's now the CIA's responsibility."

Gerald's legs froze in mid kick, and he suddenly looked like he'd been punched in the gut.

"Look, Major," said Bethert. "I really don't want to know any classified information that you might have on this Mahkeem, but he's leaving a trail of bodies behind him that I don't even think Gerald can keep up with."

"But I'm really trying." Gerald stood up straighter. It was almost as if Bethert had just challenged him.

Bethert shot a disapproving look over to Gerald and turned to Bobby. "We're going to go clean up that mess down in the garage now, but there's something big going on here."

Bobby looked directly at Bethert as he moved away from the table he had been leaning on. "I know."

* * *

Bobby felt as if it had been an eternity before the CIA and hotel security had finally cleared the seventeenth floor for them to return. He rode the recently repaired elevator back to the floor and collapsed into his bed just after one o'clock in the morning. As he drifted off to sleep, he was once again interrupted when his cell phone rang. He reached over and brought the phone to his ear, still lying face down on his bed.

"Handle." His voice was slightly muffled against the pillow.

"Bobby, it's Joe, you got a minute?" Joe's voice came through his phone extremely loud.

Bobby pulled the phone back from his ear a bit and raised his head off of the pillow. "Joe, you wouldn't believe the night I've just had." He regained a little more consciousness and restated, "Wait, actually, you of all people *would* probably believe it."

"Never a dull moment, eh? I can tell you've just been through something. You can tell me later if you got a new gray hair from it."

"Very funny." Bobby rolled over onto his back. "Now what's up?"

"I'll try to make this quick," said Joe. "I was checking out the dead insurgents from the cell that took down the Kodiak mission, and you'll never guess who I ran into?"

"Normally I'd answer you with some smart-ass remark, but I'm too tired." Bobby covered his mouth as he attempted to stifle a yawn.

"I ran into the Z-man. He didn't say much because your buddy Mahkeem shot him in the side of the head during the web-cast of the second execution attempt. But I've got to tell you, the black body bag he's in matches that fucker's beard nicely."

"Wait a minute, wasn't he the guy that I shot in the shoulder?" Bobby replied with an irritated tone and sat up onto his elbows. His men couldn't pronounce half of the names in the Middle East, so they typically assigned nicknames to just about everyone they encountered.

"Yeah, and the wound healed nicely," responded Joe sarcastically.

"Who could forget the Z-man, the bastard kept spitting on everyone. He was part of the cell that we took down in the Iraqi Green Zone last year. I was just talking about those guys with Rayburn." Bobby paused before he rhetorically asked, "How the hell did he get out of prison?"

"I don't know, but it looks like he wasn't the only dead insurgent with a history. I did a little research and traced a couple of these other guys right back to that same cell."

"What the hell?" exclaimed Bobby. "Now I know how a cop feels when a guilty perp beats the rap and walks." Things were going from strange to utterly indecipherable.

"A lot of the cells are turned over to the local authorities, but we still keep tabs on them. These guys vanished for over a year and then came out of nowhere with fissionable material." Joe sounded just as frustrated as Bobby.

The goddamned Z-man of all people, thought Bobby. *What's next, Ticar al-Udadise shows up missing?*

"Anyway, I was just saying," started Joe again, "that if we wouldn't have put this fucking group out of commission last year, they would have assassinated one of our VIPs. You remember who they were targeting?"

Bobby thought for a moment. "Yeah, now that you mention it, I do remember."

Chapter 23

Kyle leaned over, picked up the syrup bottle from the restaurant table, and flooded his plate of pancakes. He added a large dollop of butter, which quickly slid off the island of pancakes into the sea of thick, sticky, brown liquid.

Kyle actually felt good about himself for the first time in over a week. The ambush in the basement the night before, unlike the mission in Iraq, had given him a chance to pay back the radical insurgents with a shower of gunfire. He had also not only gotten a chance to see the legendary Bobby Handle in action, but had actually helped him save Ahlmed's life.

"Do you want me to ask the waiter to bring you a straw?" Laurel sat across the table from him and picked at her bowl of oatmeal. "That way you could skip the pancakes, melt the butter into the syrup, and just drink your breakfast."

Laurel had awakened with a stomach virus. She sat in her chair, slightly hunched over with one hand over her lower stomach. Her face was drained of all its color, which made her look as if she should have been in bed, not at breakfast. She had told Kyle earlier that even though she wasn't feeling well, she wanted to keep the breakfast date as a diversion from everything that was going on.

Kyle laughed. "I sort of look at pancakes the same way that the French must look at escargot."

"Huh?" Laurel shot him a confused look.

"You've got to figure that the snail is just a method to collect garlic, olive oil, and butter into one compact form that's easy to eat," replied Kyle as he stuffed a bite of pancake into his mouth. "A pancake is just a convenient way to eat syrup and butter without getting it all over your hands."

"If you say so," replied Laurel. "So what's oatmeal good for? An appropriate way to eat raisins, brown sugar, and granola?"

Kyle smiled. "Now you're learning." He took another bite and tried to think of different ways to keep Laurel smiling. He was nervous enough about the upcoming Presidential meet-and-greet and couldn't imagine being sick on top of everything else that had already happened.

"You ever try escargot?" Laurel took a sip of her nearly full glass of apple juice and held the liquid in her mouth for a moment before she swallowed.

Kyle thought about the question for a moment before he attempted his best French accent. "Actually, yes, I was in France a couple of years ago and tried it. It wasn't bad; it sort of tastes like garlic, olive oil and butter." Kyle grinned, but his French accent had already faded to the point where it had disappeared. "Although I've got to believe that the French started eating snails based on the *Little Brother Theory* of new food consumption."

Laurel tilted her head to one side. "Okay, since you're forcing me to ask, what is the *Little Brother Theory* for eating new foods?"

"Some big brother fed his little brother a snail, the kid lived, and other people started to eat them. Same thing had to happen in Hawaii; you ever try poi? Nasty shit." Kyle finished his explanation and continued to eat his sugar-and fat-enriched breakfast.

Both of them tried to keep the conversation topics light during the meal. They set basic ground rules and agreed to try to not talk about the bloodbath from the previous night. As they continued their breakfast, a hotel employee from the front desk entered with an overnight mail carrier in tow. He pointed across the restaurant before he escorted the carrier over to the table where Laurel and Kyle were seated.

"Excuse me, Ms. Crickowski." The man from the front desk kept his voice low. "This man has an urgent letter that you need to sign for."

The carrier handed Laurel an electronic signature pad. She signed the pad and handed it back to him. He then handed her a thin letter in an overnight envelope, apologized for interrupting her breakfast, and exited the restaurant.

Kyle peered over the table at the envelope as he continued to eat a large bite of his pancake. As he chewed, he opened an additional packet of butter. He bit off a small piece to add an additional accent of flavor to the half-chewed food.

"I know we agreed not to talk about anything dealing with bombs, blood, or Handle killing someone, but I have to ask you." Kyle paused to swallow.

"In your professional opinion, Hazmat Kodiak Number Two, is that envelope some type of letter bomb?"

Laurel carefully looked over the package before she picked up a knife from the table. She shrugged her shoulders and then slit the top to reveal a single folded piece of paper. She unfolded the letter and read for a few seconds before she stopped and gave Kyle a horrified look.

"Oh, my God," were Laurel's only words as she continued to stare at Kyle.

*   *   *

Jennifer knocked again on the door to Bobby's room before she turned to the newly assigned guard. "We were supposed to meet for breakfast this morning, but he never showed up." She thought for a moment about Bobby's injuries. *He's got to be okay*, she thought, but she grew more concerned. "Are you sure he's still in there?"

"Yes, ma'am. No one has gone in or out of that door for the last four hours," replied the guard.

"Well, I think we should check on him. It's not like Bobby to sleep in, and he did take a heck of a beating last night." She thought back to her experience with Bobby in Iraq. She almost expected his room to be empty. *He's probably not even in the country anymore.*

The guard nodded his head in agreement as he turned around and knocked harder on the door. "Major Handle, please answer me if you're in there."

After Bobby failed to respond again, the military guard pulled a card-key from his pocket. He slid it through the reader, and opened the door slowly.

As the dimly lit room came into view, Jennifer and the guard heard a faint rhythmic ticking sound similar to that of an alarm clock.

"Digital clocks don't tick, do they?" Jennifer gave the guard a worried look.

"No, none that I've ever seen." The guard echoed her look of concern.

Everyone was already on alert because of the second attack that had only occurred the night before. Jennifer couldn't help thinking that some sort of bomb would go off as they entered Bobby's room, but to her relief, the ticking sound turned out to be the reason that he hadn't answered the door.

Bobby sat in front of his computer with headphones over his ears. He clicked a single key on the keyboard over and over, which had created the ticking sound that they had heard upon entering the room. Jennifer pushed the door open the rest of the way and walked in.

"Bobby!" Jennifer yelled as she crossed the room.

Bobby jumped slightly after he heard his name called out from within his room. He quickly turned around and ripped off his headphones. As he removed his hand from the keyboard, he hit the *print* key by accident, which caused the contents of the current screen to be printed on the portable printer.

"Jen, how did you get in here?" Bobby looked totally surprised.

"I've been knocking for the last five minutes," started Jennifer, "and when you didn't answer . . . ." she paused and softened her voice before continuing. "Well, after last night, I just wanted to make sure that you were okay."

"I'm fine, but I'm glad you were concerned." Bobby smiled.

Jennifer turned to see the guard smirking at Bobby's reply. "What are you smiling about?" Her tone sounded overly sarcastic.

The guard's smile was instantly replaced by a much more serious look. "Nothing, ma'am." He turned his head to look at Bobby. "I'm just going to go back to my post now, if it's okay with you, Major?"

"Go ahead," Bobby replied.

The guard quickly exited the room and closed the door behind him. Jennifer walked over and sat down next to Bobby in front of the computer.

"So what's more interesting than our breakfast date? Or maybe I should start out by asking you how you're feeling?"

Bobby thought about Jennifer's question. It sounded like she really was concerned about his well being. "Like I was shot at, run over by a van, and thrown into an elevator at twenty-five miles per hour."

Bobby had already been awake for a couple of hours due to the pain in his side and calf. Since he couldn't sleep, he decided to use the time to step through the media timeline that Bleeker had prepared for him.

Jennifer motioned to the computer on Bobby's desk. "Can I help you with anything?"

Bobby took in a deep breath and exhaled slowly. "I've been going through this web-cast trying to figure out the command that was given through the field phone in the background." He rewound the video on the screen and pointed at the rebel holding the communication device. He then removed the headphones from his computer and turned the sound up.

"Listen to this."

Jennifer listened carefully to the audio that Bleeker had manipulated for Bobby. "Sounds like he's saying *yellow* or something. It's hard to hear with all of the other sounds going on at the same time." She looked at the other quadrants on the screen that contained the Monocle and chip feeds. "Nice presentation format. Did the tech guys over at the Pentagon set this up for you?"

Even though the information in the web-casts was public knowledge, the other quadrants on his computer screen contained information that was classified. Even so, Bobby reluctantly replied, "Yeah, they synched the whole timeline for me." He leaned back in his chair and attempted a stretch that was cut short by the pain in his side.

"The heat imaging is really cool. I've seen this type of technology used on television shows, but I've never seen a real-life application of it." Jennifer continued to study the screen. "I also like the way the small white dots in this other window sort of line up with the heat signatures. I'm guessing that those are the Special Forces chips that I keep hearing about. Do you have one of those things in you?"

"Standard issue for the last six years. It takes some time to get used to it, but it really gives you peace of mind when you're on a mission. If a soldier gets separated from his team for any reason, it makes the pick-up really easy." Bobby tapped his shoulder where his chip had been implanted.

Jennifer smiled. "Sounds like something that would be useful for tracking my cat when he gets out."

"As long as you're willing to pay fifteen thousand dollars for a chip and a receiver. Sure, it would probably do the job." Bobby let a little friendly sarcasm slip into his voice. "But you'd have to convince our government to sell the technology to you first." He tapped the key a few more times so that the timeline on the computer moved back a few seconds. He appreciated Jennifer's support, but he really needed to get back to work.

"You know, on second thought, I'm going to wait a few years until they come down in price." Jennifer looked at the current time displayed in the lower right of the computer screen, stood up, and pushed her chair back. "You're busy, and it looks like I'm going to have to get going. I have to meet my cameraman down at the White House to finish up a few things."

"Good luck with that. I'm going to try to catch your special tonight." Bobby turned to face Jennifer in an awkward silence as their eyes met. A half second later, Bobby looked away. "But for now, I might as well go over this one more time to see if I can make any progress." He reached over and played the clip of the video segment one more time, and then shook his head. "I am never going to figure out what the hell that word is."

Jennifer was half way to the door. "Keep working, you'll get it." She looked down at her watch again, "I've got to hurry up and get going."

Bobby's eyes grew wide as he opened his mouth in disbelief. "That's it! I know what the word is."

"Wait, are you telling me that you just figured out the word from the video?" Jennifer turned around and took a step back toward Bobby.

Bobby threw up his arms and shook his head as if the answer was always right in front of him. "Yes, it's a very common Arabic word."

*   *   *

"What's it say?" Kyle finally broke the silence that had ensued from the arrival of the overnight letter. He poked his remaining pancake with his fork, but it was no use, it had already dissolved into a sugary blob.

"It's a letter that has probably just ended my career in the United States Special Forces." Whatever color Laurel left had in her complexion was now gone. She looked as if she'd just lost a close friend.

"I need a little more info, Number Two." Kyle used the same tone he had used with her when the fissionable material had vanished from the Iraqi bunker.

"I'm sorry," Laurel apologized as she snapped out of the semi-trance she had been in for almost thirty seconds. "It's a letter from a production company in California. They want to offer me almost a half million dollars to buy the exclusive rights to my story. It also goes on to mention book rights and a possible public speaking tour next year."

"That's fantastic!" Kyle got up and moved his chair closer so that he could view the letter along side of her. "Didn't you say that your current commitment with the Army was going to expire in five months anyway?"

"My current commitment, yes, I did," started Laurel. "But I obviously wasn't planning on hanging it up a half year from now. You know how many years we've trained to get where we are." She paused and held her stomach as her face shriveled into a grimace. "I was afraid that with all of this attention my career as a Kodiak was over. I think this letter has just confirmed it."

"No way, you're too good at what you do," Kyle complimented her in a fairly positive tone. The timing of the letter couldn't have been worse, but then again, what in the past week had been timed well? *Nothing.*

"Think about it, Captain," Laurel paused for a brief moment, "the whole point of the Kodiak unit is so that we're a single team based on numbers, moving in and out fluidly without personalization or favoritism. If I go out on a mission, everyone is going to know exactly who I am. This whole event has compromised my entire career with the Special Forces. God forbid I'm ever captured again; it'll be a political nightmare for whoever is in office, just because of my name."

Kyle attempted to reply again, but stopped as a well-dressed man approached them. He looked up and recognized the man as one of the CIA agents from the hotel.

The agent bent over and spoke in almost a whisper, "You need to come with me quickly."

Chapter 24

"Well, then what is it, and what does it translate to in English?" Jennifer had already told Bobby that she had to get going, but was immediately drawn back into his room to hear the revelation.

"The voice on the field phone is saying *yullah, yullah*, or *let's go, let's go*. Which could also translate into *hurry up, hurry up*," replied Bobby. "I actually hung out with an Iraqi family of one of the parliament members when I was in Baghdad. The father kept yelling the word to his kids when they would fail to listen to him." Bobby smiled yet again. "I used to joke around with my team by yelling at them in Arabic whenever we were running behind on something." He placed both hands behind his head and stretched. The answer was so simple; he should have gotten it hours ago.

Jennifer glanced over at the clock next to Bobby's bed. "Speaking of yullah, I *really* have to run now." She opened the door. "I'm glad that I could help you out with your problem, even if it *was* by accident."

"Yeah, you have no idea how long I've spent studying that one segment of the video," Bobby thankfully commented. "I'll see you later."

Jennifer gave a quick wave and left Bobby alone once again with his computer.

He turned back to face the laptop and slid the timeline to the point that he'd been studying. He played it back and listened to it again. He shook his head and thought about the hours he had spent as a kid trying to figure out lyrics from songs on the radio. The words were sometimes hard to understand until you knew exactly what they were. *Then they're so clear that you feel like you knew them all along.*

Bobby paused the video and glanced at the portable printer that was hooked up to his computer. He grabbed the sheet of paper that he'd printed by accident when Jennifer and the guard surprised him earlier. He studied the sheet for a moment when an image flashed into his head. *Thank you, Jennifer Rayburn, you've just given me an idea.*

*   *   *

Ahlmed Mahkeem had just finished getting dressed when a small entourage of CIA personnel entered his suite. A middle-aged woman sat down across from him and opened a small notebook.

"Hello, Mr. Mahkeem, I'm agent Natalie Polburn. I've been assigned to make sure that your relocation goes smoothly. Since we're going to be working together a lot, you can just call me Natalie."

"It is good to meet you, Natalie," replied Mahkeem.

"We're going to send in a chopper to pick you up after the White House reception this afternoon. You'll be transported back to Andrews Air Force Base, where you'll pick up a direct flight to one of our military bases in Arizona. I think you'll find the weather there quite familiar." Polburn shuffled through a few papers from a folder that she'd carried in with her. "We're going to give you a new ID. I'm also going to suggest that you shave your beard, change your hairstyle, and pick up some glasses. Most of America, including the parts of country that have been trying to kill you, easily recognizes you because of your heavy beard."

"These changes will help hide me?" Mahkeem looked skeptical.

"You would be surprised what a subtle change can do. Most people have only seen you on television." She paused to hand Mahkeem some information regarding the relocation program and then continued, "In fact, most people at the military base you'll be staying at will never even know your real name."

*   *   *

Bobby quickly loaded some paper into the printer and moved the timeline to just before the first beheading. He hit the *print* key and the printer hummed to life and printed out the screen shot. When the printer finished, he took a quick look at the printout. He had printed the heat profiles from the Monocle.

The profiles were in full color on the screen, but Bobby had printed them in black and white, so that each image looked like a slightly jagged-edged circle. Each circle was about one inch in diameter on the printout. He then shifted his focus to the quadrant that contained the chip echoes. Once again, he hit the *print* button. The printout was done almost immediately because of the lack of things to print on the page. After the printer shot the page out in the small plastic holding tray, Bobby once again inspected his work. This page contained six black dots, one dot for each Kodiak in the bunker. *Okay, now I've got a printout with each man's heat signature, and one with each man's chip echo, but I really need one printout that contains the combination of the two of them.*

He took the sheet of paper with the echoes and placed it directly on top of the piece of paper containing the Monocle's heat signatures.

"Damn, the papers are too thick." He looked around the room for a minute when he spotted a large lamp in the corner. He walked to the lamp and turned it on. He'd almost positioned his printouts when his cell phone rang.

He put down the pieces of paper and answered his phone. "This is Handle."

"Major, this is Bleeker over at the Pentagon. I just wanted you to know that site 1128 has been totally abandoned along with all of the other sites that the ex-rebel gave us." Bleeker's concern was obvious as he continued, "We've already alerted the proper personnel of the change, but since we've been working together, I thought I would contact you as well."

"I appreciate the update, Private. Thank you." Bobby threw the phone onto his bed. "Now what the hell is going on?" He thought for a moment about making a few calls, but decided to finish the task at hand before delving into yet another mystery.

He retrieved the two pieces of paper he had printed and wrapped them around the lampshade. He reached down, turned on the lamp and smiled when he saw the result.

"It's a little low tech, but this should work."

*   *   *

CIA Agent Belfore escorted Kyle and Laurel down to the parking garage below the Royalview Hotel. The garage had been totally cleaned, with no sign of the fight from the night before. As they entered the garage, they saw three black limousines lined up.

"We each get our own limo?" Laurel kept pace with Belfore and Kyle, but she held her stomach as she walked.

"Not quite. With all of the attention you've been receiving, we felt that it would be best to have a couple of decoy limousines just in case there was a third attempt while you're in route to the White House." Belfore spoke in a semi-robotic tone. "This is the one you'll be riding in." He pointed at the first limousine. "We need to get you out of here quickly. Your departure time has been kept confidential for obvious reasons."

Laurel and Kyle climbed into the limo where they found two other CIA agents along with a familiar face waiting.

"Good Afternoon." Mahkeem smiled at them.

"Hey, Mahkeem, so are you ready for the big day?" asked Kyle.

"Yes. Although I am looking forward to some time alone more than anything else." Mahkeem glanced at the CIA agents who were flanked on either side of him.

"You know, we'll probably never see you again after today, and you can't exactly tell us where they're going to hide you, but good luck." Kyle had really grown to like Mahkeem over the past week. He continued to look at him and couldn't help but wonder about his future. He was basically a man without a country. *The guy saved our lives and he probably feels as if he's in a self-made prison.*

"Thank you, Captain," replied Mahkeem. "Good luck to you as well."

Kyle then glanced back to check on Laurel. She had lain down across the back of the limo. "Hey, Number Two, you going to make it? You don't look so good."

Laurel shifted her head. "With everything I've gone through lately, dealing with this stomach virus should be a piece of cake."

*   *   *

The light from the lamp illuminated the pieces of paper and made them semi-transparent. Bobby lined them up perfectly so that the echo dots were now inside each of the heat signature outlines that showed through from the other paper.

"Okay," Bobby commented slowly, "Now we're starting to get somewhere."

He walked back over to his computer and moved the timeline again so that the quadrant that contained the echoes now displayed the solar flare distortion. He moved forward slowly until the lone echo appeared on the screen. Once again, he printed the snapshot of the screen. When the printer spit the piece of paper out, it was blank except for a single black dot. Bobby placed the printout on top of the other two pieces of paper and wrapped all three around his lampshade.

"Crap." Bobby moved his face within a few inches of the paper. "Now these are too thick for the light to shine through."

He quickly went back to his desk and grabbed a black marker. He removed the sheet with the single echo on it and placed the original two sheets back against the lampshade. Bobby traced each heat signature from the bottom sheet onto the top sheet. He made sure to trace all of the heat signature circles, regardless of whether or not they contained an echo dot. After he'd traced the last signature, he removed the bottom printout that he no longer needed. *Okay, now I've got a single piece of paper with all of the heat signatures on it—and some of them have echo dots in them.*

He placed the printout with the single echo underneath his new composite drawing of the first two sheets. The echo lined up perfectly with one of the heat signatures that did not already have an echo. Bleeker had already done the same type of thing back at the Pentagon when he overlaid the images on the screen, but with one minor difference. Bleeker had used the heat signatures during the solar flare while Bobby used the images from the last non-distorted point in the timeline. The heat images had been displaced on the screen, but the echoes had never moved. They had disappeared and reappeared.

"So what's the probability that the solar flare distortion would cause a chip to line-up perfectly over another signature?" Bobby went back and watched the Internet web-cast segment frame by frame. He placed his head into both of his hands and massaged his forehead. "This can't be right."

*   *   *

"Yes, I need you to send it over to him with the letter," replied President Sumner into his phone, nodding his head in agreement. "I'll make the time whenever he's physically recovered."

Cynthia Sumner walked out of the bathroom and shot her husband a quizzical look. Sumner held up his finger to communicate that he was almost done with the conversation.

"Okay, then we're all set . . . Uh huh . . . Okay . . . Good-bye." He hung up the receiver.

"What was that about?" inquired Cynthia.

"I just wanted to confirm that our injured soldier from the mission . . . ." Sumner checked his notes to make sure he got the man's name right. "Ah, here it is, Robert Sinden. I want to make sure he receives my personal letter of acknowledgement for his service. He's going to miss the ceremony today, but I wanted him to know that we didn't forget about him. I've extended an invitation to him so that as soon as he's able to, he'll receive the same recognition that his fellow team members are getting."

"That's why I love you. You never forget anyone." Cynthia walked over and gave her husband a small peck on the cheek.

*   *   *

Bobby let the water from the shower run down over his bruised body. The wounds from the previous night hurt much worse after a few hours of inactivity, but the pain was still secondary to the current puzzle. He had already gone over the scenario a dozen times, but it just didn't seem possible.

He'd spent so much time with the data that he'd almost forgotten it was time to get into the shower, get cleaned up, and then head over to the White House. His mind jumped back and forth between the misplaced echo dot and the vacated rebel sights. *I need answers, and I'm not going to find them in the shower.*

Bobby turned off the water and grabbed a towel. He carefully stepped out of the shower and dried himself off as he tried not to agitate any of his recent wounds. He looked at himself in the mirror and thought of the conversation with Jennifer a couple of days ago when she had asked him what he saw each morning.

"Nothing," he had replied. *Maybe Jennifer is clouding me so that I can't think straight. Got to focus.*

He grabbed a small bath towel and wiped the steam from the mirror.

"Still nothing," he said to himself as he studied the multitude of scars across his body. "Wait a second—"

Bobby saw something that suddenly made the last piece of the puzzle fall into place. The words on the rebel's field phone during the web-cast now made sense.

He moved as quickly as his body would allow and walked back to his paperwork that he had gathered earlier in the week as part of his investigation.

"Come on, where is it." He flipped through the pages quickly. "Where is . . . got it." Bobby read the words on the page, grabbed his cell phone, and hit speed dial. After a few moments, he started speaking rapidly to his favorite Pentagon technician.

"Private Bleeker, this is Handle, I'm going to need another favor."

Chapter 25

"You know, it was President Kennedy who actually redesigned the Rose Garden so that it could be used as a venue for outdoor ceremonies." Sumner stood inside the Oval Office and gazed out the window into the White House Rose Garden. A number of network media people had already arrived and were in the process of setting up equipment and cameras for the forthcoming medal presentation.

Babare smiled. "Yes, and it looks like it's going to turn out to be a perfect day for the ceremony. The Weather Channel had predicated rain for this afternoon, but it looks like it's going to hold off until tonight." He took a small sip from a plastic bottle of spring-water. "The grounds crew has gone over the entire area to make sure that everything is in order, including the small stage and podium."

"Yes. Everything is coming together nicely," replied Sumner.

"And the Bridges Muslim network was thrilled to have an opportunity to cover the event today. These events are usually reserved for only the larger networks." Babare took another sip of water.

Sumner paused as General Tabler entered the Oval Office. The General gave a quick salute, which Sumner acknowledged before he returned his attention back to Babare. "It was the least we could do for them. Their network has been very apologetic about the misuse of its name in the attempt on Mahkeem's life. They've also been very cooperative in working with our agencies to track down any leads on the assassins."

"But be assured, Sir," began Tabler, "we have verified that the Bridges news crew attending today's ceremony is, indeed, a real crew from their network."

"Good. With the initial attempt on our ex-rebel friend and the bloodbath at the hotel last night, we can't be too careful." Sumner studied the media crews in the garden and recognized many of the faces. "Even though we are at an increased risk for a backlash from the JET organization, I'm hoping the ceremony shows other insurgents that there are better ways to negotiate than strapping a bomb to your chest."

"Not to worry, Sir," Tabler quickly replied. "We're monitoring everyone on the watch-lists very carefully to insure that any action against our country is stopped before it even has a chance to start." Tabler, as usual, stood in a semi-state of attention.

He opened his mouth to speak again when a White House staff member briskly strode into the Oval Office. She handed Press Secretary Babare three small boxes and exited the office as quickly as she had entered.

"Sir, the medals are here." Babare opened each box to verify that the correct medals had indeed arrived. "Two military medals and one civilian freedom medal."

Sumner moved away from the window to peek at the medals as Babare verified the contents of each box. The entire situation still left him with an uneasy feeling deep in his gut. Would a medal ceremony really make a difference? *Lives have still been lost. The nuclear material is still missing, and here I am handing out medals. Commander-in-Chief—still not what I signed up for.*

"Sir," started the General, "would you like me to hold onto those until the Vice President arrives?"

Sumner continued to stare off into space for a few moments until he realized that Tabler had just asked him a question.

"Good idea, Tabler." Sumner finally answered. "Compton is playing the role of the Best Man today. Make sure he gets them as soon as he arrives." Sumner alluded to the fact that the Vice President would hand each medal to him during the ceremony just as the best man at a wedding is in charge of the ring.

Babare handed the three boxes to General Tabler and smiled. "Try not to lose these."

*   *   *

"Excellent take, Jen," commented her cameraman.

"Yeah, not bad. But I know I can do better than that." Jennifer brushed the front of her suit with her hand to remove any wrinkles. "Let's tape another one."

Jennifer and her assigned cameraman, Allen Garrick, stood just outside the gardens at the White House. They had arrived a half hour earlier to film a few last-minute segments that would be edited into the hour-long special report that was to air later that day. Jennifer was dressed in one of her most formal, navy blue business suits with matching shoes. She had also pulled her hair back in an attempt to make her look a bit older. She always referred to this particular style as her *Prime Time* look

"Okay, Jen." Allen had the camera set up for another take. "Whenever you're ready, go ahead. We're rolling."

Jennifer exhaled and then took in a deep breath. "Less than one week ago, a United States Special Forces team was captured by the radical Islamic group known to the world as Jihad End Times." She paused for a moment and stared directly into the camera. "With little hope left, the surviving team members found themselves at the mercy of their captors. The vicious insurgents then executed them one by one until an ally arose from the rebel ranks to step in and save the remaining soldiers. The following hour-long special will chronicle the events of the last few days, including an exclusive interview with ex-rebel, Ahlmed Mahkeem. The questions that Americans have been asking will be answered, but I must warn you." Jennifer took a step toward the camera. "The conversations and events that will be covered over the next hour are very graphic in nature, and are not suitable for young children." She paused one last time before finishing. "This is Jennifer Rayburn, reporting from the White House, Washington, D.C."

Jennifer held her pose until the red light went off on the camera. She then unclipped a small mike from her suit and walked over to Allen. She handed him the small wireless device with authority because she knew the last take was perfect. *Finally nailed it.*

"Good call on the extra take, Jen, that was excellent." Allen turned and headed back toward the White House parking lot. "I'm going to run back to the van and upload these segments to the station."

"Okay, but make it quick. I want to make sure that we get back to the White House Rose Garden before it gets too crowded. I understand that the normal pool of reporters has been tripled for today's event." Jennifer knelt down to quickly adjust her shoe. Throngs of reporters were invited, but she knew that she already had the inside scoop. Today would be a day that would be a defining moment in her career.

*   *   *

"Okay, gentlemen, let's review the ceremony one last time," started Babare. "All of America will be watching this one. Remember that Jennifer

Rayburn is also doing a special in prime-time tonight, and she *is* the current ratings queen."

President Sumner, Vice President Compton and a number of Secret Service men stood in the Oval Office awaiting the final review of the ceremony events. Outside in the Rose Garden, the media personnel quietly talked among themselves as final preparations were being made.

"I think we've got it, but one more overview wouldn't hurt," replied Sumner. *Time for Commander-in-Chief-cover-your-ass instructions.*

Babare stepped forward. "I'll start out with a brief introduction, which will be followed immediately by the Vice President's speech." He motioned to Compton. "You'll then introduce President Sumner."

Compton gave a quick nod.

Babare then pointed to Sumner. "Mr. President, you'll walk out from the White House and proceed to the podium. After your speech, we'll start with the two military medals." He then directed his attention back to Vice President Compton and asked, "You've got the medals?"

"Right here." Vice President Compton held up the three jewelry cases.

"Good. And remember," started Babare again. "The military medals are in the cases with the eagle insignia on the side. The freedom medal is in the case with the profile of Kennedy embossed on it." He paused and then added, "We don't want to hand out the wrong medal to the wrong person."

Sumner couldn't help but think about the irony in Babare's last statement. *It's not like anyone is going to die if they get the wrong medal. And would they even care or notice?*

Compton inspected the three cases and rearranged them in his hands so that the two military medals where now on the top. He then doubled checked the bottom one. "Got it."

Babare nodded in agreement. "After each medal is awarded, Vice President Compton will stand to the right of the recipient. Mr. President, you'll stand to the left as you shake their hand. This is the big press photo-op, so hold the pose while the cameras have a chance to capture the moment."

Babare turned to the small group of Secret Service men. "After the presentation, three of you will remain on the stage while the President, Vice President, and the medal recipients head back into the White House for a small reception. Any questions?"

The men all grew silent in the room as most shook their heads to signal that they understood the order of events.

Compton strode over to one of the side tables in the office, placed the jewel cases containing the medals down, and opened the one that contained the freedom medal.

"I haven't seen one of these in a while." Compton admired the medals. "Nice award and quite an honor." He lifted the medal out of the case and directed a second comment at Sumner. "This medal is a bit larger and heavier than the military ones that we're handing out."

Sumner looked back and raised his hand to make a point. "Regardless of size, they both carry the same weight when it comes to a Congressional Medal of Honor."

*   *   *

"As soon as the ceremony is over, I need you to get back to the van again and send the footage to the studio." Jennifer spoke with an excited tone as the final piece of the special was about to be filmed. Allen gave a quick thumbs-up as she reached into her purse, hit the speed dial on her cell phone and raised the device to her ear. A few moments later, Curt picked up on the other end of the line.

"Curt, it's Jennifer. How did the lead-in turn out?" She hadn't been this nervous about a project since she'd first gotten out of school. Every reporter who goes on to greatness has a breakthrough story. *And this is mine*, Jennifer thought, *this is mine*.

"We've edited your opening and closing comments into the special and viewed the final, they look great. As usual, nice job," replied Curt. "You ready to finish this thing up?"

"Between the hotel blood-fests and the crazy hours, I'm ready for a vacation." *Ready for a vacation . . . unless the network needs a follow-up to this story.*

"You've earned it," answered Curt. "Are you going to come down to the station during the special tonight? A few of us are going to get together to watch it and then see what the initial reaction is from surfing a few of the Internet message boards."

"I think I'm going to have to pass. After the last few days, I'm just looking forward to going home, taking a long hot bath, and watching the special from the comfort of my own bed." She paused and then grinned. "I may even fall asleep before it's over."

"Somehow I don't think that will happen." Curt laughed into the phone.

Jennifer finished out the conversation and threw her phone back into her handbag. She looked around at the other reporters and felt the buzz of excitement that was in the air. She then glanced over at Allen. "You know, it's times like this when I love my job."

*   *   *

A lone figure stood in a darkened office within the White House West Wing. The figure watched a small television that was tuned to WNN. The reporter on the television spoke live from the White House.

"And in a few minutes, we'll be going live to the White House Rose Garden for the medal ceremony honoring the Iraqi ex-rebel Mr. Ahlmed Mahkeem." The announcer finished the sentence as the channel went to a commercial break.

A commercial about protecting endangered species came on the television screen when the figure pulled out a small remote control from his pocket. He raised the antenna on the remote and nervously cracked his knuckles in anticipation of the completion of a plan he had set in motion over a year ago.

*   *   *

Bobby waited impatiently for the elevator to reach the lobby. He had called the White House to try and stop the medal ceremony, but he had been overruled because it was already under way, with a good part of America watching. Without any other options, he had to get to the White House immediately.

A few minutes ago, he had walked out of the shower, looked into the mirror, and saw the small scar from his chip implant. He then referenced Mahkeem's medical report and realized that the lone echo from the video had not been a side effect from the sun flare distortion, but an actual Special Forces tracking chip, implanted in the Iraqi rebel and pinging on a lower frequency. The key lay in the fact that *the echoes never moved during the solar flare, just the heat signatures.* The discrepancy had led the technicians to believe that the extra chip actually did line up with one of the Kodiak implants. When Bleeker hit the lower frequency, the chips were already responding again, including the implant in the rebel. A moment later, the sun flare cleared up just as the technician returned to the normal frequency to find the other echoes present once again.

Bobby also figured out what had bothered him about the web-casts. There was one subtle difference in actions of the insurgents when comparing the two Internet media presentations to each other. During the first video, the rebels had not spoken a word, yet right before Mahkeem fired his first shot during the second, the insurgents screamed to their god, *Allah*, as if they knew they were about to die.

Bobby found it hard to believe the depth of the betrayal. He couldn't stop thinking about how dedicated the insurgents were to their cause. "They sacrificed themselves to promote one of their own. And we took the bait. Hook, line, and sinker."

The voice that had barked the *yullah* command on the rebel field phone, if Bobby had correctly identified the speaker, had then expanded the plot in a way that was almost unimaginable. He didn't understand exactly how the two parties were linked, but Joe Manelli's discovery, in addition to the lone echo, had cemented the relationship in his mind.

"Six of one, half a dozen of another—and Mahkeem makes the thirteenth echo," Bobby spoke the line under his breath in disbelief.

As the elevator came to a stop, he heard the usual ding and the doors opened. He was relieved to see that the elevator had actually stopped on the first floor instead of continuing on to the basement.

He walked through the lobby, still favoring his one leg slightly as adrenaline had replaced most of his pain. He exited the hotel and looked around.

"Where the hell are they? I ordered a car; they should've been waiting for me." He paused for a second. "Unless . . . . shit!"

Bobby came to the quick realization that he could be waiting a while when he heard a familiar voice from behind him.

"That should just about do it. Do you want to grab something to eat before we take off? You know, unless you've already got plans or something." Gerald almost sounded like he was asking Captain Bethert on a date.

Bobby spun around. "Bethert, I need to get to the White House as soon as possible, can you help me?"

Gerald's eyes lit up. "I can get you there, sir. We can take my car." He pointed to a rusted-out car from the previous century.

Bobby looked at the car and quickly shot a look for help to Bethert.

"That's okay, Gerald." answered Bethert. "I think we'll take my car."

*   *   *

Captain Anne Bethert placed a portable police flasher onto the top of her car and sped out of the parking lot. Bobby rode shotgun, with a very happy Gerald B. Orlando bouncing along in the back seat.

"This is really cool. I don't usually get involved in this stage, I usually show up after all the action's over." The grin on his face proved that Gerald was truly enjoying the moment. "Should I have brought my stuff with me, Major?"

Bobby turned around and shot Orlando a look of bewilderment. "I hope not."

"We should get you there in just under ten minutes." Bethert swerved around a U-haul truck.

"Can I use your phone for a second?" asked Bobby.

Bethert went to pull her phone out of her pocket when a hand with a purple cell phone flew into Bobby's face from the back seat.

"You can use mine, sir. I've got unlimited daytime minutes, so don't worry about—"

"Thanks." Bobby grabbed the phone in his left hand while he hit the speed dial on his personal phone that was already in his other hand.

"Bleeker, you ready on your end?"

"Yes, ready when you are."

Bobby turned on Gerald's phone. "I'm dialing the number right now, get ready . . . it's ringing."

"Satellite trace is starting . . . . now." Bleeker paused for a moment, "Got it."

Bobby hit the *end-conversation* button on Gerald's phone and turned it off.

Bleeker talked again in Bobby's right ear. "It will take a few moments. We've already got the exact latitude and longitude, now I've got to overlay the map. Hang on."

Bobby had contacted Bleeker about tracing a cell phone's location before he left his hotel room. Bleeker had explained that it shouldn't be a problem, and that the cell phone user didn't have to actually answer the call to triangulate the coordinates. The Private had contacted the cell phone company and coordinated a yellow alert phone trace. A yellow alert meant that a Homeland Security request had come in and needed immediate attention. A member of the phone company was then made available to complete the special government security request.

"Major Handle, I've got the location of the cell phone," responded Bleeker.

"Go ahead, Private." Bobby glanced back at Gerald who had leaned forward so that his head was in the front seat.

"The cell is currently in office W5, first floor of the White House, West Wing."

Chapter 26

President Sumner heaped great acclaim upon Laurel as one of those brave women who come along only so often in history. Throughout his presentation, he also made sure that he let the television viewing audience know that in his opinion, all women shared this award. As he continued to give a brief run-down on her accomplishments, he paused occasionally to glance over at her. She was slightly bent over and looked as if she were about to throw up. He looked down at his notes and decided to skip her last few accomplishments. *I don't need her getting sick on national television.*

Sumner wrapped up his comments and draped the medal around Laurel's neck. He then posed with her and Vice President Compton to allow the photographers to capture the moment. He gave a quick glance over to Compton who had also clearly noticed that something was wrong with her. After another few seconds, the press core was done, which allowed Laurel to quickly step aside and out of the spotlight. *One down, two to go*, thought Sumner. *Hopefully the next two are feeling better.*

The clapping roared to life as Laurel gave a weak smile to the select crowd, shook the President's hand once more and walked off-camera to allow Kyle, the next in line, to receive his award. She slapped him on the arm as she passed him and then reached her head up to the side of his ear. "Smile big."

"Try not to throw up on camera," Kyle whispered back.

"I'm going to find the bathroom right now." She gave Kyle a nod to the affirmative and then quickly left the stage to keep the American public from seeing yet another side of her that she probably wished to remain private.

The President did a heck of job building her up, can't wait to see how he spins my career. Kyle moved forward and prepared himself for the biggest load of bullshit he'd ever been part of.

As he stood next to Sumner, he heard his military accomplishments recited back to the entire country. A few seconds later, Kyle suddenly felt his heart speed up. *Never been much for on-stage.* He let out a slow long breath and figured it was best to just suffer through the ordeal. He did so and made his body rigid in a state of military attention. He never imagined being honored by the President, but now, he just wanted it to be over.

*   *   *

The figure in the military uniform watched the proceedings from a large office in the West Wing of the White House. He gazed at the historic event being transmitted over the small television set that sat perched upon the desk located next to the door to the hallway.

The military man watched as President Sumner gave his speeches and awarded the Congressional Medals of Honor to the Kodiak soldiers. He waited with exasperation until it was the Iraqi rebel's turn to be presented. Then he could finger the button on the radio-controlled device that would trigger the plastic explosive packed freedom medal award. The explosion would kill the President, the Vice President and almost every other person on the stage.

Tabler thought his dream aloud. "Then this country can start making the hard decisions it has to make."

He looked at the monitor once more before he stared at the remote detonator in his right hand. He swung his thumb back and forth as he waited for Sumner to finish praising Kyle. He tapped the button twice, almost coyly, but with not enough force to depress the metal triggering device.

Tabler looked back at the monitor again and then turned around as he thought he heard a noise from behind him.

Suddenly a sharp pain arose from his right hand, the one holding the mechanism. He stopped in mid-turn to see another fist wrapped tightly around the thumb that was precariously hovering over the trigger button. As the fist pulled the thumb backwards, Tabler fought back a scream as he heard the sharp crack of that particular bone being broken.

Tabler involuntarily released the device, but Bobby was able to quickly bend down and catch it in mid-air. With his body still in the bent position, the General spun around and kicked Bobby full in the side—the side that had been wounded earlier. Bobby went down on one knee with a grunt as Tabler continued his assault. He brought up his other leg and snapped his knee under Bobby's chin to drive him backwards, down to the floor.

Tabler took two steps to walk around Bobby's defeated form. He was within easy reach of the triggering device when Bobby, still groggy and vision slightly blurred, shot out his hand smacking the device. He sent it skidding along the smooth wooden finish until it traversed the length of the room. The device finally made its way under a desk where it came to a rest underneath the drapes along the wall next to the window.

A heavy shoe connected with Bobby's ribs which brought a hoarse moan up from his throat. As he looked up, he squinted to try and clear his vision. As he focused, he saw the handgun in Tabler's grip, complete with a Carswell silencer, pointed directly at him. Tabler stared back at Bobby. He rubbed his broken thumb as he grimaced from the pain.

"God damnit, Handle, can't you see that you're about to fuck up an important moment in the history of our country?" Tabler's anger seethed through gritted teeth. He straightened his posture and checked the monitor. The display showed the President placing a medal around Kyle's neck. He then redirected his attention to Bobby, who was still lying flat on his back.

Bobby sucked in a gulp of air. "You mean letting history know that people like you always fail when they try to overthrow a free government?"

With the gun still pointed directly at Bobby's face, Tabler gave another kick. Bobby gritted his teeth.

"That's right, Major, no noise or I'll empty this silenced clip of bullets into your goddamned face."

Bobby exhaled through the pain softly.

"No, Major Handle, to answer your question, history admires strong men who keep weak leaders from taking their country down the wrong paths." Tabler took a step toward Bobby and shook the gun as he spoke.

"You could have run against him last fall in the general election." Bobby continued to blink rapidly as his sight returned to normal.

Tabler threw another kick into his side. "I thought this way was easier than trying to raise ninety million dollars for a campaign."

"You've obviously been planning this since the last election, haven't you?" Bobby concentrated on the gun. He tried to use it as a focusing trick to channel and control his pain.

"You're perceptive; no wonder you rose through the ranks so quickly when you were younger. It's just too bad that Sumner had to pull you into all this; I really do respect you. You're a good soldier just following your orders." His next kick was just to let Bobby know that he could do it, not so much as to inflict more pain.

Bobby thought of the information that Joe called him about, the information about the Z-man and the captured rebel cell. "This plan of yours started when we took down the cell in the Green Zone last year."

"That's right," agreed Tabler. "That captured cell you delivered to me gave me the idea to have my own sleeper army ready to go. So I worked and I worked until I had everything fall into place." His eyes narrowed. Tabler took deep breaths as he moved his thumb from side to side.

"The Kodiak mission?" Bobby was afraid to hear what he already knew.

"The entire thing." Tabler smiled at his own ingenuity as he looked toward the television screen. The President had just introduced Mahkeem.

"All of those Kodiaks were murdered just to make your Iraqi lapdog look good!" Bobby almost spit out the words as he attempted to sit up.

"Actually, Mr. Mahkeem had a much larger role in the beginning, but your impending arrival made it clear that I had to improvise." Tabler glanced back at the television but kept his gun focused on Bobby's head.

"Yullah, yullah." Bobby repeated the words that originally had alerted Mahkeem.

"Exactly." Tabler looked to the small monitor screen again. A still photo of Mahkeem was on the screen for a moment before it was followed by a flurry of typed information that detailed his life. The information continued to flash across the bottom of the screen as the medal presentation went on.

"Why?" Bobby tried to buy time but hoped the General would not notice.

"Because I had that country right where I wanted it. I was the one who routed out most of the deck of cards that became such a common bond for our country to see that we were winning that war. In fact, you were involved in half of those missions yourself. Sure there were pockets of rebels still active, but most of the country was free and democratic, just like our good ol' America. Two more months under my military guidance and those people would have been begging for fucking hamburger franchises to be erected on every fifth sand dune. If the government would have left me alone for another half of a year I would have had the Iraqi's cracking walnuts out of their little brown asses for us, all of the time singing Yankee Doodle Dandy. But I saw the pendulum about to swing. I knew the opposing party was building up a powerful movement to win the White House, basing a large part of their platform on withdrawing our troops from the Middle East. I gave Sumner that country on a fucking platter and all he wanted to do was to pull out and let them have it back."

"It's their country, damnit." Bobby spit out the words in the loudest tone that he dared. Tabler shouldn't have been able to get the upper-hand on him, but he was too beat-up from the previous night.

Should have brought more backup. Bobby felt the pain more severely than before.

"It was never their country, you fool, it was ours. We were never liberators, we were occupiers." Tabler continued to speak through his teeth as his complexion became redder with each word.

Bobby saw the look of madness on Tabler's face.

"And speaking of occupying," began Tabler, "that's what you'll be doing momentarily." He shifted the gun slightly so that the barrel was lined up directly between Bobby's eyes. "Occupying a place in hell."

*   *   *

Ahlmed Mahkeem looked out at the media crews that had come out to cover the medal ceremony and laughed to himself. The American infidels believed that they were doing him a great honor by placing a worthless piece of metal around his neck.

"We will relocate you and protect you from the people trying to kill you," the CIA agent had told him earlier.

The foolish intelligence agency couldn't even figure out the real target of the attacks, nor could they actually protect him if he truly would have been the target.

Major Bobby Handle had complicated everything since his arrival at the bunker, but even the resourcefulness of the so-called military legend had not stopped the plan from reaching the pinnacle moment that was about to arrive. Although he had to give him some credit—Bobby Handle was indirectly responsible for giving him the opportunity of a lifetime—the chance to please his god by killing the leader of his enemies, the President of the United States. *Symbolism. There would be no greater symbol than that of killing the President.* He would stand next to Mohammed, a hero to all in the afterlife.

When Major Handle had been assigned to root out and capture the insurgents responsible for the suicide bombings in the Iraqi Green Zone, Ahlmed Mahkeem was at the University of Baghdad where he received encrypted information through the computer labs to help organize the acts of violence. A few days before the finalization of the Iraqi Constitution's amendments, he received a message that detailed the visit of an important military leader from the United States. The military man would be staying at the U.S. Army installation at Saddam's old palace, and would be attending many of the government related events throughout the week. The military enemy to be targeted for assassination was General Charles Tabler.

Tabler had been personally responsible for organizing the missions to capture key players within the Iraqi insurgency. A high-ranking military official could rarely be targeted, so an elaborate plan to assassinate the General was set into motion.

In order for Tabler to reach Baghdad, he would have to travel down the airport road. The road had already been the site of numerous suicide bombings over the last few years; most of them targeted at U.S. convoys. Mahkeem had organized a two-phase strike to take out the General. The first part of the plan was simple. Multiple cars packed with explosives would charge the convoy and detonate on impact. Mahkeem banked on the fact that they would probably be able to demolish the outer vehicles that surrounded the General's transportation. The attack would then send the car that carried Tabler back to the airport, where the rest of the cell would be waiting to finish the job.

The plan would have succeeded, but Handle's team intercepted the cell members in a local suburb of Baghdad before they could reach the vehicles that were packed with explosives. Bobby Handle had gone on to dismantle the entire insurgent organization operating within the Green Zone. He then sent all of the members to an Iraqi prison, *or so he thought.*

General Tabler, while touring the local police facility in the Green Zone, asked to speak to the men who had targeted him for assassination in private. Mahkeem had heard that Tabler wanted to look into the faces of the insurgents to better understand who he was fighting, but to everyone's surprise, General Tabler had made them an offer.

"Why kill me, when we can kill a common enemy, an enemy that in death would please your god much more than by killing an old general like me." Tabler then handed the men a disposable cell phone with a single number programmed into its memory. "Call me if you're interested," were his final words. The men were then released from custody. They owed their freedom to some behind the scene machination from Tabler, and soon returned to their brother insurgents with the General's interesting proposal.

The plan required a man who was not on any watch-list, who would have to be able to speak English fluently. This man needed to be very intelligent to pull off a deception that could fool an entire nation.

Ahlmed Mahkeem was the most logical choice, and he pleasingly stepped forward to participate in the most high profile assassination in the history of his organization. He also looked forward to personally paying back the Americans who were still occupying his country.

The members of JET gained additional trust in Tabler as he released more imprisoned cell members back to the North insurgency over a three-month period. During this time, Tabler insisted that Mahkeem receive a Special Forces implant so that everyone could monitor their key player. Tabler also supplied JET with a Pentagon chip receiver as a gesture of good faith. With both sides now confident in one another, the final preparations began.

Tabler had been instrumental in formulating the Internet web-cast where Mahkeem would save an American soldier. The JET organization then added a small detail that shocked the Americans at first. They suggested that Mahkeem should kill the entire cell of rebels during the broadcast. The men in the JET organization all prayed that they would be given the chance to die in a plot that would lead to the death of the U.S. leader, which made it very easy to find volunteers.

With the plan complete, a last minute change was made when Mahkeem suggested that if he were to save a *female* U.S. soldier, the incompetent U.S. media would probably embrace him even quicker. Laurel Crickowski was then officially assigned to the mission, compliments of Mahkeem.

The night of the Kodiak mission started out as planned. The second team of U.S. Special Forces personnel was to be hunted down using the chip receiver while the first team was supposed to be captured in preparation for the live executions. Although the second team of Kodiaks had proved much more resilient than the rebels had anticipated, the team of Americans had still been defeated. Mahkeem's primary responsibility the first night was to remove the fissionable material from the bunker as the team of American soldiers arrived.

The plan had originally called for Mahkeem to save a greater number of U.S. soldiers, but the Kodiak who spoke Arabic had to die before he compromised anything, and the soldier crushed by the falling chopper, although very pleasurable to Mahkeem, was not planned.

During the first execution, it was Mahkeem's job to act as if he was in shock by what was transpiring. He had rehearsed it many different ways, but quietly stepping back and whispering to himself in his native language seemed to be the most effective.

It was after the first execution that the plan deviated from its original course. Mahkeem was to kill his cell members, save Laurel in front of the world, and exit through the tunnel below the compound with the surviving Kodiaks. He would then help the team get back to the U.S. front-line troops, but Handle's arrival had changed everything.

General Tabler had contacted his rebel group on the field phone and told them about Handle's impending rescue. The cell then had to complete the mock-execution as fast as possible or Handle would have arrived before Mahkeem would have had a chance to step in. As it turned out, he pulled off the performance of his life, and just in time.

During the conversation with Tabler on the field phone, the General had communicated that they would be exercising the optional part of the plan—the attack in London. Tabler had decided that if the U.S. government needed more proof of Mahkeem's goodwill, there would be no better way than by stopping an assassination in an allied country. With Bobby Handle's arrival, Mahkeem waited patiently for the right opportunity to exercise the contingency plan which gave him an additional opportunity to further prove himself.

Tabler gave Mahkeem instructions to reveal the London plot to *only Major Handle.* If Handle himself were convinced that Mahkeem was for real, that could aid Tabler to convince the President, among others, to trust the rebel.

To further the deception, Mahkeem was also given a number of insurgent training sights to disclose during the Pentagon debriefing sessions. JET made sure that the sights all had some sort of activity, even if it was minimal. The sites were then to be abandoned before any U.S. offensive could take place. With the deception complete, Mahkeem only had to wait a few days until he could fulfill his final destiny.

He focused back on the present, and on the few moments of his life that remained. He couldn't wait to talk to the other cell members in the afterlife who had already sacrificed themselves. Allah had truly blessed him for giving him a chance to consummate his ultimate dream. As he continued to listen to Sumner speak about international trust and friendship, he felt sickened by the words.

Chapter 27

"You know our President, Major Handle." Tabler switched the gun to his left hand and flexed his right. The area below his broken thumb was bruised and swollen, but he cracked his knuckles through the pain. "You of all people should realize his love of history. Sumner should know that his pulling out of Iraq would only lead to another type of cold war, this time in the Middle East. I can't allow that to happen to our country."

Tabler stole a quick glance at the television screen. Sumner was reaching for the medal to drape around Mahkeem's neck. He then averted his gaze back to the floor and looked down at Bobby.

"I'm afraid your death will have to take a momentary back seat, Major. History awaits me." Tabler moved his broken thumb outward and cracked the knuckles on his right hand nervously. He then turned and strode toward the far wall when Bobby shot out his left foot and caught him hard on the ankle. Tabler's leg flew out from under him as he went sprawling to the ground.

Bobby rolled over onto his stomach and with as much speed as his aching, beaten body could muster, shoved upward with his arms which allowed him to get a knee in between himself and the floor. He pushed off hard and achieved a semi-standing position. Using what little momentum he had gained, he then leaned over in the direction of Tabler and threw himself atop the megalomaniac.

Tabler rolled over and pounded Bobby's shoulder and neck with the butt of his gun.

"You're denying me my place in history, Major." The voice came out as a contorted hiss.

Bobby was too weak and knew the deadly game of tag he'd played with the van had taken too much out of him. He also knew there was too much at stake in this fight for him to allow the pain to dictate his present course of action.

"You're grasping at straws now, Tabler, and we all know that's hard to do with a mangled hand." Bobby reached out and grabbed Tabler's broken thumb and twisted.

No sound emerged as Tabler opened his mouth to scream, just a gurgling wetness that came from deep within his larynx. His eyes glazed over for a brief second. His pupils seemed to dilate as a harsher look of madness came over him. The look made him not only unrecognizable as the high ranking Army commander that he was, but also unidentifiable as a human being.

The pain in Tabler's hand seemed only to intensify his strength as his left arm swung forward and clubbed Bobby across the face with such force that he was thrown back to the floor. Tabler repeated the motion one more time and then placed the tip of the barrel against Bobby's cheek. Tabler leaned forward and pressed all of his weight into the gun whose barrel now bore into Bobby's cheek.

He pulled the trigger.

*   *   *

Laurel wiped her face with the paper towel she had pulled from the metal dispenser on the restroom wall. She leaned over the sink and held her stomach with her free hand as the toilet behind her automatically flushed to take the contents of her stomach to another part of the city.

She swore to herself aloud, as she knew in her mind that the action, adventure, and "be all that you can be" life she had chosen was over. Her life would soon be replaced by recruitment drives and television ads, not to forget the book deals and movies of the week prospects that were already coming to her.

There was a knock on the door before it opened just a crack. "You okay in there?"

"Fine. I'm okay now." Laurel turned to see the door close. She'd left the stage in a hurry, but was escorted to the bathroom by one of the members of the Secret Service. *For her own safety,* he'd told her. *Where were you when my career ended?*

In a way, her military career was ruined even before the mission went to hell. She was a young girl; her country preferred her at the rear, rather than at the front. Occasionally she would be inducted into a unit near the front to be available to search female Muslims for possession of bombs, but her Kodiak training she felt was ill put to good use.

The thought of her wasted career made her sick in a different sort of way, but she still handled it in the same fashion. She splashed more cold water on her face.

*   *   *

The medal was placed around Mahkeem's neck as the crowd watched in silence. Mahkeem moved between the President and Vice President and shook the President's hand as they paused while the cameras went off. As Mahkeem felt the weight of the medal rest against his chest he raised his head upward and yelled, "Allah!"

Sumner shot a look to Vice President Compton as the Rose Garden fell into silence. He then looked out to see startled looks upon the face of every person in attendance. After a few uncomfortable moments, Sumner was able to compose himself, grab the situation, and make it into something positive.

"And may God bless also." The words along with the beaming smile cut the tension. "I think that's what our friend was trying to say and I agree with him." The media clapped in approval as they cheered both Sumner and Mahkeem.

That was interesting, thought Sumner. *Guess it's sort of like a musician thanking God at the Grammies, except that Mahkeem looks confused.*

Sumner studied Mahkeem's expression of bewilderment. The ex-rebel must have been in shock from all of the media coverage, because he looked as if he was totally lost in the moment.

Press Secretary Babare stepped forward and reminded the throng of reporters that a reception was to be held in a few minutes. He also told them that the President as well as the medal holders and the Vice President had to leave temporarily. Babare finished his explanation, walked to the side of the stage, and opened the door that led into the White House.

Sumner paused and gave a quick wave to the reporters before he exited into a hallway in the West Wing. Kyle and Mahkeem followed a few steps behind him along with the rest of the security team.

Moments after they'd entered the hall, Mahkeem became extremely agitated. *Why am I still here? Why am I here with these infidels? They should be dead.*

He knew by now that the plan should have been executed and he should have been granted rewards in a glorious afterlife. He'd worked too hard to earn his rewards. His personal sacrifice was to bring death to the American leaders, but the bomb did not go off. Mahkeem knew that Tabler must have missed his opportunity. *Or did Tabler change sides?*

A strong and desperate urge to find Tabler, or take matters into his own hands, came over him. He wouldn't mind if both happened. He was a soldier, and he would do whatever it took. *This is my last chance,* he thought with a vengeance.

Just then, a member of the Secret Service interrupted Sumner. The man walked up to the President to remind him that a squad of agents was ready to escort him on the pre-arranged walk through the White House Gardens, possibly with Mahkeem, to personally thank the ex-rebel before heading down to the small reception.

Sumner nodded in agreement as Mahkeem suddenly dove at the Secret Service agent. The duo slammed into the wall. As they did, Sumner, Compton, and even Kyle stood transfixed at the sudden actions of the Iraqi.

Mahkeem had seen the agent's gun, and now that he had the man pressed against the wall, reached into the inside of the Secret Service man's jacket and pulled it out of the holster. As he grabbed the weapon, he fired into the agent's stomach. Mahkeem now had the upper hand. He'd created an opportunity to kill the enemy of his people, and he was going to take it.

The agent slumped over as Mahkeem quickly turned and pointed the weapon at Sumner. He shouted something in Arabic as he pulled the trigger twice.

The bullets would have hit and possibly killed the President, but Kyle's body came into view as he flung himself between the weapon and Sumner. Kyle was also able get his hand on Mahkeem's gun. He pulled it away from the grasp of the insurgent, but not in time to keep the weapon from discharging again.

The bullets struck Kyle in the collarbone and grazed the top of his shoulder before he was able to wrestle away with the gun in hand. He then fell to the floor next to the dead Secret Service Agent and looked up at Mahkeem.

Mahkeem stared back at Kyle with a crazed expression. Sumner was supposed to be dead. He'd gained the upper hand, but lost it because of Kyle.

An infidel will die today, it's not over yet. Mahkeem, now disoriented and frightened, turned and fled down the hall to look for Tabler. *I must fulfill my mission.*

*   *   *

With all of Tabler's weight on the gun, Bobby jerked his head to the left. His sweat-soaked face was no foundation for the weapon. As the gun discharged, the silenced weapon had already slid off of Bobby's face and onto the wooden floor, where two bullets now pockmarked the beautiful veneer.

Bobby pressed his right arm against Tabler's side as he cocked his hip at the same time. He used the leverage to flip Tabler off of him and toward the door to the hallway.

Tabler rolled quickly to avoid further injury to his right hand. A second later, he rose to his feet.

Bobby also struggled to get up from the floor. *Okay, I don't know where Mahkeem is at, and don't know the status of the explosive. Just stop Tabler, and everything else should work itself out.* He knew Kyle and Laurel were with Sumner. They could take care of anything that came up now that the bomb threat had almost been neutralized. *Almost, being the keyword.*

Both of them heard gunshots from down the hall

"I don't know what's happening." Tabler turned to the television monitor to see that the ceremony was indeed finished.

Bobby had gotten to his feet and stood erect.

Tabler laughed in a deranged fashion, but Bobby knew it was the mirth of madness. "Who knows, Major, I might even find a way to blame the whole thing on you. I'm a four-star General. I'll bet I can make just about anything stick."

Tabler was still laughing when Mahkeem flew through the open door. The Iraqi rebel slammed the door closed behind him. Tabler's laughter was quickly replaced by a look of disbelief as he stared at the rebel.

"General," said Mahkeem. He was totally out of breath and could barely utter the word.

Bobby saw the medal, still hung around Mahkeem's neck. He thought back to the ploy he had used in the basement at the Royalview and turned.

Tabler saw Bobby move and a look of horror crossed his face. He raised the gun and fired.

Bobby flung himself across the room and landed on the top of the desk near the window. A bullet flew by his left ear and into the bookcase against the wall. As he slid across the top of the desk, he grabbed the front lip of the top. His momentum carried him over to the other side, and his tight grasp pulled the desk backward and over.

Two more bullets tore through the wooden frame of the office furniture that protected Bobby.

Where is it? Come on, come on. Bobby groped under the drapes for the triggering device. *It's got to be here. I saw it.*

"Where is it, where is—" he quickly found the small rectangular remote and activated it.

The ensuing explosion forced the desktop to push Bobby back into the wall where he struck his head. The last thing he remembered was a General's four-star epaulet embedding itself into the ceiling of the room directly above him.

*   *   *

"Son of a bitch, now what!" Bethert shouted as she ran from her car toward the White House proper.

Meanwhile, the suddenness of the explosion made Orlando drop his overly sweet cup of soda mixed with iced-tea. He left the drink where it spilled on the ground and ran after Bethert. The words shot out past his sticky coated braces.

"I knew I should have brought my forensic gear with me."

Chapter 28

Bobby sat silently across from the President's desk in the Oval Office. Next to him were Kyle, Laurel, and Vice President Compton. President Sumner sat on the other side of the desk and watched Press Secretary Babare pace back and forth across the office and in and around each chair. Bobby knew that everyone was still in shock after hearing his report of the events that had led to his battle in the West Wing with General Tabler two hours ago.

Bobby couldn't help but think Babare looked like some type of shark, aimlessly circling the office while he waited for someone to respond. Bobby already knew that this was going to be the part where the White House would add their spin, but as usual, he wasn't sure exactly how the truth would be twisted.

The attendees of the meeting had told him that they were amazed that he was even able to stand after the beating he'd taken earlier, let alone recall his investigation with such detail. *Guess they don't know me very well,* thought Bobby.

Bobby's new wounds had already been treated and his old ones were given a fresh set of bandages. The doctor who had worked on him made a few comments about a possible infection if he didn't rest his body. Bobby's only reply had been a head nod. *He didn't know me very well . . . either.*

Laurel, who also sat in silence, had made a number of comments on the fact that Kyle looked like a younger sibling of Bobby. Kyle's arm, wrapped in a large bandage, hung comfortably in a sling as he sat slouched in a chair next to Bobby. Both he and Bobby had walked into the office with a serious limp and matching shoulder bandages.

Like Bobby, Kyle watched Babare pace while he continued to shake his head in disbelief that Mahkccm and Tabler had worked together in a plot to bring down the presidency.

Bobby had covered everything in great detail. He had started with the discovery of the chip in Mahkeem's shoulder. He described his low-tech way of cross-referencing the Monocle's images with the chip implants by overlaying pieces of paper. He then detailed the recognition of Tabler's voice on the rebel field phone and finally, his dialogue with the General in the West Wing.

"That's basically everything that we know to this point." Bobby paused while he took a drink from a small plastic bottle of water. "In fact, the only issue we haven't been able to address is the one that started this whole ordeal in the first place, the missing fissionable material." He turned to Sumner with confidence. "But my resource at the Pentagon, Private Bleeker, has assured me that they won't rest until it's been located. He also informed me that the Interagency Incident Management Group is ensuring full situational awareness if anything concerning the material comes up."

"What about the medal?" As Sumner spoke, he motioned to Babare to try to get him to stop pacing. Babare paused for a moment, but then went back to his endless circling.

Sumner threw up both hands. "You can't expect me to believe that General Tabler was able to build a bomb with a remote detonator in the short time that the award was in his possession."

"A very good question, Sir." Bobby scratched his forehead. "Tabler must have gotten help from somewhere. If the mechanism was assembled in advance, then it may just have been a case of placing a couple of pieces together." He hesitated as he thought through what he had just stated. "Approximately how long *did* the General have the medals?"

"Less than one hour," replied Sumner plainly.

Bobby shook his head. "It does seem like too short of a time period for someone who's obviously not a weapons expert to assemble something that complicated without blowing himself up." The room fell silent again as Bobby pondered the situation further.

"The bottom line is that we're both still alive." Sumner let out a long slow breath. "We owe you our lives."

Bobby gave a quick nod and pointed to Kyle's shoulder. "I appreciate the gratitude, but Captain Bradly did a hell of job blocking a few bullets."

"That he did," commented the Vice President. "In my opinion, that tackle was the play of the decade." Compton smiled toward Kyle and then formed a puzzled look. "So all of this was basically because the General felt that our administration had undone everything that he had worked so hard to accomplish in Iraq over the last decade?"

"Exactly," replied Bobby, "although it's sort of ironic that the JET organization's victory would have been cut short when their American partner, Tabler, sent in troops to wipe them out. And with everyone in America seeking justice for the President's death, he would have had unlimited resources available to him to finish the job." A thought popped into his mind. "And I would have probably been leading one of the campaigns against the insurgents under his command." As he spoke, he once again realized how close the nation had come to losing its leader just a few hours earlier.

Everyone in the office was silent for almost a full minute before Sumner spoke. "We can easily discount anything that the JET organization may claim to have almost done, leaving the six of us as the only witnesses knowing the whole truth." He thought for another moment. "And it needs to stay that way. The media is pounding down the White House doors trying to get some answers to what happened following the ceremony today. We were supposed to host a reception, which was suddenly cancelled by an explosion in the West Wing. When the windows blew out in that office, people started asking questions. Questions that we'll need to supply with answers."

Here comes the spin, thought Bobby.

"The Secret Service blocked off the entire section of the floor containing the office where the explosion took place." Babare resumed to pace. "We're just lucky that the White House windows are not only bullet proof, but also sound proof."

Bobby squinted at Barbare's last comment. *Too bad they weren't bomb proof.*

Babare paused as he gathered his thoughts. "The media didn't hear the shots in the hallway, they only heard the explosion that followed, so we can get as creative as we need to be with our explanation." Babare sat up and was about to utter something else, but Laurel, still weak from her bout with the stomach virus, finally joined into the conversation.

"Mr. President, Sir," she began weakly. "I have an idea."

"Yes, Laurel," Sumner informally spoke to her. "Go ahead."

"Couldn't we just simply tell the truth?" Laurel now had everyone's undivided attention as she continued, "Mahkeem sacrificed his own life saving you from a would-be assassin from within the White House staff, and the General was also killed in the explosion. Nobody needs to know that the assassins happened to be the same two people who died saving you."

Bobby tilted his head to one side slightly and gave a half nod. *Not a bad spin, and it's actually . . . true—from a certain point of view.*

Sumner leaned back as he thought about the idea. He shifted in his chair, which caused it to squeak slightly, as he nodded. "You know, that might just work."

"I concur, Sir." Babare nodded his head in agreement. "Mahkeem has been a symbol of trust and friendship for us, so let's just blame the entire thing on a member of the Secret Service who was being blackmailed by the cell responsible."

"Good," stated Sumner. "I want you to put together a formal statement for the press. Keep it short and let's not take any questions just yet. I want some time to see how the media reacts, and then we can deal with them accordingly."

"Yes, Sir." Babare stopped his circular walk and headed toward the door.

Kyle and Laurel took the cue from Barbare, stood up, and prepared to leave. Kyle limped slowly due to his recent injury, while Laurel held her stomach and softly groaned as she moved.

"Hey, Number One, we're one sorry looking team, aren't we?" Laurel leaned over and gently elbowed Kyle.

Kyle tilted his head slightly. "Yeah, but right now, I'm just looking forward to a little Kyle Bradly time, Number One is officially off-duty."

"Yeah, well, Number Two is right behind you, *Kyle*." Laurel smiled again as they both walked down the hallway.

*   *   *

"Come on, agent, give me a break, you're going to have to do better than that!" exclaimed Jennifer. "I've been following Mahkeem around for almost a week and I've seen way too much happen to believe that the reception was cancelled simply because he was overwhelmed by the moment and needed to lie down for a little while. We all heard the explosion, what the hell happened in there?"

The Secret Service man closed the door to the reception area. Most of the other reporters had left nearly an hour ago, but Jennifer's intuition told her that something big happened—something that nobody was willing to talk about.

She had already checked with the Royalview staff and discovered that Bobby left in a hurry with members from the D.C.P.D. She also had failed to reach him on his cell phone. Those facts when combined with Bobby's last minute revelation from the web-casts had led her to believe that he had uncovered something about the ex-rebel. Or if not directly about Mahkeem, then maybe he had finally solved the mystery behind the repeated attempts to kill the new American ally.

Jennifer pulled her cell phone from her pocket and hit the speed dial button. As soon as she heard the party on the other end of the phone pick up, she spoke, "Curt, I'm getting nothing over here. So you'll have to go with the final version of the special that we discussed earlier."

"But you *still* think something's going on, don't you?" Curt had spoken to her a couple of hours ago after he'd finished the postproduction work for the special.

"Yeah, something's up. I was going to do a commentary on Monday's newscast about the reception following the ceremony, but an explosion cancelled the event, and I can't seem to get a straight answer from anyone. Bobby, Mahkeem, the Kodiaks, everyone has just vanished!"

"Listen, Jennifer, you've had a long week. The White House will make a formal statement, and when they do, you'll be there to hear it. You need to take your own advice from earlier today. Go home, relax, and enjoy your prime-time special tonight. As I told you before, you've earned it. Call your friend Handle tomorrow, I'm sure he'll explain everything." Curt's voice sounded like a late night DJ on a radio station that only played classical music.

I know you're trying to soothe me. Jennifer let out a long breath and very reluctantly replied, "Okay, you're probably right. I'm out of here."

"Good girl, see you later," replied Curt.

Jennifer hung up the phone and thought about the last time that Bobby had disappeared on her. The current circumstances where undeniably similar to those a year ago in Baghdad. She had attended a large media event while Bobby Handle departed, once again, presumably to go save the world. She shook her head as she walked back to her vehicle.

"Some people just never change."

* * *

President Sumner asked Bobby to stay behind after everyone else had exited the Oval Office. Babare had gone to prepare a formal statement for the media based on the results of the just-completed meeting while Kyle and Laurel headed back to the Royalview to gather their things. Both Kodiak soldiers were ready to head home and spend some well-earned time with their families and friends.

"Bobby, we've been through a lot together over the past year," began Sumner. "I know you've spent most of that time overseas in the Middle East, but I'm thinking about reassigning you."

"Reassigning me to what extent, Sir?" Bobby sat up in his chair to readjust the position of his healing calf muscle. Sumner was anti-war, so a reassignment could mean almost anything.

"This breach of security was right under my nose and I was almost killed today because I put my trust in the wrong man." Sumner removed his glasses and placed them into his shirt pocket. He rubbed his eyes and looked across the desk."

Okay, thought Bobby as he stared back at Sumner, *let's just get on with it. Where am I headed?*

"I need you here at home. I want you to head up a new team of individuals that we can trust. Your new team would report directly to me and act independently from the other branches of the military. The primary focus would be to investigate security breaches within our own ranks." Sumner looked like he was trying to read Bobby's face for some sort of reaction, but Bobby remained emotionless, which caused Sumner to finally add, "So what do you think, Bobby? You want to be close by the next time I have to take on the dammed role of Commander-in-Chief?"

"Sir, ten days ago I would have told you that I could best serve my country by returning to my unit in the Middle East. I would have also reminded you that we already have agencies here at home to perform the exact tasks that you are now asking me to assume responsibility for."

"And now?" queried Sumner.

"Now I would tell you that I totally agree with you, Sir." Bobby thought back to the depth of the betrayal within his own government and could easily see exactly why Sumner was making this request. *Not as bad as I thought, and probably no waiting.* Bobby adjusted his wounded leg again. "I've got one prerequisite before I officially accept your offer."

Sumner finally smiled, "What would that be?"

"That the first two members assigned to my new team are Kyle Bradly and Laurel Crickowski." Bobby had seen both of them under fire. He'd also seen Kyle bounce back from the failed mission quickly. Both would be good soldiers he could trust.

"That shouldn't be a problem, but do you think that Crickowski will want to continue? Her commitment to the armed forces is due to expire in less than six months." Sumner folded his hands on his desk and leaned forward to make his point. "She's going to be busy dealing with her new found fame and fallout from this mission for some time, don't you think?"

"While I agree with you, Sir, I also have to believe that once her fifteen minutes in the national spotlight have officially passed, America will forget her name, and she'll be ready to move on." Bobby thought about typical American idols. Their fame was typically gone before they knew it. *Americans are always looking for the next idol. They'll forget you almost before they get to know you.*

Sumner nodded. "I probably don't have to ask if you'll be pulling in your partner in crime." He tilted his head back and stared at him with a hard look until Bobby finally smiled.

"Yeah, my team just wouldn't be the same without the indispensable Joe Manelli." Bobby thought about Joe's key role in saving the President. He'd come up with the right information at the right time. *As usual*, thought Bobby.

"Well then, Major Robert Handle," Sumner used his most formal tone that he could muster. "Welcome home."

Chapter 29

Kyle meandered across the lobby of the Royalview Hotel. He wanted to take one last good look around before he exited the building for the final time. He'd already rented a car, courtesy of the United States Government, to drive to Philadelphia for his well-deserved break. He'd spoken to his parents earlier in the week and detailed his plans to come home after the medal ceremony, but he hadn't anticipated being dismissed so soon. He couldn't wait to surprise his parents because he knew that he wasn't expected home for at least another few days.

Kyle was near the main entrance when he glanced back one more time at the elevator in the bay that had dropped them into the garage a couple of nights earlier. As he stared for a moment, lost in thought, the elevator doors opened to reveal a familiar face. His mind drifted back to the present moment as he turned and gave a quick salute to Bobby.

As Bobby walked slowly through the lobby, he favored his wounded leg with each step.

"Hey, Major, where are you headed?" Kyle addressed Bobby by his title, but his tone couldn't have been more informal.

"I made a promise to Jennifer that I'd try to catch her special tonight at nine." Bobby looked down at his watch. "Looks like I've got about twenty minutes until it's on."

"You know, Sir—" Kyle attempted to say something, but Bobby interrupted before he could continue.

"Kyle, we're not on duty, and even if we were, I'd still tell you to call me Bobby." Bobby sounded even more informal than Kyle had just a moment ago.

"Okay, Bobby," started Kyle again. "I just wanted to say that it has been a pleasure working with you this past week."

"Well, how would you like to continue working with me?" Bobby crossed his arms and waited for Kyle's response.

"What do you mean?" Kyle shot the question back quickly. *He couldn't actually mean work with him, like on his team?*

"Look, I'm going to go down to one of my old hangouts and watch a little television and throw down a couple of beers." Bobby smiled and uncrossed his arms. "Why don't you come with me and I'll fill you in."

Kyle weighed his options, *surprising his parents, or hanging out with the legendary Bobby Handle.* He took almost a full second to make up his mind. "I'll drive."

*   *   *

Jennifer sat down on her couch and flipped on the television. She had already taken a long hot bath in an effort to try and think about something else besides Mahkeem and the man who had kept the ex-rebel alive, Bobby Handle.

She looked at the cell phone next to her couch and thought about calling Bobby to try and get a scoop on what had happened down at the White House. *He wouldn't tell me a thing anyway. Bobby would probably say that it's classified information and that I'd have to wait for the White House to make a formal statement.*

She tried to put him out of her mind and focused back on the current television commercial that was trying to convince its audience that a better flea and tick collar now existed because of another breakthrough in science. She shook her head at the sales pitch when she heard her phone.

She reached over and picked it up. "Rayburn, here."

The voice on the other end of the phone spoke as Jennifer listened intensely. As the caller continued, she became more and more concerned.

After another minute, she hung up the phone and stared into space. "This can't be happening."

*   *   *

Bobby walked through the front door of Phil's Tavern and Wine Bar with Kyle a step behind. The bar was sparsely populated with only the local regulars in attendance, but Bobby knew it would become much more crowded as the night progressed.

He saw Kyle look around the bar and hone in on a female acoustic guitar player near the back. She was in the middle of setting up her equipment on a small stage.

"Nice," commented Bobby. As he watched her, he realized that it had been over two years since he'd heard any type of live music.

Bobby and Kyle sat down at the bar and hailed the bartender. The bartender quickly approached and smiled as soon as he recognized Bobby.

"Captain Bobby Handle," exclaimed the white-haired bartender. "I saw you on television the other day dueling with those reporters over at Andrews. How the hell have you been, son?" The bartender threw his hands down and leaned over the bar.

"Hey, Phil, I guess it's been a while," said Bobby. "I actually made it to the rank of Major." He looked at Kyle and then back at Phil as he shrugged his shoulders. The sight of Phil brought back a number of memories. *And most of them involved me waiting for something to happen.* Bobby glanced back at the female guitar player. *And most of the time, nothing happened.*

"This guy's always been way too modest if you ask me." Phil directed his comment at Kyle. "Handle here is one hell of a soldier. Now what can I get you boys tonight?" Phil stood up and rubbed his palms together, ready to go to work.

"Couple of drafts, and could you do me a favor and flip on channel six." Bobby motioned to the small plasma screen that was mounted on the wall behind the bar.

Phil turned around, grabbed a couple of glass mugs, walked over to the beer taps and filled them. A few moments later he returned with the frothy beverages, changed the channel on the television, and turned up the volume.

"First round's on me, Major," said Phil with a wink. He then took off to service another group of patrons who were in desperate need of refills.

Bobby took a sip from his mug and wiped his mouth. "You know what the funniest thing is about this special tonight?" He lowered his voice to a whisper. "The entire thing is a lie."

Kyle nodded his head. "Yeah, we could play a drinking game based on the show's content. You have to drink every time you hear something that isn't accurate."

"I don't think I'd make it past the first fifteen minutes without passing out from alcohol poisoning." Bobby took another long drink from his mug.

Kyle looked like he wanted to laugh. Instead, he just shook his head with a look of disgust. "If you wanted the real truth, you'd need General Tabler's director's cut of the television special. When you really think about it, he was the real executive producer of the entire plot."

Bobby raised one eyebrow. "Yeah, but I think he was looking for a slightly different ending."

"I hear ya." Kyle spun around on his barstool and watched the acoustic guitar player for a few seconds.

"Let me get right to the bottom line here, Kyle." Bobby's tone grew slightly more serious. "The President has asked me to put together a new team right here in Washington to look into suspicious activities within our own ranks. He wants the team to be built from people who can be trusted. I want you to be part of that team."

Kyle attempted to reply, but Bobby raised his hand to show that he wasn't finished. He took another drink from his glass and continued, "You were put under an incredible amount of stress this past week, and I was really impressed with how you carried yourself. The deck was stacked against you by everyone, including your own government, but I saw you bounce back from the failed mission before you realized that you'd been set up." Bobby glanced up at the television and then back to Kyle. "I think we'd make a good team."

Kyle was speechless after Bobby had finished his sales pitch. Bobby knew he'd undergone extreme training to become a Kodiak, and the thought of moving back to a position within the States may have thrown him for a moment.

Kyle took another drink from his beer and weighed the pros and cons, but the allure of a chance to work with Bobby was too good of an opportunity to pass up.

"You can count me in. I'll do everything in my power to make sure that nobody else has to go through what we just did." As he finished, he looked over at a couple of other customers who where playing a pinball machine near the front of the bar.

"I'm glad to have you aboard. I'm also going to see if Laurel is open for a career change in a few months; I think that she'd make a good addition to the new team." Bobby motioned to Phil that he was ready for a refill.

"Yeah, Crickowski's okay," replied Kyle. He thought back to his first meeting with her on the plane over Iraq. He'd really grown to respect her. *Best damn female Kodiak solider on the planet.* He raised his glass. "To Laurel."

Phil delivered Bobby's second beer just in time for Bobby to reply. He raised his glass. "To Laurel."

Both men then turned their attention to the television, as the special was about to begin. Kyle watched as Jennifer gave her lead-in speech in front of the White House. As she finished, he leaned over to Bobby. "So you and her, huh?"

"I don't want to talk about it." Bobby shot a look of surprise back at him.

Kyle just nodded as they continued to watch the special.

"And now, we're going to introduce you to a few of the more recent Freedom Award recipients from the past few years." The overdubbed voice spoke as still pictures of past honorees filled the television screen.

Bobby watched the screen as he thought about the fact that America would wake up tomorrow to discover that its newfound Iraqi hero had been killed. He also wondered how President Sumner felt about corrupting history itself, because Mahkeem's contributions would be recorded based on falsified information provided from the White House. Not only did Sumner have to take on his least favorite role of Commander-in-Chief, but the result would now corrupt history as the President knew it.

Bobby continued to think about the past week when a familiar face on the television screen derailed his train of thought.

Kyle saw Bobby's reaction to the broadcast. "I didn't know that *he* received a Congressional Freedom Award."

"Yeah, me neither." Bobby stared at the television.

He thought about the debriefing in the Oval Office earlier and of the few unanswered questions which remained. He now believed he had the answers.

Bobby slid off the barstool and stood up as a look of astonishment washed over his face. "Kyle, I need to borrow your car."

*   *   *

Bobby had been in the car for twenty-five minutes when he pulled over to the side of the road. He activated the hazard lights and walked around to the back of Kyle's rented car. When he reached the rear of the vehicle, he knelt down and reached under the car to retrieve a small dangling object.

He examined the object briefly and gave a small nod. "Perfect. If it works."

Bobby placed the object into his pocket and climbed back into the car. A moment later, he turned off the hazard lights and drove back onto the road. He continued to drive north, and after another fifteen minutes, he saw a sign for Brookeville, Maryland, which signaled that he was just a few minutes away from his destination.

The storm that had been predicted to hit Washington earlier in the day had finally moved in. The air was notably cooler. Bobby could hear thunder in the darkening skies. He hoped that somehow he was wrong about his assumption back at Phil's Tavern, but the more he played and replayed the scenario through his head, it became more apparent that he was correct.

He slowed down as he searched for the street he was looking for. Thirty seconds later, he took a right turn onto Gold Miner's road and then another left. A few seconds later, he arrived at his destination.

A large iron gate blocked the driveway with a small intercom mounted just to the left of the pavement. Bobby rolled down his window and hit the *talk* button on the two-way communication device. A small camera mounted above the gate swiveled as a voice came over the intercom.

"Yes, how can I help you?" the recognizable voice stated over the speaker.

"Major Bobby Handle, I have some information that I'd like to discuss with you."

The camera moved again so that it was pointed directly at the windshield of the car when the voice spoke again, "Oh, Major Handle, I'm sorry I didn't recognize you. I'm opening the gate right now so that you can drive up to the house."

After a small metallic sound of the chain as it tightened on the gears, the gates opened to allow Bobby to drive though to the house beyond. As he approached the house, he took note that the estate must have been worth well over five million dollars based on the cost of living in the D.C. area.

The house was a tutor style home with brick accents set on at least ten acres of land. The long driveway was flanked by an endless array of trees and shrubs, lit by small low-voltage outdoor lights. As he drove up to the front door, multiple statues of classical figures adorned the grounds to complete the extensive landscaping.

As he rolled to a stop, Bobby turned off the ignition, took a deep breath and exited the rental vehicle. *If I'm right about this, I probably should have brought more backup. If I'm wrong about this, then I just missed Jennifer's special for nothing.*

He walked up to the front door, but before he could ring the doorbell, the door opened revealing the man that he had come to see, the Speaker of the House—Leamon Davis.

"Good evening, Major Handle." Davis had a confused, yet relaxed look on his face. "How can I help you?"

Chapter 30

Bobby stepped through the front door into the entryway of the enormous estate. The spacious two-story foyer had a solid marble floor and a number of statues from the Renaissance, including a reproduction of Michelangelo's *David*. He followed Leamon Davis past the statues and down a long hallway that opened up into a large great room. As he walked, Bobby noticed that the hallway followed the same artistic theme as the entryway. The walls were adorned with various paintings that all depicted scenes of Ancient Rome. The great room had a large, vaulted ceiling and a stone fireplace that was flanked by numerous windows on either side. A long, fully stocked bar ran across the far side of the room that was finished in a honey oak tone, just a few shades lighter than the solid hardwood floors. As they entered the room, Davis motioned to one of the barstools.

"Have a seat, Major. Can I get you something to drink?"

"Just a glass of ice water, thank you." Bobby sat down on the barstool at the end of the bar.

Davis bent down and reached under the bar to open what sounded like a refrigerator. A moment later, he stood up and gave Bobby the bottled water.

As Bobby twisted the cap open, he took a quick look around the room and noticed a number of additional pieces of Renaissance artwork. Most of the pieces focused on war, but across the room near one of the hallways, was a piece that featured Madonna and child. Bobby also took note of the openness of the floor plan. He was impressed about how the large great room flowed into an open, yet formal dining area, which in turn led into the household's kitchen. The large kitchen was cloaked in deep shadows, and except for a small digital clock built into the stove, all of the details of the room remained hidden.

"So how many pieces of artwork do you own?" Bobby motioned to the paintings around the room.

"I've lost count over the years," said Davis, "but I think I've probably collected just over six hundred. About half of them are sculptures."

"I noticed your statue of David on the way in. Is that a full size reproduction?" Bobby didn't know that much about art, but he could recognize the classics.

"Hardly," said Davis with a smirk as he opened a bottle of whiskey and poured a shot. "The actual statue of David stands at about seventeen feet tall. My reproduction is just over eight feet. So it's about half the size of the original. But even so, it's one of my favorite pieces." He paused to drink the contents of his shot glass, blew out through his lips and then continued. "We could chat about my art collection for hours, but I'm sure that you didn't drive all the way out here to discuss the brilliance of Michelangelo. So what's on your mind, Major?"

Bobby took another drink. He noticed that Davis was incredibly calm as he stood waiting for Bobby's reply. *Maybe he doesn't know why I'm here?*

Bobby put down the bottle. "Actually, I wanted to speak to you about the attempt on the President's life today."

"I'm not sure what you're referring to." Davis had a confused look on his face as he replied. "I wasn't informed of any assassination attempt."

"The White House is still working on a formal statement regarding the matter, but that's not my point." Bobby stared directly into the face of Davis. "I really started to think about the assassination plot, and realized that the President wasn't the only man targeted. I now have reason to believe that the Vice President was supposed to be eliminated as well."

"Why would someone want to target the Vice President?" Davis' expression showed little interest in the conversation.

Bobby continued to stare at Davis. *Either Davis is a great poker player, or he still doesn't know why I'm here.* Bobby thought for a moment and decided to take the direct route. "Because I believe that with the elimination of both the President and Vice President, the Speaker of the House is the next in line to become President of the United States."

Davis stiffened to the point where he looked like one of his statues with a look of confusion frozen on his face. "Major Handle, are you accusing me of being involved in a conspiracy to take over the Presidency?" Davis emphasized the sarcasm in his voice. "That would be treason. Do you know how ridiculous you sound?"

"I thought so, too, until I connected you to the assassination attempt." Bobby spoke mechanically and let all emotion drain from his face.

"What are you talking about?" Davis tilted his head and narrowed his eyes slightly.

"General Tabler and Ahlmed Mahkeem were killed earlier today when the Congressional Freedom Medal awarded to the Iraqi rebel exploded, instantly killing them both. The medal was packed with enough C-4 to execute the award's recipient in addition to anyone in his immediate vicinity. General Tabler was holding the remote detonator during the award ceremony. I stopped him from activating the bomb moments before he was about to press the button, which would have killed the Iraqi rebel along with our leaders." Bobby paused and tried to read Davis again. *Still, nothing . . . .*

"I've known the General for years," commented Davis with a shocked expression. "I can't believe Charles would have committed treason, and as soon as we're finished here, I'm going to make a few phone calls to get some more details from the White House." Davis paused with a puzzled look. "But I still don't see how this has anything to do with me?" His tone seemed to grow a bit defensive as he spoke.

"Well, sir, you were also an honored recipient of the Congressional Freedom Medal, the same type that Ahlmed Mahkeem was awarded this afternoon. I believe that you worked with Tabler to have *your* medal packed with C-4 along with a remote way to detonate it. The General then swapped the medals before the ceremony, replacing the one minted for Mahkeem with yours." Bobby had said what he'd come to say. Davis was a polished politician with enough years in service to span two generations—yet with Bobby's last statement, he'd hit some type of nerve.

"An excellent hypothesis," replied Davis smirking. He gained some of his composure back. "But I still fail to see how you've connected me to any of it."

"I guess it all came together when I found this in the rubble from the explosion." Bobby stood up, reached into his pocket and pulled out a flattened piece of gold metal. "This is what's left of the back of the medal that was awarded to Mahkeem." Bobby held the mangled award up between his thumb and forefinger. "Did you know that it's illegal to sell a Congressional Medal of Honor? That's why our government makes sure that each one has a serial number stamped into the back of it. The number, along with the name of the recipient, is then recorded over at the U.S. Mint." Bobby saw Davis swallow hard as he stared at the remains of the medal. *You've just given yourself away. Gotcha . . . .*

The House Speaker's smile disappeared and his eyes narrowed as Bobby finished his explanation.

"So I took the medal over to the Mint and looked up the serial number." Bobby closed his fist around the award. "Mr. Speaker, Sir, this is your medal."

Leamon Davis clenched his fists as the veins in his neck constricted. "I'm sorry, Major Handle, but you haven't left me any other option."

As the House Speaker finished the statement, the words had triggered a lone figure into action from the shadows of the kitchen. The figure moved forward, and using a handgun equipped with a silencer, took two quick shots that abruptly incapacitated Bobby. The first shot hit him in the upper left shoulder. The impact of the bullet caused the damaged medal to fly out of Bobby's grip toward the bar. The second shot grazed him in the back of his recently wounded calf and caused his leg to buckle. He hit the floor with a dull thud.

Bobby turned to look back in the direction of the kitchen as he bit his lower lip and tried to focus. Blood was now flowing freely from his shoulder and his calf felt like it was on fire.

The figure stepped into the light and walked across the room to join Davis at the bar. Bobby's expression toppled into a look of betrayal as Laurel Crickowski spoke.

"Don't move, Major Handle, or the next one's fatal."

*   *   *

Jennifer had just gotten off the phone with one of her inside sources on Capitol Hill. The source had informed her that Press Secretary Babare was preparing an official White House news release concerning the Iraqi ex-rebel. The source went on to explain that Ahlmed Mahkeem had been killed at the White House when a member of the Secret Service detonated a bomb. A rumor was also circulating that the agent who had set off the bomb was actually being blackmailed by a terrorist cell. The source then finally added that a military man accompanying the ex-rebel was also killed in the explosion. Jennifer immediately came to the conclusion that the military official must have been Major Bobby Handle. After she failed to get a hold of him, she decided to contact her co-anchor, Baxter Jameson, to see if he had heard anything.

"Come on, Baxter, you've got to have *someone* at the White House that can get us more information." Jennifer's voice cracked as she finished her statement into her cell phone. *Bobby can't be dead. He always makes it. He's a legend—and that's what legends do.*

"Jennifer," Baxter's voice sounded calm. "We'll just have to wait until the White House is ready to disclose the information. Can't you try to call Handle again?"

Jennifer had never sounded this desperate in front of a colleague before. She also knew in the back of her mind that Baxter didn't have an answer for her.

"I've already tried his cell three times," she replied. "I keep getting the pre-recorded message about his phone being turned off or out of range."

"What about the other two soldiers who were with him? Maybe they know where he's at," said Baxter.

"They're already gone. Bradly and Crickowski both checked out earlier today. Bradly said something about surprising his parents in Philadelphia by coming home a few days before they expected him." Jennifer thought for a moment. "I'm not sure where Laurel disappeared to, but I'll bet she's finally enjoying herself now that she can put all of this behind her and get on with her life."

*   *   *

"I distinctly remember you telling me that the medal would be totally vaporized in the blast." Davis exhaled, his brow now covered in perspiration.

"It should have been totally destroyed," argued Laurel emphatically. "The heat from the C-4 explosion should have at least melted the gold." She paused and glanced down at Bobby. "But then again, when the legendary Major Handle is involved, anything is possible."

Laurel walked over, sat on one of the barstools and looked down at Bobby. "I've seen what you can do even when you're hurt, so if you even look like you're going to try something, I'll kill you without a second thought."

Bobby looked up at Laurel with disgust. "I don't know how much he's paying you, but I hope it's worth it." He thought about all the clues he'd gotten from the video, the chips, and of course, God's Monocle. *But I missed a big one*, thought Bobby. *No sexual assault.* There was always some type of sexual abuse when a woman was captured, but in this case . . . *they wouldn't assault someone who was on their own team.*

"Shut up, Handle," Laurel spit the words at him. "You have no idea what it's like to go through years of Special Forces training and then be assigned basic duties like searching Muslim women for explosives at various checkpoints." Laurel stood up again and aimed the gun directly at Bobby's face. "I risked my life everyday, praying that some suicide bomber didn't take me out before I got a chance to prove myself on a real assignment. When I finally got the opportunity to make a difference as a Kodiak, Sumner pulled the carpet out from under me. I've lost too many friends because *our* President decided to remove most of our forces." Laurel finished her statement and turned to look at Davis.

"You figured out that Mr. Mahkeem was our inside man on the Iraqi side," started Davis, "but I also needed someone I could trust on the Kodiak team. I had to make certain that Captain Bradly fell short of the mission objective. Since the intent was to retrieve hazardous material, I needed to make sure that the Kodiak Number Two assigned to the team could control the mission's final outcome." Davis paused and glanced back in Laurel's direction, "Ms. Crickowski's skills have come in handy for a number of things that we've needed to accomplish."

Bobby's body seized up in pain as he commented hoarsely, "So you were the one who put together the bomb, not a member of the cell?" The missing pieces now made sense. *A weapons expert—the second clue I missed.*

"It took a military weapons expert to put that device together," Laurel was almost bragging. "Your typical cell member wouldn't have the first clue about how to assemble a mechanism that sophisticated." She paused when Davis raised his finger toward his lips.

"I still give you a lot of credit for figuring out as much as you have," said Davis. "JET was, of course, going to take full responsibility for the exploding medal, but I couldn't trust the actual construction to just anyone. Remember, Major, these people are very adept at building crude devices used in suicide bombings. This bomb needed someone with a bit more training."

"So JET would've taken the credit for building the bomb, when in reality they would just be covering Crickowski's work." Bobby closed his eyes and shook his head. Davis was right. The electronics would have taken someone with more expertise; he should have made the connection to the female Kodiak. *Damnit, I should have seen it.*

"Yeah, just another bunch of idiots taking credit for my work. Although I really didn't mind it this time," said Laurel confidently. She leaned back onto the bar as she relaxed her grip on the gun slightly. She must have been able to tell that Bobby was in no position for a counter attack.

Davis walked over to where Bobby was laying on the ground. "I purchased this rug in Italy, and I'm not sure if blood will come out of it." He then checked to make sure that the slowly growing pool of blood surrounding Bobby wouldn't reach his area rug that was a few feet away. After he studied the situation, he decided to err on the side of safety as he kicked the rug away from Bobby.

"You know, Major, there is a book called *The World of Art,* in which Robert Payne wrote about the statue of David. After seeing it, he described David as a god who had descended to earth in order to chastise the mighty and to tear kings from their thrones. Davis pushed his area rug back further as he continued his lecture. "He also went on to say that the youthful body that was sculpted stands in absolute composure, conscious of its own strength and power to accomplish whatever the intelligence demands."

"You see yourself as David?" Bobby shook his head. "Then you're just as crazy as Tabler."

"No, I think you misunderstood my reference." Davis bent over closer to Bobby. "I'm willing to fight against whoever I need to in order to protect our country." He paused and let out a long, slow breath. "General Tabler was going to be my personal choice for the next Vice President. You know, the General loved this country as much as I do. It's too bad it didn't work out for him. When you consider all things, the only person that really ended up getting what she wanted was Ms. Crickowski."

Laurel gave a sarcastic laugh. "I've got a book deal, a made-for-TV movie, and a future in public speaking engagements. You asked me earlier if I was paid, let's just say that I banked on the American media to take care of my monetary needs. They've given me fame and money; two things which I can use to help the rest of the country understand how hard it is for women to be respected in the military. I guess I need to thank Jennifer Rayburn the next time she interviews me."

"I'm glad to see that things worked out for you," commented Bobby sarcastically. "And I see that your stomach is finally feeling better."

Laurel looked at Davis and then back at Bobby, whose shirt was now totally soaked in blood. "Mahkeem isn't the only one who can act, but I will admit to taking a number of pills that are designed to induce vomiting. I think the drugs are actually for victims who have been poisoned and need to discharge the contents of their stomach."

Laurel then changed the direction of the conversation as she addressed Davis, "It's sort of ironic isn't it. You sent multiple assassins to take out Major Handle. I even instructed you on what type of weapons we could get past the CIA filament scanners back at the hotel, but I'm going to end up doing the job myself."

Bobby closed his eyes—*something else I missed*. He'd lost count, but it was at least the third thing he should have connected.

Davis nodded. "I agree that our JET counterparts failed miserably to kill the Major. I would have hired a team of Kodiaks to take him out, but the problem with Americans is that you have to pay them too much and then you have to worry about them talking. All of the Islamic cell members came fairly cheap; seventy-six virgins in the afterlife and no witnesses left alive to question."

Davis returned to the bar to pour another drink as he continued, "In fact, the six Kodiaks in the second team almost took out the entire convoy. The U.S. military then actually recovered the goddamn chip receiver from the insurgents." He shook his head, "We basically put bulls-eyes on the Americans, and the insurgents still barely managed to kill most of them."

Bobby tried to shift his leg, but Laurel motioned with her sidearm to dissuade him from any attempts to move. He knew that Laurel would kill him in an instant and decided to remain still. "And the fissionable material?"

Davis smiled. "I did get into a bit of trouble for running a few days behind on the retooling of one of my nuclear power plants. You just can't find good, enriched uranium, so I borrowed some material from my plant for a week. But don't worry, it's back safe and sound, supplying power to paying customers." Davis motioned to the lights in the room as he took another drink of whiskey. "The bottom line was simple, Major Handle. I had an agreement with the insurgents in the North. I was ready to give them their own nation, North Iraq. My administration would have recognized the new country and offered them aid, leaving the oil resources in South Iraq available for my overseas companies to exploit." Davis grew smug as he continued, "In exchange for help from my administration, the Northern Insurgents guaranteed that they would pull back from the South as long as we kept off of their soil."

Davis raised his hand and pointed at Bobby. "We would have finally been on our way to true peace in the Middle East, and you could have been part of it." He shook his head as he looked into Bobby's eyes. "It's actually a shame, we would have worked well together. I'm sure that by now you must understand that this was the only way to get the support from the American public to continue our military campaign. After seeing our own President killed, we would have been able to return not just to Iraq, but to the entire Middle Eastern block of countries and rebuild them in our own image."

"Yeah," agreed Bobby through clenched teeth, "the image that Washington and Lincoln leave on bills. You could have left the Iraqi people to their own devices after the pullout. I'm sure they would have worked things out, but you traded patriotism for greed, screwing everyone involved." He took a deep breath. "I hope you didn't spend a lot of time working on your inauguration speech."

Davis stood in silence, probably thinking of how the plan had gone to hell. He then motioned to Laurel. "I believe that Major Handle's time is up, just be careful of where you shoot him, I really don't want any of his blood to stain my Italian rugs."

"People are going to be looking for me," replied Bobby in a desperate attempt to stall for a few more seconds.

"You've got enemies all over the world," taunted Davis. "I don't think anyone will be surprised when your body washes up tomorrow morning on the banks of the Potomac."

Laurel leveled the gun and pointed it directly at Bobby's forehead. She pulled the trigger, but the silencer failed to work as the explosion of the black powder in the gun's chamber echoed throughout the entire room.

Chapter 31

Laurel's face froze as she looked across the room at Kyle. He held a firearm that was pointed directly at her. She had intended to pull the trigger of her own gun when a bullet struck her in the upper chest. Her expression never changed as her lifeless body collapsed to the ground.

Leamon Davis, in shock from seeing his allied Kodiak soldier fall, stood in silence as his eyes darted between Laurel, Kyle, and finally back to Major Bobby Handle. Kyle, who also looked as if he were in shock from his own actions, walked across the room and kept his gun trained on Davis.

Bobby had given Kyle very specific orders before they had arrived at the Davis Estate. Kyle was to wait in the trunk of the rental car for exactly twenty minutes. If Bobby had not returned to the car within the given amount of time, he was to enter the house. As he entered, he must have followed their voices through the house, down the long hallway, and into the great room where he found Laurel about to kill Bobby. He must have only had a few seconds to decide on whether or not to pull the trigger, but his quick action had clearly saved Bobby's life.

"Bobby, are you okay?" Kyle moved swiftly across the large room.

"I've had better days. Can you help me up onto that couch?" Bobby could only imagine what was going through Kyle's mind. His team had been lost in Iraq, and now he'd taken down one of the last survivors.

Davis watched in horror as Kyle helped Bobby onto the leather couch. Bobby shot a look back at him. *Let's see you get my blood out of this, you bastard.*

Davis watched for another moment before he gazed down at the remains of the Freedom Medal that Bobby had been clutching before he was shot. The battered award was still on the ground near the bar. He reached down and picked it up slowly.

"What the hell is this?" exclaimed Davis under his breath. "This isn't a Congressional Freedom Medal; it's a half mangled military medal!"

Bobby looked at Kyle and shrugged his shoulders. "I guess that I brought the wrong one. It looked like a Freedom Medal to me."

Bobby had asked Kyle for one small favor as they exited the bar back in Washington D.C. He wanted to know if he could borrow the military medal that Kyle had just been awarded. Bobby then proceeded to slam it in the car door five times and drag it for thirty miles from the trailer hitch on the rented vehicle. Kyle had commented that he couldn't believe that he'd so easily given up his medal awarded to him by the President of the United States just so the Major could destroy it—but from the current success of the deception, it had been worth it.

Leamon Davis suddenly looked like a man who had just gotten a reprieve from death row. His mood changed as he put his own political spin on the last half-hour of events. "Thank God you came in when you did, Captain Bradly. This woman was working with the cell that attempted to assassinate President Sumner." He glanced at Bobby as he continued like he was giving a re-election speech. "She must have followed Major Handle here in an attempt to kill him before he discovered her involvement in the secret scheme." Davis looked at Bobby again as he slowed down to emphasize his words. "A secret that must be kept from the American public. We wouldn't want them to find out that Mr. Mahkeem was a key player in a plot to assassinate the President."

Bobby's face remained emotionless, "What are—"

"Major Handle," interrupted Davis, "with all of the pressure you've been under lately, not to mention the loss of blood from your wounds, I'm sure you may have misinterpreted a few things that were said over the last twenty minutes or so."

Bobby looked back at Davis and thought about what the politician had just said. He had no real evidence that linked Davis to the assassination attempt. In addition, he knew he couldn't talk to anyone except the President without potentially unveiling the entire plot to the American media. Finally, Davis had incredible influence and wealth, so any attempt to prosecute him would also compromise a secret that the White House so desperately wanted to protect. *And take years in the process, not to mention millions of tax dollars.*

"You have a point, Mr. Davis," commented Bobby. "But Mr. Mahkeem is still a hero in the eyes of America, and Sumner is still our President, so you've failed."

Davis noticed Kyle shoot Bobby a confused look and then quickly filled the silence. "I don't know what you're talking about, Major Handle." Davis' expression grew concerned. "We've got to get you to a hospital; you've lost a lot of blood."

Bobby reached into his pocket to retrieve his cell phone. "I'm just going to dial 9-1-1 and get an ambulance. It seems that you were right, Mr. Speaker, I have lost a lot of blood."

Bobby saw Davis smile. *He knows that I understand the situation,* thought Bobby. *If I even think about taking him down, the entire plot would be revealed and President Sumner and his administration would look like fools.*

Bobby turned on his cell phone and it immediately rang. He gave a surprised look to Kyle and answered his phone.

"Handle, here."

"Bobby, thank God you're okay," exhaled Jennifer into the other end of the connection. "My contact at the White House told me that Babare was preparing to make an announcement that Mahkeem and a high ranking military officer were killed earlier today after the ceremony. I just thought that it may have been you, and when I couldn't reach you, well—"

"I'm fine, Jen." Bobby stared back at Davis who had already poured himself another drink, this one possibly in celebration. "Look, I've got to go. I'm in the middle of something right now. I'll talk to you tomorrow."

"Okay, but you'd better actually call this time!" Jennifer sounded like a great burden had just been lifted from her shoulders. "And what about—"

Bobby interrupted, "I can't talk anymore, but I will call you—bye."

He hung up the phone. "On second thought, let's just skip the ambulance." He moved forward to the edge of the couch. "Come on, Kyle; help me get out of here. I'll live for another fifteen minutes, but you're going to have to drive this time."

Kyle lowered his gun for the first time since he'd entered the room and helped Bobby off of the couch. Bobby threw his uninjured arm around Kyle's good shoulder as they both walked toward the hallway that led to the front door.

"I'm glad we were able to come to a reasonable solution, Major," Davis called out from behind the bar. "Maybe we'll work together someday under more favorable conditions."

Bobby shook his head. "Yeah, favorable."

They continued to head for the front door when Bobby stopped and turned his head to look back at Davis. "But then again . . . ."

Chapter 32

"That would probably explain some of the conversations that Davis and I had after Mahkeem saved the lives of our soldiers," commented President Sumner. "Looking back, General Tabler and Leamon Davis basically double-teamed me."

Twenty-four hours had passed since the medal ceremony had taken place. Kyle had spent most of the night at the hospital as multiple doctors attended to Bobby's latest injuries.

Bobby had phoned the President from the emergency room to fill him in on what had transpired. After he had finished his explanation, the President insisted on a face to face follow-up meeting in the Oval Office with both Bobby and Kyle to discuss their next steps.

"I take it that you've talked to Joe Manelli about his new assignment," asked the President.

"Joe is headed back to the States as we speak, Sir," answered Bobby. "He's ready for the challenge, but he's also glad to be coming home."

"Good." Sumner nodded his head. "I spoke with the Prime Minister of England this morning about the Secret Service agent that made an attempt on my life. When the media broke the story, he called me immediately to make sure that I was okay. He also asked me if there was anything that he could do to assist us in our investigation. As you both know, Great Britain still hails Mr. Mahkeem as a hero because of his role in saving the Defense Minister's life." Bobby and Kyle nodded their heads as Sumner continued. "We're going to keep your new team small for a while. Based on what happened with Laurel Crickowski, I don't want to involve anyone else at this point." The President put up his index finger and addressed Bobby. "The first thing that you, Kyle, and Joe need to do is identify anyone else who would have been involved with either Tabler or Davis. I want a thorough investigation. Go back as many years as you need to." He paused and raised another finger.

"Second, if anyone ever mentions Laurel Crickowski, the official line from the White House is that she requested an extended leave and cannot be reached for comment."

"Yes, sir," answered Kyle somewhat despondently.

Bobby was impressed at how Kyle had responded to Laurel's involvement in the plot. Kyle had explained that while he felt betrayed, at the same time he was relieved that the Iraq mission failure wasn't his fault—and that the mission really hadn't ended until just a few hours ago. *With a much better result*, thought Bobby. *We know what happened to the fissionable material.* He looked around at the electrical devices in the oval office. *Each and every one of them is probably powered directly by the Davis family.*

"I know it's been a tough week, Kyle," said the President as informally as he could. "I'm proud of you, and I'm glad to have you working with Bobby." Sumner paused and smiled. "Don't worry, I'm going to go ahead and get you a new medal as soon as I can."

Kyle finally smiled as he responded, "Thank you, sir. I'll try to be more careful with who I lend it to in the future." He looked over to see that Bobby was now smiling as well.

"There's one last thing, gentlemen," announced Sumner as he stood up. "The Prime Minister of England is also putting together a small team that will function similar to yours. We actually discussed the possibility of coordinating our efforts should the need arise."

"Depending on where our investigation takes us, we may need them sooner than later," commented Bobby. "Do you have a contact name yet?"

"Actually, I do," responded the President as he shuffled a few papers on his desk. "The senior member of the team is a Mr. Bart Hobbs, Jr."

*   *   *

"So you need a lift anywhere, Bobby?" asked Kyle. They stood outside the White House in the restricted parking area as they continued their conversation. Both of them had matching slings to go along with their comparable shoulder wounds. Bobby, in addition, was using a single crutch under his good arm to improve his somewhat limited mobility.

"No, Jen's doing a live report tonight and then we're going to dinner."

"Talk about living dangerously," chided Kyle.

"What do you mean?" Bobby honestly asked. *After what we've been through in the last week, I feel like I could do anything.*

"With what you know, but can't say, and with what she doesn't know, and would probably like to ask." Kyle paused when Bobby gave him a look of total confusion. "I guess what I'm trying to say is . . ."

"What?" Bobby interrupted.

"You just better not talk in your sleep, if you know what I mean," said Kyle with a smirk.

Bobby shifted his weight to his good leg. "You're going to have to learn some respect, you know that?"

Kyle pointed to a news truck as it pulled into the parking lot. "I guess I'll start working on that when I get back from Philly. Your girlfriend's here."

Kyle gave a quick salute and headed to his car as the D.C. media truck pulled up next to Bobby. Jennifer hopped out of the vehicle and gave Bobby a quick glance. "Are you going to make it through my live report? It's only going to take me about thirty minutes, but you honestly look like you could pass out at any moment."

Bobby looked down at the sling on his left arm and thought of the two painkillers he had swallowed thirty minutes earlier. "No, it doesn't hurt as much as it did an hour ago. Take your time. I'll just go check out my new office in the West Wing."

"Well, I'll try to hurry anyway." She gave a quick wink before she turned to walk away.

Bobby thought back to the time that he'd spent waiting for the pain of his parents' deaths to go away. He thought of the long waiting between missions and the painful waiting of being alone that he saw on the horizon of his own future. Now, as he stared straight ahead to the beautiful woman in front of him, he saw possibilities for the two of them that no longer made the anxiety of passing time excruciating for him. Bobby looked into Jennifer's eyes and exhaled. "I can wait."

*   *   *

Bobby sat in his new office and watched the news on his new computer. He was patiently waiting for Jennifer to finish her segment so that they could go to dinner.

"Now we're going live to the White House where Jennifer Rayburn is standing by." The voice of the national evening news anchor, Jeff Kovitch, went silent as Jennifer began her report.

"Thank you, Jeff." Jennifer moved the cordless microphone closer to her mouth. "I'm standing live outside the White House where the staff has officially announced the building of a new International Friendship monument in honor of the Iraqi ex-rebel responsible for saving the life of President Sumner, Ahlmed Mahkeem."

The screen then split down the center so that Jennifer was on one half while Jeff Kovitch was on the other.

"Jennifer, how is the general mood around Capitol Hill today?" Kovitch had a serious look on his face. Then again thought Bobby, *when doesn't a national news anchor look serious?*

"Well, Jeff, it's really a mixed bag at this point, especially with the sudden passing of Leamon Davis just last night." She paused a moment, almost like she was staring right into Bobby's mind from within his screen. "His death from a heart attack has shocked all of us here in the Washington, D.C. area. We're all going to miss him."

Bobby listened to Jennifer's description of the House Speaker's death and thought about the statement that Kyle had made earlier in the parking lot. Kyle had been right; if his relationship with Jennifer progressed, he'd have to make *sure* that he didn't talk in his sleep.